Imprisoned by Love

C. S. Brahams

London | New York

Published by Clink Street Publishing 2020

Copyright © 2020

First edition.

ISBN:
978-1-913340-82-7 paperback
978-1-913340-83-4 ebook

This book is dedicated to the individuals suffering from dementia and their close family members affected by this cruel and unyielding illness.

The author would also like to express her gratitude to her parents, her husband and her daughter, for their support.

Inspired by *King Lear*

"Who is it that can tell me who I am?"

*"O, let me not be mad, not mad, sweet heaven
Keep me in temper: I would not be mad!"*

*"I am a very foolish fond old man,
Fourscore and upward, not an hour more or less;
And, to deal plainly,
I fear I am not in my perfect mind."*

And a special note of appreciation to Iris Murdoch, a writer of great worth, robbed of her greatest skill. In her own words:

"We live in a fantasy world, a world of illusion.
The great task in life is to find reality."

Chapter 1
The End of the Long Hot Summer

It is extraordinary how quickly a summer holiday can pass without incident or argument. It has been blissful. Nine days in Croatia, basking in the intense heat, cooling ourselves off in the tranquil water. Michael, the twins and I, are celebrating our last summer together before they go off on their gap year to Australia and we return to work effectively as *dinkys*: double income no kids *yet*. Except that we have kids. Expensive ones. We made rash promises when they started the Upper Sixth: straight A grades and you can have £1000 each. Straight A* and you can have £2000 each. We underestimated our own children. But we are so proud of them. Neither Olivia nor Eddie ever imagined doing this well. They have deferred their entry to Exeter and Warwick universities and are now considering Oxbridge. I hope this is all that they have to worry about. I don't know whether to encourage or discourage this. It's easier to advise other people's children.

Eddie is the spitting image of his dad, only thinner. He is well over six foot now; quite muscular and tans effortlessly. Michael, who was much the same when I met him at Durham University, is still an attractive man. He is forty-nine and hasn't let himself go, too much. His dark hair and blue eyes have been passed onto our son. I'm disappointed that he has given up on his contact lenses: too much of a faff, apparently. He wore them for twenty years, but now he struggles to use them. I only wear sunglasses. But I know that as I approach fifty, things are going to change.

We are treating the twins, and ourselves, to a last minute, all-inclusive stay at The Sun Gardens Hotel, Dubrovnik. Technically, it's not located in the old city; it is too hot and too crowded there, so we are relieved to be on the coast. Neither Michael nor I like crowds whilst we're on holiday; we have enough of London's urban buzz to contend with on a day-to-day basis. It's idyllic here. The twins have never stayed in a five-star hotel before and I suspect it will be many years until any of us do so again. It is a far cry from our spontaneous forms of travel. I have spent so much time in the water, racing the twins and losing, that I am wrinkled; if this is a taste of what's to come, I don't know if I want to be that old. It's Michael's turn now. He's an outstanding swimmer. If anyone were in difficulty in the water, he would be the person who could save you. Despite working ludicrous hours, he has always been there for both our children, never favouring one over the other. I watch him now, peering over my Kindle, and smile as he pretends to be a shark, just as he did when they were five. He is less inhibited than I am. I find it endearing.

In the evening, we sit in a beautiful little restaurant, over-looking the sea, clinking our glasses with our grown-up children. Olivia looks like I used to: petite with long, straight fair hair and green eyes. She has little freckles that are allowed to dance on her pretty little face whilst we're on holiday; at home, they're hidden beneath a thin layer of face powder. I take my mobile out and ask the waiter to capture our happy, perfect family. I feel blessed. I know I am. I instantly send it via WhatsApp to our "immediate family group" which includes all of us. Everyone laughs and mocks me for being efficient on holiday as well as at work. I can't really help it. I'm enjoying the freedom Croatia has given us. We aren't rushing in the mornings or berating each other for the most trivial things. We are happy. And it's lovely. It's all a bit too good to be true. I pinch myself. I'm lucky to have Michael in my life. Lucky to have my twins. Sometimes we need a little unhappiness to know when we are happy.

It is slightly different when we are at home in London. Michael's work is relentless. He toils away for long hours. He hasn't slept well for years, particularly the last two, and I fear that he will have a heart attack unless he slows down. The twins and I work in six-week cycles; that's schools for you. He doesn't. I want him to work less. Slow down. Reduce his hours. He has been a little absent-minded lately; I put this down to exhaustion and stress. Unlike me, Michael spends hours in front of three screens, analysing data and liaising with high net-worth clients. I spend my day with adolescents. He's an actuary and I'm a Senior Teacher; this means he earns more money than I do though I am a member of the Senior Management Team (SMT). I take a cursory look around the hotel complex, hoping that I don't see one of my colleagues or pupils here.

Our nine days have nearly expired. I can feel the weight of the journey and my return to school, sitting on my shoulders like the proverbial albatross. I don't like flying and I fear most forms of public transport. I'm dreading going home but I'm dreading the end of our holiday more. I know that my job will fill me with distractions – many good ones at that – but it won't be the same without the twins. The house will feel empty. And Michael will be back at the office where only his colleagues and clients will benefit from his quiet charm and sharp intellect; it's all spent by the time he comes home.

Michael can almost read my mind. He puts his large and caring hand over my shoulder to reassure me. He squeezes my shoulder to the point that it hurts a little; he's unaware of his strength. Olivia and Eddie wander off to talk to other teenagers. They are confident and polite. I'm proud of the way we have brought them up. But they are still naïve. It is natural to worry about one's children but I have an irrational fear that our perfect foursome will be shattered. I need to practise what I preach: cut the umbilical cord; let them fly into the distance. And the day before I return to my school, they will be flying to Australia for their well-earned gap year. I can't quite get my head around this. Both of them. Together.

September's Inservice Training

The twins left for Sydney yesterday; it was both tearful and joyful. We all cried. I won't relax until they're back in London, of course, whereas Michael will focus on his work, or me. He won't worry the way I will. I can derive some comfort from the second leg of their trip, when they're in Melbourne, as they will be meeting up with cousins. I remind Olivia and Eddie to look after each other. I don't need to do this as they've always been close. Although I know that I am going to miss them, it is strangely liberating for me. Eighteen years is a long time to be around children 24/7.

So here I am, back at work. It's as if the summer never happened.

It is neither money nor ambition that makes me sit in my twenty-fifth INSET day since I qualified as a teacher of English. Teaching is a vocation. I'm not sure that I still have *it* though – I will tell you at the end of this academic year – but my twenty-fifth INSET anniversary has been a surprisingly enjoyable one. It's hard not to be cynical. I have sixteen years left before I retire, that's if cancer doesn't get me first. Don't be alarmed. I don't have the big C, insofar as I know, it's just the way we teachers talk. We are all counting down until our retirement, even those of us who love what we do. I started my countdown at twenty-two.

"If you're going to fail, fail fast; that's what they say in business." We don't say it here. Failure isn't an option. Not for the pupils; not for the teachers and certainly not for me. Our ethos currently follows the Dodo: *"Everyone has won and all must have prizes."* We even have a prize for the member of staff who has completed the most covers; that's supervising other people's lessons, not preparing complex plates of carrots cooked three ways in Gordon Ramsey's restaurants! Last year's prize was a £25 Amazon voucher. Michael wouldn't roll out of bed for £250. We live in different worlds.

I am the Deputy Head of an allegedly "outstanding school" in Central London. I am partly responsible for our ethos: success breeds success. It was slightly borne out of the marketing campaign focusing on "Education" dating back to Tony Blair's reign as Prime Minister: *"No one ever forgets a good teacher. Could you inspire young minds?"* It was a memorable advertisement. But very few of us were taken in by this romanticised vision of teaching whilst throwing back the popcorn in our local cinemas. Back in the late 1990s, I was working in the state sector. We welcomed the attention. But we still felt underpaid, undervalued and overwhelmed. We caught pupils mimicking the advertisement in their breaks, changing the pithy tag line to: *No one ever forgets a bad teacher. Could you inspire young criminals?"*

As any practising teacher knows, the INSET day is both heaven and hell. The bells ring every forty-minutes. This is followed by a contented silence pervading the corridors. The staircases aren't littered with boisterous teenagers and even the new school café is spotless. Heaven. But hell is only twenty-four hours away and we all know it's coming. The relentless stream of challenging pupils; the unyielding battle with the demanding parents and the continuous supply of regurgitated essays replete with the standard excuses – barely changing year-on-year. Why teach? I wouldn't do anything else. I told you. It's a vocation. It is utterly and totally enveloping. I do try to see my friends but usually we catch up in the holidays; that's how it is for me.

Today, however, is my turn to listen. Take a backseat for about an hour. I should just make the most of it. Jack Baldwin is leading the INSET. He's in my department and technically he is the number two. The second in command. The General's Lieutenant. And he's smug with it. Jack is practically an albino; wears expensive tailored suits; well-polished shoes and looks more like a Bond villain than a Bond Street teacher. Jack is unashamedly ambitious. The first PowerPoint slide is up: TRANSGENDER ISSUES (& IN

OUR SCHOOL). This immediately takes me by surprise as he was scheduled to speak about preparing for our "forthcoming inspection." We have been preparing for it since the last one. I don't recall receiving an email about the switch.

Jack is the *only* person wearing a suit today. We dress down for each other and up for the pupils. The pupils dress down for their parents and up for their teachers. We live in an up and down sort of world. I notice a small coffee stain on his otherwise pristine double white cuff. The PowerPoint is prescriptive. We "learn" about gender dysmorphia and transitioning, mainly. There's also a slide about Mermaids, a charity that "supports young people with gender variance". Jack has clearly done his homework. There are plenty of statistics. The penultimate slide is a picture of a unisex toilet. There's a quick straw poll to see if we think our school should have one. Our disabled toilet is already unisex. The vote is an overwhelming "no" mainly because it would result in re-allocating an existing staff loo – already much in demand – and assigning it to the pupils. We all consume far too much caffeine to be this politically correct. Besides, there's nothing unisex about peeing into a beaker when you're desperate to relieve yourself.

The session ends a bit abruptly as the Principal wants to cut-in. Two of our pupils – *both girls* – are now identifying as "young men". I already know this because I receive most of the same emails as the Principal. Joanna is to be known as Jeremy (seems an odd choice in the light of Corbyn's unpopularity at the moment) and Chloe is to be known as Kris with a K. I find this bizarre. *He* could at least keep the same initial. Both pupils are entering the Lower Sixth this year. Jeremy will be in my A Level English set. Kris has chosen three sciences in addition to maths. There's also a boy called Jake, who is in Year 9, whose is "gender fluid". We have been told to use the pronoun "they" as much as possible. As a teacher of English, I find this a bit annoying.

The bell rings and we ignore it; it's the only day that we

can. The Principal, whom we all affectionately call Principal Peter, is still up on the podium. He is an imposing figurehead. I'm wondering whether he is 6 foot 6 or 6 foot 7; this is about 1 meter and 98 centimetres, for those of you that are the same age as my children. Peter is much taller than the door frame against which he is leaning. He is wearing dark blue jeans and a red and white checked shirt. He looks like an American cowboy even though his native country is Canada. He spends his life correcting people. His deep transatlantic voice is in sync with his manly appearance. I find him quite attractive though not as good looking as Michael. He regales us with stories about the plethora of positive meetings he has had over the holidays; the much-awaited and now state-of-the-art STEM lab that has been financed by our "generous sponsors" and best of all, we officially have "a waiting list of desirable pupils". This is amazing. We are, quite frankly, not an "outstanding" school at all. We celebrate middle-class mediocrity. For the first time in the school's twenty-five-year history, we are oversubscribed. I have been tasked with analysing our data for the past three years. Apparently, I need to produce a spreadsheet and present this at the next Governors' meeting which I'm told is imminent. I'm not really the right person to do this. I am appalling at statistics. I take everything home and my brilliant actuary of a husband, Michael, does it all for me though lately he has complained that it's become too much of a chore. I am grateful. I offer to iron shirts but I don't think this is the reward he was hoping for...

The morning comes to a close. I don't have time to sit with my colleagues. I have a long "to do" list and everything is either "urgent" or "important". I miss my old job as the Head of Sixth Form, a position I loved. My office is no longer on the top floor – the Penthouse – it's on the ground floor, two doors down from the Principal's. It is also next to the room with the photo-copier in it; this is both a plus and a minus. I put a sign on the door saying "Room 101".

After lunch, the staff are allocated two hours to make their form-rooms look "inspiring". Fortunately, I don't have one this year. The other teachers are running around earnestly, relieved that they're not tasked with analysing spreadsheets. I open up the one that Michael had prepared for me in the holidays, and save it on the SMT drive. It looks all right but I haven't had time to check it. I prop my door open with the elaborate iron doorstop (which I bought from a second-hand shop in Islington) and head down to the staff room to make another mug of tea. I sniff the milk that has been left out on the draining board; it already smells, so I venture out to the Sainsbury's Local to buy another one. I like fresh air. Besides, once the students are back, I won't have a spare minute.

At 3 pm I have a meeting with all my tutees; there are ten of them this year. At 4 pm I have to attend the English Departmental meeting; this is led by Harry, the HOD. He's an old Harrovian. We're the largest department in the school and rather female-dominated. Harry finds this difficult but he "manages" us quite well. He is embarrassed that the number 1 and number 2 in the department are both forty-something men. The other members, except for me, are all in their late twenties and early thirties. I am grateful that I am *not* the HOD. I hated that position. Just because you like books, doesn't mean you want to run a department. The admin is horrendous. All those acronyms and syllabi; they're enough to make any do-gooder misread the almost invisible asterisk; this is the evil little marker that denotes a play or a novel coming off the syllabus in January as opposed to June.

At 5 pm we are officially "dismissed" and told to get a good night's sleep. Some people laugh. Others feel patronised. I don't care either way as I need to return to my sanctuary. Principal Peter returns to his. We speak to each other on the phone as neither of us wants to disturb the other's important reading. I suspect my taste in fiction is rather different from Peter's. Finally, I get a chance to print out and photo-copy everything I need for Week 1; this is utterly tedious but wholly necessary. Last year, I did battle with the photo-copier. There's a small dent in the machine where my Gabor boot hit it. There's a CCTV camera in that room now.

It's 6 pm and I feel the weight of the week to come and decide to head home. I change into my "cycling clothes" and mount my black hybrid bicycle; it's pretty old now but I love it. I don't love the traffic and I particularly dislike being trapped behind a bus. The advertisements of cheerful students don't ring true to me. Their smiles look too forced and their teeth look too white. But they make me think wistfully of Olivia and Eddie. I wonder where they are right now and am desperate to talk to them. Michael thinks we should let them contact us first. He reminded me not to become a heli-copter parent; it won't benefit the children. They need to be independent. He is right, of course. We compromise on five days, otherwise I will turn grey with worry.

I am home at 6.45 pm. The door isn't double-locked so I assume that Michael is in. He isn't. Careless. Out of charac-ter. There are several messages on our answering machine; piles of brown envelopes to open and little in the fridge, even though I have been off school for about eight weeks. Well, we have been away... I feel guilty. I pick up my mobile and open the Ocado App. It's so easy. I book a delivery slot for 8 to 9 pm the next day. I check the school calendar for dates. Nothing.

I have six text messages from Rosie and Emma; we have been friends since we moved into the area. They want to arrange a girls' night out. In principle, I agree but can't commit to anything until half-term. Neither of them is a teacher. They both work part-time. Both are artists. Emma's husband is stinking rich and has bank-rolled their pottery and ceramics business for the past five years. I have no idea if either of them ever makes a profit. Their plates and mosaics are pretty though; we have quite a few of them in our house.

Michael is home *very* late. I don't bother to tell him that the door wasn't double-locked. We talk a bit about our respective days. His is full of responsibility and analysis. He is rather a back-office sort of guy. Naturally reserved though occasionally outspoken and loud in his own defence. Not a risk-taker. Doesn't ruffle other people's feathers, not as a general rule. Michael isn't motivated by money – though he likes to earn it – he's motivated by success. He is well-liked by *almost* everyone in the office. I think this is remarkable, given his level of responsibility. And the levels of stress that he is frequently under. I am the opposite to Michael. I like the front line. I *am* a risk-taker. I like to think that I am well-liked (like him) but I use humour to engage and am not permanently on the charm offensive. I am a team player. Michael isn't. Back office. Front office. That's us. We are the team. But some of our friends call us the "dream team" which we find embarrassing. I know I am lucky. Michael may be a little reserved; he may not be the funniest chap at the dinner party table, but he's my husband. And I love him, unreservedly.

We go to bed with our books. Mine is *The Collector* by John Fowles, which I am teaching this term. I have taught it once before. Michael is re-reading *Freakonomics* which he has read five times and counting. He has a copy of *Capital without Capitalism* on his bedside table; it was birthday present which he said he wanted. We switch the light off at 11.30 pm I can hear Michael rummaging around for a Rennie which he finally chews nosily. He says it tastes like chalk. Gaviscon was my constant companion during my pregnancy. He thinks it's for women. Between the two of us, Michael usually falls sleep first; perhaps his conscience is clearer than mine. We lie together, slightly out of sync, as he breathes out, I breathe in. I never tire of the soft sound of his gentle snoring.

I am surprised how pleased I am to see my pupils. They've all blossomed and grown-up over the summer holidays. They are completely re-energised. The Lower Sixth are thrilled to be in the Sixth Form and even Freddie Adebayo, who just scraped enough Level 7s in his GCSEs to stay here, is focused and relatively smart though he has taken to wearing black shirts as well as black jumpers. We have no uniform in the Sixth Form. Just guidelines; these are mostly ignored. We have to pick our battles; this isn't one that I wish to embrace.

I am quite keen to start teaching my A Level set. Joanna-cum-Jeremy is in it. S/he is very bright. Emotionally intelligent. Strangely intuitive for a sixteen-year-old. There are seven other students. None of them is as bright as the transgender student but each of them has his or her own talents. I have two external students joining the set: William (Wills) and Louisa (Lulu). Both had been attending single-sex schools and were desperate to switch to co-ed. We start with some background on Romanticism and move onto Mary Shelley. They can't quite fathom that she was only fractionally older than they are now when she wrote her novel. Everyone has read *Frankenstein* over the summer. I have taught it three times before and know it well. Besides, my text is heavily annotated, just in case early onset dementia sets in …

For some reason, I suggest we see Mel Brooks' *Young Frankenstein* as a Christmas outing. It's on at the Garrick Theatre. At least the risk assessment won't be too onerous. My dream lesson is interrupted by the shrill sound of the pulsating fire alarm. It's a drill, of course, as we always have one in Week 1; however, why it has to be in my favourite lesson and not when I have Year 9 is something of a minor blow.

We stand outside, in the half-mild, half-cold weather. It's early September but it is neither summer nor autumn. The pupils file out quickly and quietly, in addition to them are: the staff; the cooks; the administrators; the peripatetic music teachers and the burly caretaker, Joe. He has a small and elderly ginger cat draped casually around his neck. Half the school is able to fit into the mews around the back of our grandiose classical building; the other half spills onto

Bond Street. There is some muttering and resentment by passers-by. I am secretly impressed that everyone is quiet. Liam (the Academic Deputy) stands with his red clipboard, and keeps a note of the start and finish time of this drill. We have beaten our record. Once the excitement is over, the staff and pupils dutifully file back into school. The bells rings joyfully and happily it's break.

Emily, the new and rather intense and earnest maths teacher, makes me a cappuccino with the pristine Nespresso coffee machine. We *all* feel a bit uncomfortable about the damage we're doing to the environment. Annie – the Head of Art – has been working on an installation using the empty coffee pods but even so, once the inspection is underway, the Nespresso may have to hide in the cupboard, along with the its brightly coloured pods.

I have a meeting with two different sets of parents; a conference with Principal Peter and two sponsors from the pharmaceutical company. I also have to observe Benedict White, our new history teacher. He is straight out of college and looks about twelve. Luckily, the observation lesson is third period. I print off an appropriate form from the teachers' drive and another, just in case I mess up the first one. I should have been a Scout leader.

I arrive at the same time as Year 11. They form an orderly queue outside the Room 12C and Benedict ushers them. No one misbehaves. He hands me the copy of his lesson plan which is almost identical to the pro forma on our database. Good for him. I decide to sit at the back, next to a girl called Fran. She's going through a Goth stage at the moment. It doesn't suit her. I notice that she's wearing a very baggy black jumper – not the school one which has a distinctive double red line to mark the V shape – and that her white shirt is very long. Much too big. Her nails have been painted black. I am on the verge of reprimanding her but can't. Not now. She gives me a half-smile initially but ignores me for the remainder of the lesson. Benedict entertains the students with clips from YouTube; *Blackadder* and even has excerpts from old films. Seemingly effortless. All of this is achieved whilst referring to the GCSE assessment objectives. Benedict is adept at all things technical, as are all millennials. He sets them an essay for homework. No one grumbles. I notice that his blue shirt is untucked. I congratulate him on the quality of his lesson and offer to buy him a drink on Friday. He readily accepts. He doesn't look much older than my son, Eddie.

The morning disappears as quickly as it appeared and we are already into the afternoon block of lessons. I have a double with Year 10 followed by a single with Year 9. Liam O'Riley, the other Deputy, is in charge of the timetable. He lives in a one-bedroom flat near Warren Street and walks into work. It takes him twenty minutes. Liam could easily sleep in his office; it's big enough, and he has all manner of things at his disposal: a shaving kit, an electric razor, spare shirts and ties, three pairs of shoes, socks, mints, toothpaste and a toothbrush, boxes of Alpen and his own expensive coffee. He also has a sleeping bag tucked away in his cupboard. Liam always looks smart. Professional. He could be a pilot for Aer Lingus.

Almost everyone goes home by 4.30 pm I don't. And neither does Liam – King of the Timetable. There is always something to do. I'm reading through some of the pupils' SENCO reports, ensuring that each one has an up-to-date statement. I'm not trained in Special Needs but somehow this falls under my wing as the Pastoral Deputy. I don't mind. There's a polite knock on my door. It's Abbas. We have both been in the school for ten years. He is Iranian; approaching sixty-three and is the kindest man in the school. He had a heart attack in the classroom last year, so it has been agreed that he should have a very light timetable. I really want him to go part-time but Principal Peter wants him to take ER: early retirement. Ironic. Despite being very capable, he is not management material. He dislikes computers and is rather old-school. Abbas teaches Religious Studies. The subject is oversubscribed at both GCSE and A Level. I appreciate and

value his friendship. The feeling is entirely mutual. I sometimes feel guilty when I am with him. He's such a warm
and caring man. I can't explain what we have but there is
definitely something between us. We connect. He pays me
compliments with ease, unlike Michael, but I can never tell
whether he is truly genuine, which Michael always is. We
are just friends. Colleagues. We will never be more than this.

We mainly talk about our children; their A Level results;
their plans for the future and ours. We also chat about our
current and existing students here but can't help focusing on
the transgender ones. He bemoans the loss of Joanna-cum-
Jeremy's beautiful long blonde hair; it's brutally short now,
with a slightly floppy fringe. *He* is thin and languid. Could
be a model. I tell Abbas about the evening course I took at
The Tavistock Clinic. He gives me a wry smile. He updates
me about the chatter in the staff room – for which I am eter-
nally grateful – and agree that it was more fun in the old
days. We pity the new recruits. We simply weren't under the
same scrutiny in the twentieth century.

Finally, I befriend my bike. The traffic is chaotic. I
swerve and swear my way through London's commuter and
post-commuter traffic. The adrenalin dump barely makes
the ride home worth it though I vow that I will stay later
tomorrow. I might even see what time Liam goes home. *When*
I get home, the door is double-locked but Michael's keys are
still in the lock. We live in Daleham Mews, Belsize Village.
I can't believe we haven't been burgled. Michael and I have
lived here since the twins were four. Now they're eighteen
and half way round the world. I miss them.

I immediately turn on Radio 4. I am uncomfortable with
silence. I start unloading various items from my backpack.
My bespoke Bond Street School A4 planner is substantial. I
like to enter my whole timetable for the academic year; this
takes quite a long time (as it's a page a day) and if there's a
change to the schedule, I have to make endless amendments.
I never learn!

There's a text from Michael saying that he's leaving work early; it's 8.30 pm. He has made two typos in his two-line text. I throw some tuna, fresh tomatoes, chopped onions and sliced black olives into a pan and stir in some ready-made tomato sauce from Waitrose. I put the pasta on at 9.15 pm Michael comes home around then. He divests himself of all his outer clothing and takes his socks off for good measure. He forgets to put his slippers on; this is part of his routine. The smell of the freshly grated parmesan morphs into Michael's slightly sweaty size ten feet. I try not to notice. He looks exhausted. I am too tired to snipe at him. He rarely snipes at me. We are quite tolerant of one another. It will be interesting to see if we will remain on our best behaviour without the children present.

The next morning, we both wake up feeling exhausted. We talked too much whilst in bed and I am not enjoying re-reading *The Collector*. Miranda is trapped in the cellar but still desperately trying to manipulate Frederick (her abductor) from there. The book has made me worry about Olivia. She's miles away and there's nothing I can do from here other than Facetime or text. I know the ending of the novel but I'm still rooting for Miranda. Michael didn't sleep well either. He is definitely troubled by something. I try to ask him but he brushes it off and makes various plausible excuses. He seems a bit absentminded. More than usual, perhaps. But he's busy at work. I know that's what it is. We peel off in two different directions. Michael walks to Belsize Park tube station and I cycle towards Swiss Cottage and continue south. I used to sit on the underground, wedging myself underneath people's armpits. But I don't do that anymore. I suffer from taphephobia; it's a fear of the underground and a fear of being buried alive. It's not completely irrational.

When I veer up to the school entrance, I notice the plaque has been removed. There's a trace of black spray paint around the edges of where it had been pinned to the entrance. The plaque was a shiny gold one, quite discreet, but probably more suited to a dentist's practice than an independent co-educational school. Joe, the caretaker, whose cat is not swathed around his neck this time, is fumbling about with an Amazon package. His nails are dirty and his hands look rough. We chat a bit about the graffiti incident (on the plaque) and he complains, again, about the litter in the Sixth Form common room. I don't disagree with him. I let him flirt with me. I don't know why.

I chain up my bicycle against our own railings – even though I am conscious that this annoys Principal Peter. I don't really know where else to safely stow my precious hybrid. Yesterday I left it in the disabled toilet. I'm not very popular right now. No one dares suggest I take the tube – something everyone who lives in London really has to grapple with – they know that I can't do it. Not even after copious amounts of counselling. Liam wants me to attend a course but thus far I have refused. I think the money would be better spent on updating my safeguarding knowledge; after all, we live in a litigious climate.

I have a free period first thing; this is great. Everyone else is pretty much timetabled. The staff room is empty. I help myself to a clean mug; it has our school emblem and motto on it: *"Laboris Gloria Ludi"* which means "work hard play hard"; that's how we interpret it anyway. Our school colours are red, green and black. Mostly black. A bit too distinctive for town. We are thinking about scrapping the green, red and white tie. Too many of our pupils have been bullied on their way home from school. I prompt the staff to remind all the pupils to remove their ties at 4 pm I try to use the coffee machine but we don't have one at home, so I don't really know how to use it. I shove a random Nespresso coffee pod into what *looks* like the appropriate slot. It should be child's play. It isn't. There's a faint sound of percolating but this transpires to be the milk heating up. I end up with hot milk and no coffee. I try to extract the coffee pod but it has been arrested. I Google the price of a new machine.

It's extortionate so I quietly slink away back to my office. I really ought to know better but at heart I have always been a bit of a rebel without a cause.

I have 109 emails. Liam has emailed us the cover of the day. Luckily, I am not "on cover" for period 1. Mind you, not even deputies are exempt. I notice that Abbas has been assigned an additional lunch-time duty. I think this is mean. But I suppose a light timetable leaves you open to a plethora of tedious obligations. Lunch time duty is the worst. We become Epsilons. And since our previous inspection, those on duty have been instructed to wear a red and white overall. I have conveniently developed an allergy to the material. I am no one's "Handmaid".

One of my 109 emails is a complaint. It's about Emily, the new maths teacher. I am surprised that any parent can justify a grievance so early on in the term. I read it twice and print it out and highlight the main points for good measure. I am a born teacher. Apparently, the young maths teacher has no empathy. Emily was the best qualified candidate whom we interviewed. She has first-class honours in maths from Birmingham University. She seemed normal. Not autistic. Not even on the spectrum, if you know what I mean. Young though. Mind you, everyone looks young to me these days. She's new and doesn't appreciate how weak some of our pupils are. She is taken in by the clipped accents and their veneer of sophistication. They might be blessed with inherited wealth but this doesn't mean that they've inherited their parents' intellect. My *mole* has already told me that the bottom set "hate" her. I detest this part of my job – and think it should be Liam's, but we agreed that complaints, even about academic matters, stray into my pastoral territory. I forward the email to Principal Peter, just to keep him in the loop, and email Emily to ask her to make an appointment to see me today. I tell her not to worry. I send her a text message as well. I like to think that I am efficient.

On Thursday, I will be conducting tours of our school. We

do these on alternate Thursdays. This is my favourite thing to do as it doesn't feel at all like work. Principal Peter says I have more gravitas than him, so he happily delegates the walking tours and coffee mornings to me. I think the truth is that he's bored with saying he's not an American. He leads the assemblies. And he is very good at them. Apropos of my busy schedule, I mark out the new route, taking in the refurbished classrooms; the airy and spacious art room; the modern laboratories and our new café area. I make a point of avoiding all the scruffy classrooms and don't want to take prospective parents up and down too many stairs. After all, they're not going to be doing them. I decide to email my designated route, complete with approximate stopping times, to "all staff" and mark it "important". No one needs to be caught with their pants down.

I'm just about to tackle a few more of my emails when Emily's neat little figure pops her head round the door. She is dressed for an interview. I think this is respectful. I push the doorstop away with my right foot and close the door behind me with the other. I gesture towards one of the two Victorian antique armchairs facing my desk and she sits down quickly, folding both her arms and legs simultaneously. She is wearing a navy suit with a fitted white shirt. She's all buttoned up. I ask her an open question about how she thinks she's getting on, especially with Years 7 and 8. She is obviously new to this game. Somewhat breathlessly and with overwhelming honesty, she admits to all her failings. I was only aware of one. I make a few notes and listen sympathetically. I offer to make her a cup of tea. I can't offer her a cappuccino as someone has broken the coffee machine. Selfish! Emily is rather tearful and on the verge of resigning. I strongly discourage her. This is not what we want at the beginning of term. I'm going to observe one of her Year 7 lessons (the bottom set) and Liam will have to do the same with Year 8. I tell her about some disastrous lesson I had when I was in my first year of teaching. She laughs. I think I have won her over. She leaves with her dignity intact and I am relieved that I am not twenty-three anymore.

We have a weekly staff meeting at 4.15 pm designed to flush out the teachers that escape from the building before the pupils do. There are various apologies from teachers with young children. I used to be one of those. I remain sympathetic to the working mother. Liam makes a list of all the attendees which he will dutifully add to the notes of the meeting. Absentees will also be conspicuously noted. Tea, coffee (instant) and a packet of plain digestive biscuits are placed on the large oak table in the Randolph Room; this is the only place that's suitable for staff meetings so we always have them in there. Principal Peter has been for a lunch time swim and looks a bit dishevelled. He ploughs his way through a very long agenda in which he calls on his key staff, including me, to give our input. At least there is no AOB. It all takes ages. Whilst I am not speaking, I take a moment to observe my colleagues.

Benedict is sitting next to Emily. They're the two fast-track graduates. Both are good looking. It didn't take them long to find each other. Their knees are almost touching. The whole science department is present – good show on their part – but they're all huddled together. I can't quite make out whether they're being subversive. Abbas is sitting quietly at the back so that he can make eye contact with me, and I notice that only three members of the English department are present. We finish at 6.15 on the dot. I don't think this is too late but everyone else is grumbling and grousing. Oxford Circus and Bond Street will be horribly overcrowded and teeming with people of all ages, shades and denominations. No one can gain entry or exit after 6 pm I don't miss it.

Eventually I go outside and find the front wheel of my bicycle missing. I feel deflated and disproportionately upset. It's an inconvenience, not a disaster. I need to show more resilience. One day, I might need it.

There are no brightly coloured Lime bikes in sight – they're always loitering around street corners when you don't need them – so I return to my office and take off my cycling garb; change back into my work clothes and start walking towards the bus stop. The 13 will take me to Swiss Cottage and I can easily walk home from there. The queues for the bus are dreadful. I can't get on the 13 or the 113. Eventually I walk home. But not before making several purchases along the way: a new purse from Accessorize; a pair of sensible shoes from Clarke's (which I change into) and a very expensive bottle of water from Starbucks.

When home, I am surprised to find Michael unloading the Ocado order which I had completely forgotten about. He puts things away – though mainly in random places – but I'm just grateful someone was in to open the door. We go through our usual routine; watch the ten o'clock news and collapse into bed. I don't feel like talking and neither does Michael. He falls asleep straight away. I don't. I decide to go down to the kitchen and switch on my laptop. It's midnight. I already have 37 unread emails. Some of them seem quite important and I dash off responses. I know that I should be more circumspect. Our mews house is eerily quiet at this time. Normally, we can hear people dragging their wheelie bins out on Wednesday night but today there's nothing but solitude. I should cherish it. We never have this at school. I decide to sit downstairs, in our kitchen, and read. There's a framed photograph of the four of us, in Croatia, which the twins gave us before they left for Australia. We all look so happy. It's as if we're mortgage free, which alas, we are not. I sit for quite a long time until I feel drunk with exhaustion.

I decide to take two Night Nurse capsules; they're easy to swallow. I return to bed. Michael is snoring quietly and regularly. He's in a diagonal position now, right across my side. I squeeze in behind him, and drag the pillow towards me and rest it under my neck. Although he is asleep, he stretches his arm out towards me, and pulls me in next to him. I'm not sure if he thinks I'm the spare pillow or his wife. He is definitely asleep.

I regret taking Night Nurse at 1 am. I feel as though I am completely hungover. I'm up and out of the house at 6 am. I catch the 13 and sit at the front on the top deck. I have the whole bus to myself. I am the first person to arrive at Bond Street School. I poke my nose through Liam's door, just to check that there isn't a camp bed *in situ*. Although I have conducted many tours over the years, I always have a rush of adrenalin a minute or two before I commence. It's as though I am appearing in a West End production. We start at 9.15 a.m. so that all the pupils, even those that are slightly late, aren't out of breath. And, more importantly, the subject teachers have had time to demonstrate their ICT skills. I send out a reminder: school tour this a.m. No need to blow up the science laboratory. Do parents really expect to see Bunsen burners these days?

I look around at the tour group. There are twelve people, mostly couples, including two handsome gay men, also a couple. There's one woman in an expensive Chanel suit. I think she might be a grandma but it is impossible to tell these days. Her forehead is rigid. I've learned not to assume anything. When Michael and I did the data analysis on who was paying our fees, we found that a fifth were either entirely paid by grandparents and another 10% of these were making significant contributions. The Grandparents' tea is a new date in our annual calendar. I overruled the initial title: The Vintage Tea. Some of the grandparents are only in their sixties.

We set off on my golden route. Lots of "oohs" an "aghs" as we pass the splendid and vibrant art room and the well-designed modern science laboratories. I avoid the nasty spiral staircase and stick to the royal blue carpeted one. "Feels like a hotel" and "Gosh, it's like a Tardis inside, isn't it?" are the most frequent comments. People are so predictable. I laugh politely. I would have said the same thing in their position. I deliberately end the tour in our twenty-first century, state-of-the-art STEM laboratory. It has literally just opened.

And it's massive. It is our USP for now. I am obliged to mention our sponsors – a leading Biotec company – but none of the parents cares two hoots. They're looking forwards to their coffee and biscuits. I generally refrain from imbibing on these occasions, just in case I drop something down my expensive suit.

I explain the registration procedure; remind everyone that we have a waiting list and escort them back into the Randolph Room where they're greeted with tea, coffee and biscuits from Fortnum & Mason. I ask Linda, our Admissions Registrar, if she's retained the tins. The morning ends well. Lots of parents fill in a registration form and part with the fee of £125. The Chanel suit fills in a form sitting down. I can see now that her ankles are a little swollen and her hands have tiny little age spots. "For my grandson," she says. I smile at her and we shake hands; they're soft and clammy but her handshake is firm, like her forehead.

Friday comes and goes. The vast majority of the teaching staff, even the ones with small children, make it to Jak's bar in South Molton Street. It's this term's new haunt and last term's summer party venue. The DJ was one of our former students. Wayward but fun. South Molton Street is heaving.

I stumble into the house to find Michael slumped on our blue sofa. His navy-blue suit camouflages him well, and I have to switch the light on to see him more clearly. He's visibly upset. I sit next to him and nuzzle myself up against his left shoulder. He admits to making a terrible mistake at work. The firm's best client has sacked him from his account. Everyone in his team is aware of his error: total humiliation. I can't quite believe it. I am married to one of the most capable mathematicians in the country. Michael doesn't make mistakes. Not thus far, anyway. On the other hand, I am not sure I would know. I am no mathematician. Perhaps I should check the spreadsheet he drafted for me after all?

Silence switches into a full-blown crisis of confidence. The last time I saw him in a state was when his parents died.

I look at him. He is trembling and tearful. I am afraid. I tell Michael that we can and will cancel our plans for the weekend. It hasn't been the same since our twins went to Australia for their gap year. I already miss them. *We* miss them. But it's not that. Michael seems a bit depressed. Less organised than usual. Rather confused. Is this a new thing? Perhaps I have missed something. We have all been so busy. I try not to overanalyse him. I will be kind. I won't ask too many questions. Men don't always want to talk about their problems. I know that in the same situation, he would be supportive to me. He's a caring and loyal husband. I must be the kind and loyal wife back.

We don't go to our friends' dinner party in Notting Hill Gate. I was rather looking forwards to it but I hide my disappointment. I have to make up some lame excuse about us both having food poisoning. We venture out to Retsina, the unashamedly *all-things-Greek* restaurant in Belsize Lane; it's literally two minutes from our tiny house. Neither of us eats much. We drink quite a lot instead. We go to bed. Neither of us can fall asleep. I tell Michael not to worry, just as I did Emily earlier this week. He has an excellent reputation. One small mistake isn't going to wreck his career. I spend the next hour reassuring him. He thanks me. He admits to losing control at work. This is out of character for him. I don't probe him further. I wonder whether he should become a consultant: advise rather than work. He doesn't need to work under pressure anymore. We aren't badly off. My parents are well off.

Chapter 2
The Vortex

On Monday morning, Michael appears to be quite cheerful. He isn't visibly depressed at all. I'm relieved. "Thanks, Sophie," he says, quite casually, and we part company at 6.45 a.m. He doesn't call me by my real name very often. He has an embarrassing nickname for me which dates back to when we were eighteen.

I've had the audacity to take the whole weekend off. No emails. No small talk about school. I feel worryingly detached. I enter the staff room to check my pigeon hole for post; take what there is, and make myself a cup of tea. Everyone is talking. I can't quite make out the main topic of conversation but I know that there is one. Abbas and I leave the staff room together conspiratorially and walk to my office. I tell him about Michael. He tells me about his wife.

I return to my office where the end of the queue for the photocopier is occupying my space. I don't comment. I switch on my computer and immediately punch in the password. I've recently had to change it to include weird symbols and numbers to meet the school's security requirements. I have 137 emails. All unread. I swear out loud, much to the amusement of the queue in front of my office. I have been told by a friend-of-a-friend that Highwood School have issued an edict to parents: that under no circumstances should parents expect to receive a reply from staff after 7 pm and before 7 am. In fact, the staff are banned from sending emails in the evenings, unless they're strictly on duty. Neither Liam nor I would ever be able to adhere to it.

There's one email that particularly alarms me; it's entitled "My Resignation" and it's from Jack Baldwin. I never thought he would leave. He has been offered the position of Deputy Head at one of our competitors in town. Damn. He knows all my PR tricks and is bound to actively use them at his new school. I immediately wonder whom he used as his referee. We need to find a replacement for January. My old Principal used to taunt me all the time, saying that English teachers were ten a penny. We will see. Perhaps we should have an internal promotion? But none of the others are committed enough.

I find it extremely difficult to achieve anything today other than just teach. I am anxious about Michael and worried about the twins; the text I received from them was very brief. Teaching is a welcome distraction from my family and also from the demands of management. I'm a natural communicator and a good listener. I'm not one of those teachers who have to go on an ego trip. I think Michael and the twins knocked me off my pedestal years ago. I just love literature and want my pupils to as well. I regret setting homework so early on in the term. Year 7 pupils are *so* keen. I have issued an edict that all subjects (except for maths) must use file paper instead of oversized exercise books. Last year, the two most common reasons for staff absence were neckache and backache. We can no longer expect teachers to lug half a tonne of books around with them. We could all do with being more environmentally friendly: less paper, more electronic attachments.

We are a Central London school. No one can have the luxury of driving in and out. We don't have a playground, let alone a car park. Besides, marking everything in school is unrealistic. Part of me hopes that the whole batch of Year 7's mini-autobiographies will accidentally fall into the recycle bin. Part of me is desperate to read them though; their honesty is so revealing at this age. Last year's Year 7 cohort included several celebrities' children, all of whom admitted to having swanky apartments all over the world.

I text Michael to see how he is faring. He doesn't reply until 3.40 pm and does so somewhat nonchalantly. He appears to have recovered well from Friday's disaster though I suspect this is probably male bravado. After nearly twenty-two years of marriage, I still don't fully understand my husband. I am not sure I need to: we have a mutual misunderstanding of each other; that's how we have lasted.

Once again, Michael is home before I am. He is busy making us a colourful salad. He has meticulously chopped up three different types of lettuce; red onions; cherry tomatoes; baby carrots and mini cucumbers. There's no protein. There's a started bottle of Pinot Grigio on the table and two glasses. There are four sets of cutlery strewn across the work surface. He has forgotten that the twins aren't here. Force of habit, I guess. I sprinkle a few pine nuts onto the salad, add some dressing and we sit down to eat. I put a small basket of bread next to the salad alongside a saucer of olive oil and balsamic vinegar. He asks me why I added the pine nuts. And why have I disturbed him in the kitchen? We have "cooked" together for twenty-years. I appear to have invaded his territory. Michael is normally so mild-mannered. An English gentleman. But this evening, he is different: moody, depressed and rather sarcastic. If my father were sitting here, he would condemn him on the grounds of coming from the Midlands. We sit at the table without talking. It's not pleasant. I miss the camaraderie that we have when the children are here. I don't want to get used to this marked change in our relationship with each other. Something doesn't feel right.

I dread going to bed. I wonder whether to use one of the twins' bedrooms. Michael reappears an hour later. He is drunk. He doesn't know why he's lashing out at people at the office (this is news to me) and he doesn't know why he feels so angry all the time (this is new to him). I ask him if he might lose his job. Tempers flare up. I massively regret the whole conversation. I retreat like a wounded lioness. There was no sign of this distress on our holiday: how can he be so different here? I want the old Michael back and I tell him this.

The next morning, I wake up early as Olivia's bedroom doesn't have blackout blinds like we do. It has only been a few days since she slept in this bed. She has a lovely room. The walls are covered in striking postcards of famous book jackets including *A Clockwork Orange*, *Brighton Rock* and *The Room*, besides many others. She has a small desk under the window; this has a large ceramic bowl on it, full of makeup and cotton wool buds. She also has a noticeboard with silly photographs of herself, mainly posing with friends in photo booths. There's a sweet one of her with her twin, Eddie. I miss him too. He is a foot taller than her. Only her head is visible in the picture whereas his whole torso is. They complement one another. There's a Chinese-style dressing gown hanging from a hook on the back of the door, and a pink old-school hoodie draped on her desk chair. I clutch it and raise it to my nostrils, breathing in her scent. I wish she was back in the UK. I send her a text suggesting when we could Facetime. I resent the time difference.

Within minutes, I creep out of our house like a thief and mount my bicycle which has been repaired by the Bike Fairies. It is nearly light but no one else is up and about. My journey to work is cathartic. Liam (the other Deputy Head) is already at his desk, and invites me into his office. We chat a bit. He doesn't have a partner at the moment though I know that won't last. He is quite attractive. I'm noticeably distracted but try to distance myself from home. It was only one silly argument. I'll apologise later and Michael will too. Everything will return to normal. Liam is updating today's cover; it's an awful job and makes him unpopular. Two members of staff are "off sick". I think it's a bit early for absenteeism. He agrees. We listen to the answering machine in his office. Both the offenders *appear* to have lost their voices; anyone would have thought they had hours to live. The first offender is Tim Brown, a fifty-something maths teacher. The second offender is Alison, our drama teacher. She is only thirty. Between them, there are sixteen lessons to cover. Deputies don't do much of this chore, to be honest, but sometimes we have to. I offer to do Tim's Year 10 maths lesson. Liam raises an arched eyebrow but I insist. Anything is better than teaching drama. I am so busy that I forget about Michael. The feeling appears to be mutual.

Whilst in the maths lesson, I take the opportunity to view Year 10's maths exercise books. The pupils have already worked hard. It's not them that I am unduly worried about. Several pages of x's and y's are strewn across the sheets. But the marking is minimal. I return to Tim's desk and carefully open the top drawers; they're full of the usual things: marker pens; spare pencils; throat sweets; post-it notes; reward slips and punishment slips. We don't even use those anymore. Everything is done on spreadsheets these days. The class is working so conscientiously that I dare myself to open the bottom desk drawer as well; this is locked. I am immediately suspicious though my suspicions may not be warranted. I'm just about to log onto the computer on the desk when the bell rings. I can't believe I have just wasted forty minutes.

There's a bit of sighing and grunting; requests for the lavatory but no one actually moves from their places. They have double maths. I feel for them. It was always my least favourite subject at school. It's ironic that I married Michael. I wait for the second cover teacher to arrive before leaving. It's Emily. As I close the door behind me, I can hear the pupils' disquiet; the scraping of chairs and loud chattering. I hesitate, just for a moment, before returning to my office. I don't want to undermine the young teacher. She will have to find her own way through this. Youth is no excuse. I was more draconian in my twenties than I am now.

I return to my office; it's such a relief to have my own

space. I deal with the usual admin, and see a reminder pop-up from my to do list. I need to send an electronic letter about the forthcoming Harvest Festival. It sounds harsh but I have to dissuade the parents from donating hampers and expensive items placed carefully into fancy wicker baskets. Instead, we respectfully request tins of soup (vegetarian), tins of tuna fish, baked beans, dry pasta, dry spaghetti, dried fruit and cereal without nuts. Even the homeless have allergies. This year, we are collecting for The Passage, a charity in St Vincent's Square. Our students and their parents are generous. I don't know why this surprises me. I telephone our contact at the charity, and ask her to speak in one of our assemblies. She agrees. I follow this up with an email. I am not sure what I will do when these are phased out, if they ever are. I also ask permission for our school to show The Passage on our Twitter account to which she gives her consent. We dare not breathe without it.

I have another double English lesson with my lovely A Level set. We are making quite good progress. I instigate a discussion about dangerous knowledge and ambition. We talk about Prometheus and hubris. The bell sounds for the end of the first lesson and I allow the students to get a coffee from their common room; this is a new concession. I vow never to touch their precious gadget. The SMT recognise that we have to treat the students like undergraduates, otherwise they will vote with their feet and go to a Sixth Form College. There are plenty of good ones from which to choose: MPW and Ashbourne in Kensington or Woodhouse if you live in North London. Before they depart, I hand them each a white and black branded collapsible cup; they graciously accept them. I note their disappointment when they see the school logo.

After double English, I am mindful that I need to pop into Principal Peter's office before his pre-emptive strike on mine. I'm usually on the phone to my mother when he does, so this time, it's my turn to embarrass him. I walk in with two instant coffees swimming about in our new collapsible cups. He smiles at me. I sit down on one of the Victorian chairs (reupholstered in the same fabric as the ones in my office) and place my coffee cup neatly on the coaster placed conspicuously on his partner's desk. It's huge, like him.

We talk about replacing Jack. There's an exchange of ideas including promoting him, trying to persuade him to stay, increasing his salary, enhancing his status. But it's no good. Jack is definitely leaving at the end of this term. We invite Liam into the office; he offers to update the job description and manage the whole process. It is agreed that I will conduct the first interview with Harry-the-Harrovian. We all know – though we can't say – that we need to replace Jack with a woman, and make her the number two in the department. We agree on a fairly short deadline and throw a perk into the mix: this job will come with an additional £1000, provided that the person is willing to take on the School Magazine. Harry-the-Harrovian is no longer interested in doing it. I suspect his resignation will be next. We ought to promote him before this happens. I don't want to lose my job though: how many deputies does a small school need?

We are barely into the second week of term when our first crisis happens.

Fran – the Year 11 Goth pupil – is pregnant. I haven't taught her since Year 7, and apart from sitting next to her in the history lesson that I observed, she has kept herself below my radar. Until now, that is. I immediately look her up on our database. She has just turned sixteen and is, fortunately, *old* for the year. But it takes no mathematician to realise that she must have been fifteen when the great act of passion occurred. I am immediately concerned. *Was she raped? Was the sex consensual? Is the partner at our school? Do her parents know? What should I do? Do I need to contact social services?* Google and I are best friends. I have lost my appetite and immediately feel relieved that my daughter didn't cause me this sort of grief. I am not ready to be a grandma.

I don't want to raise this delicate matter in an email. I walk along the corridor to Principal Peter's office. He is with prospective parents. He acknowledges me with his massive bushy eyebrows and I grimace at him, looking stressed. I return to my office which is slightly smaller than his. His interview with Mr and Mrs Lewis ends rather abruptly. I can hear his heavy stride pounding down the narrow corridor. He's always polite. Principal Peter shows the couple to the door, and shakes their hands enthusiastically, cupping his left hand over the right hand, Bill Clinton-style. The double handshake. It seems to work. "Such a warm guy," they say, "So different from what I expected," and "Didn't expect an American Principal." As I said, he's Canadian.

I have quite a busy day ahead with plenty of lessons, despite being on half a timetable. It's par for the course: multi-tasking, that is. Fran has become my priority and this time; her problem really does fall within my remit. Peter advises me to "extract" her from the science lesson. I do what he suggests. I scrutinise her. I can see a small bump protruding over her black school trousers; she has tried, quite successfully until now, to conceal it using the oversized jumper which is probably her father's. She looks at me as if to question my authority. I adopt a matter-of-fact tone and bluntly ask her whether the sex was consensual. I am relieved to find that it was. She is five months' pregnant. The baby is due in January when she should be doing her mocks. It's all relative, I suppose.

We decide to support Fran. I ask her who the father of the child is and straight away she tells me it is Freddie, the student who scraped into the Sixth Form. Freddie is mixed race and so is Fran. His father is Nigerian. His mother is from Suffolk. I have never met Fran's father but her mother looks like me. Will she want to proceed with her GCSEs? She looks at me as if I have asked her the most ridiculous question. And, of course, her mother *is* aware that she's pregnant. They share a flat in Bayswater, West London. I feel a bit of an idiot and decide to tell the rest of the staff, before the rumour-mill lands one of the male teachers into hot water. I feel a bit disloyal. Issues pertaining to safeguarding prevail.

I am resolved to get as much done as I can before lunch. I would really be quite happy to eat a sandwich or a little tray of sushi at my desk but Principal Peter insists that we mix with the rest of the staff. And the new staff canteen was very expensive to build. We are all told to use it. I telephone Fran's mother, Dr Enderby. She's a psychiatrist at the Tavistock. I remember this because I bumped into her a few times whilst doing my evening course there. She apologises for not alerting me and claims that Fran only admitted to being pregnant over the weekend. And what a lovely weekend it was! We discuss what we're going to do to support Fran. Obviously, she can't take her mocks with her peers. The timing won't work. We suggest that she sits them early. Dr Enderby has already phoned an agency and booked a maternity nurse and a home-help. She isn't ready to be a grandmother either. She is the same age as me: forty-nine.

I am bursting with information: new and old. I decide that having lunch with others will be a good thing and besides, I am now ravenous. I choose the tomato and basil soup, and take a piece of bruschetta to go with it. I sit with Abbas, who is sampling the vegetarian curry, and Annie (the Art teacher) who is on another diet. She's eating an apple, very slowly. She takes out her mobile and opens up the gallery. She shows us a picture of the coffee pod installation she's making out of our recycled products here; we tell her it's amazing. Funny how some adults still need so much reassurance and praise. She's a typical-looking art teacher: all beads and ethnic jewellery, nothing like me. I can't remember how old Annie is. She has barely changed in the eight years she has been here. I realise that I know very little about her. Luckily, Abbas is the font of all knowledge. He tells me that she is going through a nasty divorce. Can a divorce ever be nice?

I decide to leave work quite early today; it's 5 pm Liam

isn't even here. Principal Peter is still in his office – pretending to do some work – and the staff room is empty. The army of cleaners has arrived. I only know one by name; that's Margaret. She's lovely. I am amazed to discover that she has five children aged between four and seventeen. She works three nightshifts a week at St Mary's Hospital in Paddington. I am full of admiration.

I am feeling quite weak, despite lunch, and can't face cycling home. I decide to browse around the shops near Bond Street tube station and pop into Zara to buy some clothes. I'm an impulse shopper. Always have been. I never bother to return anything, even though I make quite a lot of mistakes. Margaret benefits from them, at least. Either that, or she sells them on.

The atmosphere between Michael and I isn't congenial at the moment. I am annoyed with myself but find it hard to forgive his recent outbursts. He has become increasingly irritated at the slightest thing. I put it down to stress. Although I don't feel like cooking, I do so, and this time, make a chicken stir fry with all his favourite vegetables. I marinate everything and put the bowl of food back into our undersized fridge. It's just about all right for the two of us; it was pretty desperate when the twins were here. I have no idea when Michael will be home. We normally text each other several times a day but today we haven't exchanged a single word.

We have lived together for a long time; and during that while, I have never been through his pockets, other than to check for items before taking his suits to the drycleaners. I have never suspected him of having an affair. Our relationship has always been built on mutual trust. We respect each other's space. But this evening, curiosity has got the better of me. Perhaps it was Tim's locked drawer at work that has aroused my suspicions. Perhaps I have a taste for detective work: I am a compulsive reader of thrillers. I start with his bedside drawer. There is nothing interesting in it: aspirin, a started box of Rennie (minty), a ballpoint pen, a few small golf pencils, an unopened packet of Durex and little bookmark made by Olivia, aged 9. I open the second drawer down. I don't know what I am doing. I don't know what I hope to achieve by snooping. I am disgusted with myself. Again, there's nothing interesting in there and I return to the kitchen and lay the table. I decide to make a salad whilst listening to The Archers. I have no idea what's going on. I'm just relieved that Rob Titchener has been written out of the script; listening to how he controlled his wife, Helen, had me shouting at the radio. I don't know why she stayed with him for so long. There are still no texts from Michael. I realise that I shouldn't take him for granted.

I return upstairs to our bedroom; it faces the mews. I take a cursory look out of the window. No one is around. I close the white and blue curtains, casually, and decide to look in Michael's suit cupboard. His suits are arranged from black to grey to navy. He's much neater than I am. Only my books are in alphabetical order and he knows better than to mess about with my vast collection. I decide to approach the pockets methodically, moving swiftly from his fifty shades of corporate to his more casual clothes. The grey suit hasn't even been worn yet. The pockets are still sewn up. I'm about to give up when I reach the navy suit; it's his favourite. There's nothing in the main pockets but there's a small bulge coming out of the inside one. There's a wallet with ten pounds in it; two business cards; a photograph of the twins and even one of me. It's about fifteen years' old. I am touched that he has kept it all this time. I look much younger. I feel a pang of guilt and carefully stuff the wallet back into his hiding place. I can hear the sound of the key in the lock. Michael is home.

We sit down and have dinner. It's civilised without being warm. I apologise first. I tell him about Fran and Freddie. He makes a stupid comment about my school being synonymous with EastEnders. The last time I watched it, Dirty Den "Done it" and I tried to justify my viewing by equating the sleaze-ball with a character from Dickens: a cross between

Magwitch and Fagin. We only watch Danish-cum-Swedish thrillers these days. And *Endeavour*, of course.

Michael offers to do the washing up and I accept. He's always been very domesticated. I don't take this for granted. I still feel very preoccupied about Fran. I phone my mother for some guidance. She is full of advice but it's not what I want to hear. We are generations apart. My mother (Sheila) asks me if things are all right at home and whether I have heard from the twins. I only talk about them. I'm not prepared to discuss the highs and lows of my marriage this evening. Eventually, Michael takes a long shower; changes into his blue dressing gown and slumps in front of the television. We watch the news. There's only one topic of conversation: the aftermath of Brexit.

He asks me if I am going to return to our bedroom and I do. I close Olivia's bedroom door by way of confirming this. It's a slippery slope, not one I intend sliding down. I am convinced that Michael isn't having an affair. And I know that I am not having one either. We make up and all is well. His bedside drawers remain firmly shut though.

In the morning, we kiss and I'm worried that he will make me late. It's all right for him. He's the King Pin in his office. And most of his client meetings don't start until 10 am or they're held over expensive lunches in wine bars or swanky watering holes in the city. I am usually dealing with my third crisis by then. I feel much more at ease now and promise myself that I won't be rummaging through his drawers or jacket pockets again. We are both too good for that. I vow not to stoop so low again. At least I got away with it once.

I decide to pay Tim (the maths teacher with the sore throat) a visit. He apologises for yesterday's absence. I don't hold grudges. I see the pile of red exercise books on his table; they're all open on the correct page, waiting for the intervention of his red pen. I am interrupting his marking time and feel a sense of power and guilt all rolled into one. Tim's absenteeism last year was a cause for concern. He was given a verbal warning. But maths teachers – particularly good ones – are hard to find, so we haven't taken matters further. As I'm about to leave, I notice that here's a small key in the bottom drawer of his desk, the one I wanted to open whilst covering his dreary lesson. He sees me looking at it, and pushes the drawer closed with his polished black shoe. I should mind my own business.

I return to my office and look at my schedule. I have a very busy day: several lessons, two meetings, a staff meeting, one interview and some Oxbridge references to write. It's all go. I'm feeling restless though so I decide to walk down to Robert Dyas, the hardware shop, in my free period. It takes me much longer than I expected and I find myself grabbing one of those Lime bicycles to get myself back to school on time for Year 9. The seat is uncomfortably high; I am too inept to lower it. I really don't want to be late for that riotous class. I have bought myself a small, shiny red fridge; it can hold up to four cans of Diet Coke or two cans, an apple and a yoghurt. I am pleased with my purchase and plug it in straight away. It's conspicuously noisy, much to my horror. I bang the top of it – the way we used bash the old hired television – and it quietens down immediately.

I am about to teach Year 9 when my mobile buzzes in my jacket pocket; it's Michael. I feel surprisingly anxious. Year 9 are waiting for me to walk in. I step into the classroom and confidently instruct the pupils to start reading Chapter 3 of *To Kill a Mockingbird*. I know this is a waste of time as they will have to re-read it all with me when I'm back in the classroom. *Phone me asap. Got a problem.* I can't, of course, but I text him straight back, saying that I will be in touch in forty minutes. Year 9 can't wait. I engineer a discussion about Scout's first experience at school; how she beats up Walter Cunningham and also focus on the role of Calpurnia, the black housemaid. I am mindful that we have two black pupils in the class and don't want to offend either of them. I set a very simple homework. I even award them two house points each. I slightly regret this momentous act of generosity as it involves logging into a spreadsheet; it's called *Rewards* and is not to be muddled up with *Punishments*. On a previous occasion – when the screen was linked to the interactive whiteboard – I accidentally gave Freddie a demerit for smoking cannabis. His mother was outraged. His father was amused.

I dash to my office and phone Michael. It goes straight to voicemail. I leave him a curt but polite message and switch my phone back onto silent. I have to interview a prospective teacher of English now. Harry-the-Harrovian has appeared, just in time, and the two of us confer before inviting the first of the three shortlisted candidates to come in. Two are women and one is a man. The first one, a woman, is very strange. She has squeezed herself into a navy dress; has unkempt hair and her shoes need re-heeling. Harry doesn't warm to her either. Her interview is very short to the point of rudeness. Next, we interview the only male candidate. He has an impressive application but his manner synonymous with a ring master; his banter is excessive to the point of irritation and his three-piece suit is pretentious. Neither Harry nor I consider him a contender which makes it easier for us to reject him. Finally, we meet the third candidate. Her name is Samantha Fox – not the buxom model from the tabloids– and she's ideal. We spend a disproportionate amount of time discussing literature; the AQA syllabus; her style of teaching and how she differentiates when the classes aren't in sets. Her answers are straight from a textbook. I ask her whether she is prepared to take on the School Magazine; no one else in the department is foolish enough to agree to it two years running. I might as well hold a pistol to her head. She agrees. Harry-the-Harrovian comments on her sleek black dress and her high heels. I remark on her suitability for the department. We invite her back for a second interview on Friday. She will also need to teach a lesson. I decide to give her my Lower Sixth as she has taught *Frankenstein* before. I'm considerate that way.

After the interview, I try calling Michael again; it still goes straight to voicemail so I have to give up. I need to allocate some time to our four Oxbridge students, all of whom are worthy candidates this year. I take the time to read through their personal statements and try to extrapolate any anomalies or oversights. I can only find one. I sort through the Oxbridge references in my inbox and print them out. I find it hard to use my screen the whole time. I am conscious that my recycling bin is almost full. Other people's bins are almost empty. One of my students is applying to read Maths at Oxford. This is an extract from her personal statement:

UKMT Olympiads served as an introduction to sophisticated problem-solving and taught me to link distinct areas of the mathematical realm. The second time I competed in the British Mathematical Olympiad, when participating in BMO2, I had to prove that a real-to-real functional equation was a polynomial, and, further, that it was linear. Here, my knowledge of bijective and surjective functions enabled me to make significant progress.

I feel a complete fraud. I have little concept of what she's talking about but know that it's erudite. I extrapolate what I can from the various teachers' references and make the whole thing sound like it's from me. I add a note in my calendar on my mobile: buy croissants for the Oxbridge meeting.

I have back-to-back meetings with parents of existing pupils and also with two members of staff. Nothing sensational. I sit back in my swivel chair and relax. I open my new miniature fridge and remove a very cold Diet Coke; it tastes so good. I look at my mobile under the desk. There are three missed calls from Michael. I immediately phone him back. We finally talk. It transpires that he has made another mistake. I am beginning to think that I should check the spreadsheet he prepared for me, otherwise the Governors will think that I am incompetent and suffer from dyscalculia. But Michael doesn't make mistakes, not significant ones. Neither of us can believe it. Previously he was so defensive when I tried to intervene that this time I listen and nod. He is anxious that his job is at risk. He has been at his firm for over twenty-years and has a remarkable track record. I'm no employment lawyer but I suspect he will be due a decent pay-off. I start having visions of an early-retirement and holidays in the Seychelles. A bell rings and I am sharply brought back to reality.

I'm itching to go home but I have one more meeting at 4.30 pm It's with Dr Enderby, Fran's mother. I'm dreading it. She tells me that Fran has recently become very religious; she's a born-again Christian, and that Freddie (the sperm donor in this case) has too. I'm completely shocked. Don't observant Christians desist from anything below the waist? I wonder how long this phase will last.

Fran's mother talks a great deal for someone whose pro-fession is mainly listening. I think she finds it liberating. She notices my unfinished Diet Coke and gives me a slightly dis-approving look. I feel about ten. The psychiatrist – mother – soon to be grandma, requests a great quantity of homework; past papers; revision packs and a list of all her daughter's teachers' emails so that she can liaise with them directly. I feel as though I am part of a police investigation. I readily concede to all her demands.

I am anxious to return home and talk to Michael face-to-face. I don't want him to do anything rash or stupid. People do. I can see from my Life360 that Michael is already home. It's beginning to be become a habit.

October

It's nearly half-term and the twins have been away for five weeks. We have received countless messages since they arrived in Queensland – a contrast to the beginning of their adventure in Sydney. I am delighted to see so many pictures of both Olivia and Eddie. They're mostly with other young people, none of whom I recognise.

It will be half-term soon. I can't wait. We seem to lurch from one catastrophe to another at Bond Street School.

Jeremy-cum-Joanna is having a personal crisis. S/he isn't convinced that she's in the wrong body anymore and regrets cutting off her hair. I try to be sympathetic but I am not sure what the right reaction should be. I offer Jeremy three complimentary sessions with the School Counsellor. Kris, however, has started hormone treatment and is receiving counselling. Jake – the gender fluid child – has joined a Transgender Group for Teenagers. I am a bit alarmed about this and fear that he will be on hormone blockers before the end of term. I am neither in favour nor anti trans people. I just think thirteen is too young to make a lifelong decision. I am not alone in this.

My main concern today is Fran. Her waist has disappeared and the rumour mill has circulated the news: she's pregnant. She is taunted, regularly, and sadly very few of the pupils seem to appreciate that carrying a baby is a huge responsibility for a sixteen-year-old girl, let alone an adult. She can't even vote yet. I find her at break time and invite her into my office. I offer her a glass of water, in a real glass, not a horrible paper cup. She's going to be a mother, after all. I ask her a few questions about her pregnancy – insofar as I can – and I tell her about mine, albeit many years ago. I try to imagine Dr Enderby's face in the hospital ward. I can't. I ask Fran if she wants to stay in the Sixth Form and, to my surprise, she does. I reassure that we will do everything we can to accommodate her. She's very pale. I tell myself that her dyed black hair makes her look anaemic but then wonder whether she is. I send her back to her lessons and decide to email Fran's mother. She fobs me off with a hasty email (she's with a patient, so can't send a more detailed one) and tells me to concentrate on Fran's academic work, not her personal health. I feel a bit affronted. I was trying to treat Fran as if she were my own daughter. She isn't. And I won't. Note to self: stay professional.

It seems ages since we were reclining and relaxing in the Croatian sunshine. Michael and I have just about come to terms with living as a couple, like we did before the twins. It's a major adjustment. I tell myself that it's for five months. It's not permanent. We don't know what to talk about other than our work. It's grim. He is still wandering around the house like a wounded puppy. He cries quite a lot too but he doesn't know why. We still have a loving marriage but I am not hopeful. We spend less and less time being intimate.

Whilst at work, Michael is busy and focused. But at home, he can't concentrate on anything, not even the television. He is restless to the point of being irritating. I suggest he takes up running. We both should. But I would never be able to keep up with him; his stride is double that of mine. He has decided to leave his firm. Twenty years is enough. I am very troubled by this. It would be better if he were made redundant. I urge him to hold on. Think of the redundancy package. We aren't mortgage free yet, and we still have to fund the twins through university. I love Michael but he is stubborn. He is a kind man but occasionally I feel he throws his intellectual weight around. He knows that I cannot compete with his mental agility and that I do not understand the complex nature of his work. In contrast, he thinks he knows plenty about mine. Everybody does, of course. Everyone has been to school.

Another week passes by and we celebrate the Harvest Festival at school though the majority of pupils tell me that Halloween is more important to them. I sympathise. Halloween was always a big deal in our house. I have a very lengthy parents' evening at school and don't manage to leave until 9 pm. I am always the last to finish. Most of the parents are easy to talk to and appreciate my input. Freddie's father is charming but his aftershave is overpowered by the distinct odour of marijuana. He erroneously thinks I am too square to recognise it. I am not.

I finally leave the building just after 9.15 pm. Mercifully, there is very little traffic. This is the ideal time to cycle home. All the lights are blazing. Michael is hunting for his passport.

41

I ask him if he's going on a business trip. I am sure that he isn't. He looks confused. I notice that he is unshaven and he is wearing odd socks. He admits that he quit his job today, totally against my advice, and is apparently going to Rome for a three-day break. He will look for a new job after that. For the first time in twenty years, I feel that he has let me down. And that his behaviour is selfish. What with Brexit and all the instability, I find it almost incomprehensible that an actuary doesn't bother to assess the risk factor of being unemployed this year. And yet, the truth is, I am not sure if he is genuinely capable of holding down any job, let alone a high powered one. But despite this feeling, I resent him for giving up. Michael knows that I totally disapprove of his self-inflicted jaunt. There is something childish about his expression. He looks crestfallen and hurt. I am not sure what I have done to offend him. I wrap my arms around his neck and shoulders and kiss him, gently. I suppose it must have been unbearable for him. He immediately responds with caresses and cuddles; it's like the old days. Just for a moment. But the passport hunt rears its ugly head again. He won't rest until he has found it. I take it out of his desk drawer and hand it to him. I tell him that it would be nice to go to Rome together but for some bizarre reason, he has to go now and can't wait. He has already booked a ticket online. He leaves tomorrow. Apparently, *he* is on half-term.

I have been so wrapped up in other people's problems, particularly those of my pupils', that I have failed to give Michael the attention he deserves and needs. He has been a faithful and generous husband for more than twenty years. And a good father too. Until recently, he was well liked at the office, and much respected. I am beginning to think that there is something wrong with him and that it's not depression. I decide to make him an appointment with our GP. Michael says the appointment is something to look forward to when he returns from Rome. At least he still has a sense of humour.

He leaves the next morning. Suddenly I am bereft of both my children and my husband. I am not sure if I deserve this. I try to bury myself in my work; this is what I usually do. Sometimes the work buries me. Everyone at school is worn-out. It has been a long six weeks. Most teachers have broken the back of the syllabus; half-term tests have been set and marked; parents' evenings and induction afternoons have come and gone. Fran is looking huge – I wonder if she is expecting twins – and no one has been suspended for drug offences.

It's Friday and half-term is nearly upon us. There is talk of going to Jak's Bar later but I decline. Michael should be coming back tonight. I am wondering whether I should plan a romantic weekend away together. Something spontaneous. I decide to look into this: a castle maybe? I log onto TripAdvisor and read some reviews. I also re-read my own. I have 147 followers. I don't think this is much. Peter is gesturing to me through the glass panel of my office door. I quickly switch the screen to my emails. The enormous man looks agitated. Something has happened in the Art Studio. It's Fran. She has fainted, fallen off the stool and landed awkwardly. The ambulance and her mother have been called in that order.

There are twelve First Aiders in our school but I have the most experience, first and second hand. Besides, half the staff aren't much older than my children. I rush up to the Art Studio. Fran is lying on her back with her bump protruding over her unbuttoned trousers. We all fear the worst. There is a small pool of blood. I immediately establish that the blood has come from her head, and not the baby or babies. It's a very small cut. Someone fetches the First Aid kit off the wall; it's above the sink, and I press down on the open wound with a white pad. The blood seeps through and makes a perfect red spot; it's like the rising sun on the Japanese flag. I enlist the help of Annie (the art teacher) to help me roll Fran into the recovery position. She's breathing quietly. She doesn't respond to us verbally but she squeezes my hand. I know she's conscious.

Within minutes, two jovial paramedics arrive. It's obvious that they're highly experienced which inspires everyone's confidence in them. They check her vitals; go through the same routine that I did, and Fran responds to them with a weak reply. They easily lift the Year 11 pupil onto a stretcher and cover her with a thin red blanket. She is ushered into the school lift and blue-lighted to University College Hospital (UCLH). It is not my first visit to UCLH nor will it be my last. I am not sure whether to hold Fran's hand or not. The female paramedic suggests that I do whilst she places an oxygen mask over her patient. Fran is so pale. I'm surprised her blood isn't white. She has a very flat nose – I had never noticed it before – and I wonder whether this has impeded her breathing.

Dr Enderby (Fran's mother) arrives. She is understandably flustered. And annoyed that she has had to leave her conference. I am slightly agog at this and wonder what her priorities are. As soon as the doctor gives Fran the "all clear" – though some additional tests are suggested – I feel that I can leave. I give Fran a reassuring smile. Dr Enderby looks a bit jealous of our rapport.

Back at school, there is only one conversation. I tell the teachers to bring all their Year 11 pupils into the hall, fifteen minutes before the end of their lessons. A few additional and curious staff appear at the back– even though they don't teach Year 11 – and some of them don't even know Fran, but they're concerned for her welfare. I update everyone. I hate false rumours. There's a sigh of relief all round. We are a small community. Everyone knows everyone else's business; and if they don't, they think that they do. That's small independent schools for you. If you want to be anonymous, work in an academy comprising two thousand pupils. One day, I might just do that.

Half-term officially begins at 4 pm today. There's much

talk of holidays abroad; long weekends; sleepovers and hanging out with friends. I tidy up my office; switch off my computer and go home. I make contact with both Olivia and Eddie. I needn't feel concerned. They're having the time of their lives. I enjoy looking at their pictures on WhatsApp. Eddie has let his hair grow a bit wild. Olivia is looking blonder and browner. I'm pleased to see that neither of them has acquired an ugly tattoo that they might later regret.

I'm not really sure what to do with myself. I find a copy of Michael's itinerary on our kitchen fridge; he's stuck it down with blue tack instead of a magnet. He will be flying into Heathrow at 7.55 pm I briefly wonder whether I should meet him at the airport. I'm too tired so I don't. Instead, I switch on the television. *Pointless* is on. I don't' know what the point is as I've never watched it. I'm never home alone this early in term time.

I feel restless and decide to have a bath even though my ride home doesn't exactly bring me out in a sweat. I light candles and place them precariously around the edge; pour in copious amounts of Radox and luxuriate in my surroundings: paradise. I have Radio 4 for company. My mobile buzzes offensively; it has a horrible sense of urgency about it. I have to get out of the bath to answer it, just in case it's Michael. It isn't. It's a cold call. I'm awfully rude to the woman on the other end of the line. I tell her that I have **not** had a stupid accident and I **don't** have whiplash. I tell the caller to "get a life" and add a few expletives whilst in the process. I am not proud of myself. I block the number. I step back into the bath, looking forwards to luxuriating once more, but the experience is no longer enjoyable. The water is barely lukewarm.

I put Michael's blue bathrobe on instead of mine; it makes me feel closer to him. I am a romantic, really, beneath my hard carapace. I retrieve my slippers from under our bed and find various unexpected objects and papers. There's a small carriage clock with the battery missing; an old copy of the *Observer*; a buff coloured file containing random documents and our wedding album. I obviously don't look under our bed very often. The wedding album is quite dusty and doesn't look as though it has been opened in a while. I lie on our bed and open each leaf carefully. It was a lovely wedding. Simple but profound. I wore white. I didn't look like a meringue. We had two little bridesmaids, both of whom wore white with turquoise sashes. Nothing too fancy. My whole family came. None of Michael's did. He only has one brother, and he lives in an institution somewhere in Newcastle. He chooses not to talk about Ian. And Ian is incapable of talking about him. We have been together since we were nineteen and married for over twenty years and yet I know so little about Michael's family. His parents died in a car crash when we were at university. I barely knew them. There's no "history". No heart attacks. No strokes. No cancer. Nothing. They were too young.

I look at the photographs of our friends; they were all from university. It's not quite *Four Weddings and a Funeral*. No Duckface. No Hugh Grant. But the clothes are similar and the church is nearly as pretty. We had lovely flowers. I spend ages reminiscing and probably doze off as it's 11 pm when I hear the news pips coming from our bathroom. Boris Johnson has prorogued parliament. We have all learned a new word. I carefully return our wedding album to its new resting place, and wash my hands. Michael still isn't home. No missed calls or messages on either my mobile or our landline.

Instead of calling the police, I visit my next-door neighbour, Matt. He's a writer and spends huge amounts of time sitting at his computer at home. He has a small white dog – a Shih Tzu – which is as fluffy as it is yappy. I ask him if he has seen Michael. He invites me into his mews house which is identical to ours only the mirror image. He lives there on his own. I am so tired that I gratefully take up his offer of a drink. I move a stack of magazines and old books off the armchair and place them carefully onto the rug near my feet. I didn't know a single person could make so much chaos. He sees me examining the room and is immediately rather defensive. Apparently, it's a creative mess; helps his juices flow; it isn't normally this bad. I apologise for appearing to be judgemental. I'm just concerned, that's all. Worried about Michael's whereabouts. He's gone on some mystery tour around Rome. As I say it, I know that it sounds ridiculous. I'm worrying about a forty-nine-year old man who is probably having a mid-life crisis. Why didn't I think of that?

I return to our empty little house and brush off the dog hair that has attached itself to my clothes. I open the fridge and start preparing something for supper. I prepare for the two of us. Whilst I'm listening to the radio and chopping up vegetables, I receive a phone call from the police station at Heathrow Airport. My breathing quickens. The phone call is not prefaced with "There's nothing to worry about" or anything like that. Sergeant Jameson establishes that he is talking to Sophie Boswell (that's me) and that I live at 12 Daleham Gardens Mews, NW3 etc. I concur. My heart is still beating too fast. I am immediately worried that Michael has been attacked. Perhaps he has provoked someone? He has been acting rather strangely lately.

I am wrong. *He* hasn't been attacked. It is rather worse than that. He has been arrested for indecent exposure. I am flabbergasted. Michael is being held at Heathrow Airport Police Station. The Sergeant gives me the precise address: Unit 3, Polar Park, Bath Road, UB7 ODG. He has to repeat it three times. He explains to me that Michael was "under the influence of alcohol" and admitted assaulting the woman before exposing himself. The Sergeant speaks to me as if English is my second language. Now that he has sobered up a little, Michael is suitably contrite, ashamed and embarrassed. I offer to pay the bail tonight but Sergeant Jameson is inflexible. I have to collect my husband tomorrow. He thinks he should stew overnight, like a casserole.

Despite having the bed to myself – the whole house in fact

– I hardly sleep at all. I ignore two phone calls from Olivia and one from Eddie. I can't lie to them. I text them to say that I will definitely call later. I try not to alarm them. I dress fairly conservatively as I know that I will be judged on arrival. I wear dark jeans; a navy jumper; a white shirt and very little jewellery. Nothing ostentatious. I wear ankle boots rather than trainers. I take an Uber from our house all the way to Bath Road; it's nothing like Bath, unfortunately. It's very industrial. I still haven't got used to not paying the driver. My Uber account tells me that the journey cost £48. I can see a long line of miserable looking people, hanging around the Police Station. Wives, mostly. They're all smoking.

As I enter, a very junior looking Police Constable takes down my details. He asks me to hand in my mobile and any sharp objects. I don't think he wants me to produce my manicure set or my emery board but I do. I have never been to a police station before. I empty out the contents of my handbag until the young constable is satisfied. He admires my Mont Blanc fountain pen. After a few minutes, the same young constable escorts me to Michael's cell: number 3. I am immediately struck by how bright it is. But not in a good way. There's something harsh about the light. The walls have been tiled in small creamy coloured squares. There's a large and heavily barred window that not even Peter-the-Principal could reach and a bed-cum-bench arrangement with a very thin plastic blue mattress on it. There's also a metal toilet. I can't see a wash basin or any loo paper. The cell is clean but characterless; clinical but cruel. There's a lot of shouting and bawling on either side of Michael's cell. He can no longer hear it; it must have been going on all night. It has become white noise to him.

Michael stands up as soon as he sees me. He looks dishevelled: a broken man. I don't say anything. I just embrace him and he envelops me like an eagle caressing its prey. We don't need to talk. We have permission to leave but our feet are rooted to the linoleum floor. After what seems like hours but is really only minutes, we collect our things from the Duty Sergeant. Mine are stacked neatly on a black tray. Michael's are stuffed into a brown jiffy bag. He also has a small black rucksack with him; I presume this has his clothes and wash-bag inside. I notice that his eyes are welling up and I can see that if I don't get him out of here soon, he will cry uncontrol-lably, just like he did a few weeks ago.

I pay the exorbitant bail: £750. The Sergeant won't let me leave until this transaction has been fully processed. I order another Uber and tell Michael not to say anything until we are at least two miles away from the Police Station. The Uber driver is Algerian and his English is limited. We feel able to talk and do so. The worst thing for Michael was having nothing to do, nothing to read, nothing to watch, nought to focus on other than four sour walls and a metal toilet. He has no wish to tell me about the assault. Or the indecent expo-sure. I don't press him but I hope to extract the information from him eventually. Offenders usually feel the urge to con-fess; I know this from school. Everyone has to tell someone. Michael might as well talk to me. Seven hundred and fifty pounds is practically two weeks' pay for me. I have decided that he's clinically depressed and no longer in control of his sanity. I tell Michael that we need to bring his appointment with the GP forward. He doesn't argue with me. He offers to reimburse me for the Ubers and the bail: out of the joint account. It's almost funny.

Now that we are home, I feel that I can phone the twins except that it's too late. I send them both a text and insist that we speak whenever they want to, even if it's 3 am in the UK. I just want to hear their voices. I've rehearsed a story with Michael and I write down the key points onto square yellow post-it notes. His short-term memory isn't what it used to be. I am struggling to come to terms with the change in his behaviour and personality. He seemed so normal last summer.

Michael hasn't washed in days and his smell is becoming

more of a stench. I run a bath for him – even though he prefers showers – and add bubble bath so that the room doesn't smell of him, Rome or the police cell. I'm not convinced he even got to Rome. He hasn't mentioned a word about it. It is as if he is living in a virtual world and I am not in it.

After his bath and a shave, which he doesn't do precisely, Michael reappears dressed from head-to-toe in Eddie's clothes. They don't fit him properly and make him look fatter than he is. He sees my expression and runs back to the bathroom to cover himself up with his blue towelling robe. He looks even more ridiculous now. I offer to help him shave as his hands are trembling. I hope I'm not making him feel insecure in his own home. It's as if he's in a vortex, spiralling out of control. Although it's Saturday, Daleham Health Centre is open and the receptionist takes my call. I tell her that I need an urgent appointment for my husband. Today, if possible. I'm too late, because the surgery is about to close; however, she will give Michael an appointment at 11 am on Monday. She is clear that this is a very good offer. I immediately accept it.

I feel it's only fair to inform Matt-the-neighbour, that Michael is home. I tell Michael to stay on the sofa and watch the news. He seems very out of touch for a man that has only been out of work for a week. I ring Matt's doorbell and almost fall into his hall-cum-sitting room. I'm a bit suspicious and think he might have been eavesdropping on our conversation. After all, he is a writer. God knows what he might put in his next book. He clears his throat and perches on a barstool. Matt's face is unshaven. The grey stubble is not unattractive. He has something to tell me. And I am not going to like it. Before he speaks, I explain that I am feeling quite fragile. I can see that he finds this hard to believe. He thinks I am always in control; this could not be further from the truth.

Matt drops a bombshell. He thinks Michael is gay. I immediately dismiss this as rubbish. I have known Michael for thirty-one years and in all that time, he hasn't even looked at a man in that way. I am so annoyed that I appear to be homophobic. I am not. He tells me that my response is "telling" and that I should be ashamed to call myself a Deputy Head. I can't see what this has got to do with him. I am so angry. I walk out of his house and straight into mine. Michael is drinking water out of a large coffee cup. I snuggle up next to him and cry into his chest. I feel safe in his care. I am no longer his gaoler.

The whole week has taken its toll on me. I have been desperate to talk to someone about what's going on at school; the problems with Fran; the stresses and strains of monitoring all the staff and pupils. But sadly, I am starting to fear for Michael and for myself. We don't seem to talk anymore. He is loving and kind one morning and angry and volatile the next; it's no way to sustain a marriage. We used to talk about everything and now we talk about nothing. We just cry all the time.

I cannot wait until Monday morning. Thank God it's half-term.

Chapter 3
Half-Term

I have never looked forward to a Monday morning with so much apprehension and trepidation. And it's half-term. It's fairly mild outside but the rain is teeming down like tears. The Google doctor has given me a diagnosis for Michael's condition but I can't bring myself to repeat it. I want the real doctor to diagnose him. Not me. Michael appears in the kitchen looking relatively normal. He's wearing a blue tailored shirt and his navy suit trousers. He looks professional and respectable. I tell him this. We eat breakfast: porridge and raspberries. I regret the porridge as it sits heavily on my stomach. We gulp down mugs of tea and brush our teeth. Michael needs a surprising amount of prompting even for the most basic tasks. I still can't quite get my head around this. His deterioration has been rapid.

We have plenty of time before the appointment. I suggest we walk down to Roni's café in Belsize Lane. We normally reserve this treat for Sundays and read the papers cover-to-cover. Michael is remarkably acquiescent this morning. We stroll down to the village; it's so pretty and quaint. The café is swarming with people. Doesn't anyone work these days? I buy two coffees – which neither of us needs – and we take the *Guardian* off the newspaper rack and split it up between us. There's an amusing caricature of Boris Johnson on page 5. We talk about what's going on in the news; which year it is and everything that's current. I know that I am prepping Michael and I absolutely shouldn't be doing this. I am in denial. The café is full of women. Michael is outnumbered. Not that this bothers him in the least. As I said, he's totally uninhibited.

It's ten past ten. Unexpectedly we are having to run to the doctor's surgery. I can barely keep up with Michael's long legs. We arrive, slightly out of breath, even though it's not exactly a marathon in distance, and we sit in the reception. There are stacks of magazines to read; a large goldfish tank with carp in it and plenty of patients. All of them are either elderly or pregnant.

The receptionist calls Michael's name. Michael Boswell? and says it as though it were a question. My friends used to say that I only married him for his surname. They were so jealous. We make our way to Dr Blackstone's door; it has his name on it. He's not our regular doctor. He is looks too young to be in General Practice. Or perhaps he has sold out before he has really started? He is taller than me but shorter than Michael. He is boyishly slim. He's wearing a white shirt, no tie, a burgundy cashmere jersey and jeans. Doctors are so casual these days. He invites us to sit down but speaks directly to Michael. I am determined not to be a backseat driver in this appointment.

The doctor starts with a few simple questions about Michael's health; his workload, whether he is stressed, sleep-deprived, any changes in his blood pressure, eating habits, relationships and mood swings. Michael answers all his questions succinctly. He explains the mistakes he has made at work, and how these are totally out of character. Dr Blackstone nods reassuringly and tells us that everyone is human. I hope this doesn't mean he is going to make a mistake too. He takes Michael's blood pressure; it's much higher than usual, and he feels for his pulse. He can't immediately find it but perseveres.

At the end of what feels like an interview, the young doctor writes out a prescription and tells Michael that he is suffering from Major Depressive Disorder (MDD). In layman's term: depression. There's nothing to worry about. It's completely normal to be going through a mid-life crisis before you reach your fiftieth birthday. He notes that Michael's birthday is on the 1st January. Dr Blackstone can't be more than thirty. At this point, I want to intervene. I ask him if he's absolutely sure of his diagnosis. He says he's 100%. Michael has all the classic symptoms: low self-esteem, loss of appetite, sleep deprivation and low energy. Part of me is relieved. The other part disappointed. I know that there is more to Michael's erratic behaviour than this. He writes out a prescription for Fluoxetine (Prozac to you and me). He rapidly explains the potential dangers and side-effects of the anti-depressants. We know they're not Smarties. And I honestly don't think Michael is suicidal. Depressed: yes. Unemployed: yes. Suicidal: no.

We emerge from the surgery as if we have been to separate appointments. Michael is optimistic. I am pessimistic. I still don't think this is the correct diagnosis. But Michael is keen to swallow the pills and get on with his life. He rings up an old friend of his and arranges to play golf. So, it's going to be like this, is it? I will end up being the breadwinner on course for a stroke whilst my husband plays house, plays golf, plays at being a husband and generally plays around. Tommy (Michael's friend and his best man at our wedding) is, by coincidence, free tomorrow. He will pick him up *en route* and they will drive out to somewhere in Hertfordshire where he is a member. I am pleased for Michael but envious of him too. I am keen for him to seek employment sooner rather than later. He has lost interest, for now.

Tuesday comes and Tuesday goes. The golf day is an utter disaster. It's not that he has forgotten how to play but he has forgotten that he was never much good at it. Neither am I. Playing Crazy Golf in Brighton is one thing but playing pitch and putt on a proper 18-hole golf course is quite another. I don't say *I told you so* because I know how irritating this can be. But I think it. At least the Thought Police haven't invaded our home, yet. I try to comfort Michael by suggesting that we go and see a film but he's too tired. Exhausted, in fact. He goes upstairs and throws himself onto our bed. He keeps his shoes on. Part of me wants to cuddle up next to him and tell him that I love him. Part of me wants to shake him up and tell him to look for a job. I hate this part of myself.

The rest of the week is unimaginably dull and it seems to last forever. I am really looking forward to going back to school; this is a first for me. Before I do, I spend an hour on the internet with Michael, helping him to register with appropriate agencies. He's got to find something to do before we both lose our minds. He has never known quite what to do with himself when he's at home and the children aren't around. He has never had to. Michael doesn't have many hobbies. His whole life has centred on our marriage; our children and his work. He is too young to retire. *I* am too young for him to retire.

Michael registers his impressive CV with ten top agencies based in the City and the West End respectively. He takes two of his favourite suits to the drycleaners in the village (Belsize, that is) and buys a bar of Green and Black's organic dark chocolate as a reward. He seems very pleased with himself. Not depressed at all.

Chapter 4
Back to School

Half-term is over. I leave Michael sleeping soundly in our bed; eat a paltry breakfast and cycle into school. It's a miserable day. Winter is kicking in early. So much for climate change. Joe is polishing our new door sign; various members of staff are drifting in, dangling their keys, and even some of our pupils are arriving well in advance of the first bell. I linger on the doorstep and chat to the caretaker about Michael being unemployed. Even as I say it, I regret it. The whole school will know my business in a day or two.

I'm slightly anxious about leaving Michael at home as he has nothing to do today. I'm doubtful as to whether he will remember to take his Prozac and worry about the knock-on effect of this. I have no choice. He doesn't need a babysitter. I head straight to my office. It seems like years since I was in it. I thought I would have plenty of me time in half-term but it transpires that I haven't had any. I catch a glimpse of myself in the mirror. I look thinner but older and my highlights need doing. As I said, no me-time. I'm also getting a slight pain in my back tooth and hope this isn't going to result in root canal treatment. I would rather have an extraction.

I log on for the first time since last week. My inbox has a record-breaking number in it: 467 emails. I get up and put a *Do Not Disturb* sign on my door; it's the one I usually use for examinations held in my office. I read all the emails with little red flags on them first; these are marked priority so I don't have to mentally prioritise anything. I am not on cover today: that's a relief. We have 100% attendance. That's unusual. I have two scheduled meetings later on this afternoon and a few lessons. Nothing too demanding. I manage to process the vast majority of emails, hoping that I haven't missed anything important. It's so easy to do. I print off the agendas for the afternoon meetings and do a bit of research on my areas, one of which is implementing our new appraisal system. Peter, Liam and I have agreed to split the appraisals three ways. We will start them in January. No point getting ahead of ourselves.

The rest of the day drags. I teach my lessons using my impressive stock of PowerPoints but I feel as though I am short-changing the pupils. A Year 9 girl asks me if I am all right. I am so overwhelmed by her emotional intelligence that I almost cry. I tell her that I had flu over half-term. She tells me that's bad luck and smiles. How kind. I set quite a demanding homework – one that will take them all week – just in case I encounter a crisis at home and have to take time off from work. I'm probably being overzealous. I decide to look for Abbas and see if he's free. I need to talk to someone that is not Joe. Abbas is in the middle of teaching the Lower Sixth. The title of their discussion topic is scrawled on the whiteboard: *Philosophy of Religion* and *Is there a God?* Abbas sees me through the glass panel (we all have to have them these days) and invites me to come in. He embarrasses me by saying how honoured they are to have me in their lesson. The thing is, he means it. He's so kind. I really want to cuddle him and for him to cuddle me. Instead, I make do with sitting next to him. I join in. It's great fun and for a split second, I wish I was teaching Religious Education too.

I am so absorbed in someone else's lesson that I make myself late for the SMT meeting. I apologise. Principal Peter is a born scientist and mathematician. Everything he does is systematic. When he goes abroad, he even works out how many books he should pack by multiplying the number of words in an average book with the number of words he thinks he might read per day. I decide to buy him a Kindle for Christmas. The meeting is very productive. We even agree on a new appraisal system based on eight different competencies. I won't bore you with them now. They're pretty fundamental to teaching and learning. The pupils all drift off home, as do some of the staff. Principal Peter is going for another swim – he's trying to avoid having a Pacemaker fitted – and Liam is on the telephone. All's Quiet on the West End Front. I don't want to go home. I feel comfortable now, back in my sanctuary, and I am not keen to leave it. I procrastinate for so long that I eventually clear my whole inbox; do all my filing; mark anything on my desk and even tidy up the pens and pencils in my drawer. My desk is clear, even if my conscience is not.

The school is so quiet that I take the opportunity to send long messages to Olivia and Eddie. They're in Melbourne now. I'm pleased about this because I know that they're staying with cousins of cousins. They will be well looked after. And safe. I check in on my Facebook page (which is friends with theirs by mutual consent) and see numerous postings of the twins. There's a dramatic picture of them posing on the Eureka Skydeck which is much more impressive than the London Eye. There's a photograph of Eddie leaning precariously out of the window of the narrow steam train – the Puffing Billy – as it curls around the Dandenong Ranges National Park. I yearn to be there with them.

I'm surprised that Michael doesn't say what he wants. He appears to have lost his insight. Shouldn't he have a say in his future? I'm afraid for him. Afraid for us.

Chapter 5
The Grim Reaper

The week has passed without incident – which is nothing short of a miracle at our school – and Michael has two interviews lined up. The first one is tomorrow and the second one is on Friday: Halloween. I must admit, I thought it was game over for Michael, so this is really good news. I almost have a spring in my step.

He *thinks* the first interview has gone well. The "firm" were very impressed by his client list and also with his reputation amongst other actuaries. We celebrate rather prematurely and open a bottle of champagne that one of my students gave me for Christmas last year. The plonker wrote on the label so we couldn't re-gift it, even if we wanted to. And to show that I wasn't completely ungrateful, we raised a toast to Joshua, the champagne-cum-graffiti artist. Whilst Michael is in the shower, I take a look inside his bedside drawer. There's only one Prozac left in the packet. I'm sure he's supposed to make them last until mid-November. I need to monitor him more carefully.

I help Michael lay out all the clothes and papers that he needs for the next day, just as I used to do for our children when they were young. I do it in a supportive way and don't make a big deal of it. It's not a big deal. I think I want him to get a new job. I know that he will be happier if he's gainfully employed. But at the back of my mind, I am fearful. What if he can't cope with the pressure? What if he makes another catastrophic mistake? No one wants that for their husband.

I find myself standing stock still. I am not sure what to do, what to advise, what to say.

Instead, I return to Michael and we watch the news together. We mess around and imitate Donald Trump; he's so easy to mimic. By 11 pm we are fairly sober again and the thought of tomorrow fills me with anxiety. Michael pops a pill into his mouth; it's not a Rennie.

I have to go into work early on Friday as in addition to all the usual lessons and meetings, I also have to make an appearance at the Sixth Form Halloween Party at 6 pm I think we are the only secondary school in London, or even the United Kingdom, that allows its students to have a party on the premises. I have bought a black lipstick and black nail varnish for the occasion. I refuse to humiliate myself any further and reject any invitations to dress up as a vampire or a devil. Principal Peter is a good sport though. There's no way he can do a *meet and greet* with the parents whilst he has a green face; jagged scars and a massive rubber nail sticking out of both sides of his head! Last year he was dressed up as the Incredible Hulk.

The party is a raucous event. The fancy ceiling spotlights are off. The only light in the room is emanating from two Halloween lanterns. We have the same ones at home. Our students have gone overboard with their decorations. There are black and orange garlands hanging from the ceiling; miniature witches stirring imaginary potions in cauldrons and heaps of food, mostly coloured green, black and orange. There is an inflatable of the Grim Reaper hanging from the ceiling. I feel as though I am on a film set in Hollywood Studios. Principal Peter feels at home. After all, they say "he's American!" I congratulate the students on their costumes and give them a huge cauldron of sweets (which I reassure them is a one-off) – they immediately plunge their hands into it, greedily. The music is loud, pulsating and verging on frightening. Most of our students are dressed as zombies. I look around the common room and notice that Fran is blending in. She shouldn't be there, of course, but Freddie has his arm wrapped around her shoulders. No one dares eject her. Not even me. She's in her normal Goth clothes but her face is as white as a geisha and her lips are blood-red. Her bump is twice the size it was before half-term. It must be hard to be a pregnant student in Year 11.

The party goes on for four hours. We have to finish at 10 pm otherwise Joe the caretaker will demand double time. I'm also a little worried about how the students are going to get home. I insist that they text their parents before setting off; however, most of them are greeted by one, if not both of them, so I need not have been so anxious. I have always been like this. Even before I had children of my own.

Principal Peter takes about thirty minutes to remove all his green makeup. I give him a packet of wet-wipes which I keep in my desk drawer in case I spill my Diet Coke; this happens quite often. We decide to leave together. He lives in a flat in a beautiful building near Regent's Park. I cycle past it twice a day but I have never been inside it. I'm intrigued. I start to imagine what his apartment looks like. His office gives nothing away.

Now that the party is over, I feel tired and impatient to be home. I'm also hoping that Michael's interview – his second of the week – has been a triumph. It has not. I can tell straight away by the way that he is slumped over the kitchen table, hands glued to the sides of his unshaven face. There's a crumpled-up email, which he has managed to print off, and it is a polite rejection from the first interview, the one that allegedly went well. I ask him if he's all right. I boil the kettle. I'm desperate for a mug of tea. I wonder how long he has been sitting there. There are three empty bottles of beer on the table; an apple core and some soggy Cornflakes in the bottom of a cereal bowl. He hasn't cooked and appears to have eaten breakfast for supper. I haven't eaten anything, yet.

He doesn't ask me how I am or how the Halloween party has gone. I find this so depressing. I have been spoilt in the past. But now, the effort is all one-way. I feel so lonely. I long for the confident, arrogant Michael. I just don't understand how depression can be so consuming. And soul destroying. I have been too wrapped up in my own career and the twins' A Levels to notice Michael's downward slide.

I sit down opposite the shadow of my husband and reach out my hands so that they touch his. He instantly grasps them and covers them protectively. I ask him what's happened to us and he shrugs his shoulders. He admits that he has finished the Prozac and that he thinks he has developed a bloody addiction. He is swearing much more than usual. I suggest that *we* (which means me these days) make another appointment to see the GP, preferably our usual one this time. I leave an urgent message on the Health Centre's emergency number; it's answered by an actual person. Amazing. Michael is offered an appointment for 10 am on Saturday morning. God bless the National Health Service.

I am so relieved. I eat two pieces of toast with marmite; have a quick bath and go to bed. I open up my new book: *The Testaments* by Margaret Atwood. I can't understand why I want to read about oppressed women in Gilead but I do. I have waited thirty-five years for the sequel to *The Handmaid's Tale*, as have millions of others. Michael isn't one of them. Sadly, he has temporarily lost his reading habit, much to my disappointment. He rolls over and moves his legs around restlessly. I make a mental note to add Restless Leg Syndrome to his symptoms. I am barely into Chapter 1 but it's impossible to concentrate. My husband is making it difficult for me to leave the confines of our bedroom. He is whingeing about the interviews and the associates on the panel. I'm not entirely clear what he's saying as it sounds so convoluted; besides, as he has told me many times, I don't really understand his line of work. I'm worn out but I am too tired to fall asleep. I shut my eyes and imagine that I am in Olivia's bedroom.

In the morning, Michael forgets to shave and wears two

jumpers, one on top of the other. I think it's pretty obvious that he needs to do a cognitive test. This time, I'm not going to take no for an answer. I decide to let him turn up at the surgery in his natural state. I'm not going to talk about current affairs or remind him which year it is. He will have to fend for himself.

The surgery is packed with just about everyone we know from the area; this is utterly disconcerting. Even Matt (our grumpy neighbour) is ill. Apparently, we are on the verge of a pandemic. Nothing feels real. Everything feels surreal. I motion Michael towards the back of the waiting room so that we're directly opposite the goldfish tank. He watches the orange carp as if his life depends on them. The surgery is running fifteen minutes late. Michael starts tapping his feet and moaning out loud, drawing attention to himself and to me. I am much more self-conscious than him. I pick out a magazine for him to read; it's *The Week*, his favourite. He starts to look at it but the pages turn so quickly that I know he isn't taking anything in. He says "Fuck me" a few times, especially when he sees pictures of Angela Merkel and her cronies. I am not sure why this particular article has made him so angry. I look at my mobile. The same sing-song questioning tone of the receptionist announces my husband's name. We enter the doctor's inner sanctum and sit down on the two white Keeler chairs. As soon as we do so, Dr Daniella Goldstein, whom we know quite well, opens up her notes on her computer. I do most of the talking. I explain all of Michael's symptoms, including Restless Leg Syndrome, and say that he is incapable of shaving. She tells Michael that he needs to do a cognitive test; it will help illuminate matters. The sooner the better. At least we're making progress.

Daniella asks us questions centred on life before Croatia. She probes him about work issues and whether there have been any little mistakes, ones that he has made without noticing but subsequently was able to correct. With hindsight – that gloriously annoying word – I think Michael's downward slide may have started months ago. It's just that none of us had noticed it. Daniella explains that the clinical cognitive assessment is to establish whether someone has dementia; it will include an examination of attention, concentration, orientation, short-term memory, long-term memory, praxis, language and executive function. I don't know what all this means. Michael looks very relaxed. He likes tests. As a student, he achieved as close to 100% as he could. Triple A grades at A Level; a first in maths at Durham. He was top in the Institute and Faculty of Actuaries examinations. I used to wonder why he didn't attempt Oxbridge. *That's easy,* he would say, *it is too posh for a lad from Staffordshire.* What he didn't appreciate, however, was that Durham was almost entirely made up of privileged pupils like me. At least we used to laugh about it.

Daniella doesn't waste any time. She explains that Michael could be assessed at the ironically named *Memory Clinic*; however, there is also a GP's assessment test which she can implement straight away; it's called the General Practitioner Assessment of Cognition. (GPCOG). I am on a steep learning curve. She will also arrange for Michael to have a blood test and a brain scan. Things feel as though they're moving fast.

The GP prints off the test and puts her glasses on to read it. She picks up her fountain pen, poised to complete the questionnaire. If only it were that simple. She starts by asking him which year it is. Michael is quite hesitant but gets it right though it is a painfully slow process. The next question is about time. *Without looking at the clock, or your watch, roughly what time do you think it is?* Our appointment was scheduled for 10 am and the surgery was running fifteen minutes late. It's now 10.30 am He is hungry and thinks it is lunch time. I'm afraid both the doctor and I smile at each other but we don't laugh. It is far from funny. The questions come thick and fast. She gives him an address: 22 Markham Square, SW3. It seems quite arbitrary. Michael struggles to cope with the change of direction and the pace. He is unable to count backwards from

100 to 80, and he can't say who the current prime minister is either. I find this particularly distressing. We are news junkies. He does manage to make a joke though, remarking on how many PMs we have had over the past few years. He is not completely out of touch. The GP asks him if he can remember the address that she mentioned earlier. He can't.

The deterioration of his brain is marked. Soul destroying. It is remarkably rapid; this may be linked to his relative youth. Daniella is pretty sure that Michael has some form of dementia but she isn't finished yet. She finds another test (not an official one) that involves looking at pictures. I try and do the test at the same time. It flashes up pictures in sequences. The first one is of a river. The second one is of a man fishing by the river. The third one is very similar but there is a tree in the background. We return to the first picture, of the river. Michael has to use the mouse and right click every time he thinks he has seen a picture before. It's an exacting test. I think many of us would fail it.

The strain of appearing to be normal has drained Michael of all his energy. We are both emotionally spent. But I know this is just the beginning. We are going to have to face test after test, blood test after blood test, scan after scan, appointment after appointment. It will be relentless. And if our GP is right, our future is bleak. There's currently no cure for dementia. I pray that the doctor is wrong. She asks about Michael's family history. He *can* answer this as it's in his long-term memory. He explains that his parents died in a car crash whilst we were at university. They were young – in their late forties – and extremely fit. No strokes. No heart attacks. There's no family history. That's the point. A huge lorry had veered into their lane on the motorway. Their Fiat didn't stand a chance. His parents were killed instantly. Michael explains, quite candidly, that I had been a substitute mother for him. I feel uncomfortable hearing this. We're the same age. But I guess I was there for him then as I am here for him now. I was under the erroneous impression that he fancied me back then.

The doctor says she will make all the necessary arrangements for the first round of tests and the MRI scan which will be at the Royal Free Hospital near Hampstead Heath. Nothing is instant though. There's no point booking any time off just yet. Everything will take weeks. I ask Michael if he still has his health insurance as this used to be one of the perks from his old job. He hasn't. I wonder what else he has allowed to lapse, other than his faith.

I ask Daniella's advice: should I tell the twins about Michael's condition? I feel so dishonest. She tells me to wait until we receive confirmation, just in case she's wrong. She's certain it's early onset dementia. She repeats: there is no cure. But I fear that by the time our children return to the UK in January, their father won't recognise them. The doctor reassures me that even early onset dementia isn't that quick. But I am beginning to wonder how long he has really had it. We're not talking weeks or months. Michael is so clever that it is possible that he has compensated for his deterioration in other ways. Our preconceived ideas about people rarely change.

Before we leave the surgery, I ask for sleeping pills. Daniella doesn't give me lecture; instead, she simply writes out a prescription. I haven't taken anything other than Night Nurse since the twins were born, and even then, it was only for three days whilst I was recovering from the caesarean. Daniella and I start chatting but Michael is anxious to leave. He feels claustrophobic. As I turn to the door, Daniella puts her hand on mine. She urges me to confide in my friends. This is going to be a difficult journey, not just for Michael but for me. She has tears in her eyes when she says this.

I suppose I have been in denial until now. Until now, I had little knowledge of dementia, let alone early onset dementia. What will this diagnosis mean for Michael? For me? For my children? A million questions enter my head. If the condition is hereditary, how will this affect my children's lives? Will they give up before they have started really living?

Chapter 6
November

It is a crisp, clear day in late November. Not at all dreary. Although we still have three weeks until the end of term, the reports are almost done. Most of the academic lessons are over. All the neighbouring offices and shops that flank our building have already adorned themselves with their Christmas decorations. There's a false optimism shining out from Regent Street; this year's lights are strings of blue angels with silvery white halos. Hardly anyone is actually shopping though. At Bond Street School, we don't allow decorations until the 1st December. We have only just recovered from Halloween.

We are, however, rehearsing for the end of term School Revue and also the pantomime; the former involves the whole school and the latter is written and performed by the staff. Participation is mandatory. It makes a welcome break from editing reports and also from chasing the part-timers for theirs. I do feel sorry for them. This year, we are putting on our own version of *Cinderella*. Principal Peter and Liam have been coerced into playing the ugly sisters. Emily is Cinderella (naturally) and Benedict is Prince Charming (who else?) and I have been cast as the Stepmother. I am not sure whether to take this as an insult or a compliment. It's definitely more fun to play a villain than a two-dimensional goodie, so I take this on the chin. Rehearsals start at 5 pm tonight. We have to meet in the drama studio upstairs. Other members of staff have fairly minor roles but they're all keen to take part. I think this is a more productive exercise in bonding than the over-priced "away day" we had at the Langham Hotel last year (lovely though it was).

Over the next ten days, we spend a considerable amount of time rewriting the script so that it isn't full of lewd insinuations but even Principal Peter allows us to slip a few in. He understands British innuendo well enough. His wife is an English rose. He's acquired some British humour via osmosis at least. He's been here for over thirty years. We rehearse three evenings out of four in the first week and four evenings out of five in the second. It's such fun. I have completely immersed myself in the process. We have also decided to rehearse some of the key scenes in our costumes because it's easier for us to stay in character that way. Abbas, who can't act at all, is given a special role as the narrator. He delivers it in a completely deadpan voice.

We're just rehearsing our final scene when Louisa, our faithful receptionist, comes running into the drama studio. For a split second I think she's going to tell me that Fran has given birth to her babies prematurely. But it's not that.

Peter and Liam are flashing their bloomers at the rest of the cast. It's total mayhem but the atmosphere is one of fun and hilarity. Louisa singles me out; I know that it's bad news. My husband has been sitting on the steps outside the front entrance of the school. She has no idea how long he has been there. I immediately feel a sense of dread and dismay in equal measure. Until now, I have only discussed Michael's condition with my parents and the doctor, Daniella, who has become a personal friend. I sweep out of the rehearsal room, dressed head-to-toe in my preposterous long black and green ensemble, and dash down the stairs, trying not to put my shoes through the long dress. Michael is sitting in the reception. He looks terrible. I am ashamed to admit it but I am not at all pleased to see him invade my professional space: my inner sanctum. I try to tidy him a up a bit, pushing his hair back over his forehead; it's become quite wild, like

Eddie's has, only it doesn't suit him. His shirt isn't buttoned up correctly and one of his shoe laces is undone. I suddenly see Michael as other people might see him: he looks old and depressed; hungry and homeless. I barely recognise him.

We have almost finished the rehearsal so instead of abandoning it, I invite Michael to come and watch; it might cheer him up. He follows me down the corridor and up the stairs. He leaps up them, taking them two at a time. I ask him to wait for me. It's difficult to run up the stairs in my cumbersome costume. He shows me no pity and rushes ahead of me; even this is out of character. I miss the old chivalrous Michael.

My colleagues are friendly and greet Michael with considerable enthusiasm. The new members of staff, who don't know him, look on uncertainly. I don't think he's at all what they expected. But Abbas, who knows Michael fairly well, Principal Peter and Liam and a few of the others, all shake his hand and make him feel welcome. I am touched by their warmth. Abbas fetches him a glass of water and gives him a plate with a couple of biscuits on it. He gobbles them up like a child. The rest of us bring the rehearsal to a close; tidy up; change out of our cumbersome costumes and file off into different directions. Everyone except for the three of us: Michael, Abbas and me.

I suggest we go for dinner somewhere local to Bond Street. Abbas texts his wife, Leila. He won't be home for dinner. She has made "abgoosht" (an Iranian delicacy of meat and soup) which we gather is his favourite. I feel an overwhelming sense of guilt. He assures me that the abgoosht will taste just as delicious when it's microwaved tomorrow night. There are very few places that aren't exorbitant around Bond Street so we head back towards All Soul's Church, near the BBC's Head Office, and find a table inside Pizza Express. Abbas orders a pepperoni pizza because his wife isn't there to tell him not to; I have a chicken salad and Michael has a pizza Fiorentina. At least he remembers his favourite food.

He eats the fried egg with a dessert spoon. When he's about half way through this humungous pizza, Michael goes to the Gents. I take the opportunity of giving Abbas a truncated version of our lives and how Michael has started to affect them. He scolds me for not confiding in him before. I'm not sure why I didn't. People will understand. We order coffees and ask for the bill. I offer to pay for the three of us but Abbas is too much of a gentleman to accept so we split it. Michael produces his black leather wallet and removes his debit card. The waiter brings over the PIN machine. Michael goes through the motions of keying in the required numbers; but they don't work. He tries three times. He says it's a new card but I know that it isn't. I am a little embarrassed by his swearing but the waiter thinks it's amusing.

After this fiasco, we make our way back towards Bond Street. Michael tries to persuade me to take the tube with him; it will be quicker. I feel as though I should accompany him but I can't bring myself to. I haven't been on the underground since 7/7. As a concession, I escort him to the entrance of Bond Street and manage to walk down the stairs to the ticket barrier; this is as far as I can go. He is angry with me and seems to have forgotten about my phobia. He says I should grow up. His voice is loud and I am embarrassed by the attention that we have attracted. I can already feel my heart beating faster and a full-blown panic attack coming on. I have to get out of there.

I almost jog back to my bicycle (currently chained outside the school building) and struggle to move the numbers on the padlock into their correct position. I need to clear my head. I'm breathing rapidly now and gulping in too much air. My mouth is inexplicably dry. I start to feel dizzy and faint. I still can't align the numbers on the padlock. Everything looks a bit fuzzy. I'm desperate for a drink but my rucksack and water bottle are in the office. The building is alarmed and I don't think I can manage the code. This is not the first time I have had a panic attack since 7th July, 2007. I have had copious hours of counselling. I have been taught numerous strategies for circumstances like these. I know that I have to concentrate. I have been taught what to do. I won't be defeated, especially outside my own school building. Not here.

The first thing I do is slump to the pavement. I know that if I don't, I will collapse, despite having just eaten. I've been taught to focus on one thing such as a lamppost or a shop. I concentrate on the red post box opposite our school. I breathe in very gradually. I breathe out very gradually. Inhale. Exhale. Focus on the post box. Look at the man walking past it. Keep breathing. In and out. In and out. I slow my breathing right down. I am not having a heart attack. It's *just* a panic attack; this won't kill me.

I will be all right.

I know that I am all right.

Panic over.

Michael is home before me. He is in a good mood. There are several letters still on the door mat. One of them has a light blue NHS franking mark on the envelope; it's addressed to him so I recommend that he opens it. It's confirmation of the MRI scan with a follow up appointment with the consultant, Mr R Patel. But the letter instantly angers and ignites his temper like a ravenous wolf deprived of food. The sudden change in my husband's temperament is distressing; it takes me completely by surprise. He has never been a volatile sort of man. He has spent his life being calm and composed; it has been his trademark throughout our marriage. And I loved him for it. I do love him for it. He is still alive. Part of him is. I already feel as though I am grieving for Michael. He is slipping away from me day-by-day. The tide is coming in. Fast. It's relentless. It never goes out. I am like King Canute, the Danish King of England. Like him, I know that I can't hold back the waves and that saving Michael from the onslaught is an impossible task. No one should have to endure the mental and physical anguish that dementia brings. No one.

He screws up the offensive letter and hurls it at me. I pick it up off the floor in total silence. I don't berate him. It's not him; it's the condition as we have been calling it. I repeat to myself: Michael is *not* a violent man. Michael would *never* hurt me. I can't pretend that I don't feel threatened by my own husband. He looks unkempt. Overbearing. Dangerous and wild.

The rate of my breathing increases and I instantly recognise the signs of a second panic attack coming on. This time, I stumble towards him, hoping that he will catch me in his outspread arms, just as he used to do when playing with our children. He was such a lovely, hands-on father. He always tried to make up for the late evenings by reading the twins back-to-back stories or teaching them how to do acrobatic dives in our local swimming pool on Saturdays. He *was* a great father and a loving, supportive husband. I keeping finding myself using the *past* tense.

There is no comfort or peace here. No sign of my loving, loveable husband. Michael's anger is unrelenting. I am bashed and battered repeatedly on my chest, arms and head. He is bellowing at me with his deep, gravelly voice. I used to find it attractive. Now I find it menacing. He can't stop himself. He continues to pummel me as if I were a punch bag. I stumble onto the kitchen chair which promptly over turns. There are spots of bright red blood on our tiled white floor. I am breathing too quickly now and can't get a word out. He tells me that he hates me. He wouldn't treat me like this. I don't know what I have done. I don't know what more I can do. I can't argue with him. I still can't speak. I just lie on the floor and surrender my body to his abuse. He kicks me in the stomach and the thighs. I put my hands over my face. I can't go back into school with visible bruises. Is this my new life? Is this how it's going to be for the next six or seven years?

I need help.

He needs help.

This can't go on.

Chapter 7
Telling the Twins

It is nearly the end of term; the festive decorations are up; the enormous tree has been decorated and the pantomime is almost upon us. We seem to be hurtling towards Christmas.

But Michael has his MRI scan this afternoon and I really have to be there. I have reorganised my day and set cover for my lessons. It's nearly the end of term anyway. My parents have agreed to stay in our house for a few days. They have their own set of keys and I remind them of the alarm code (though lately we haven't been using it). They're taking the train down from Hove as the parking here is impossible. They will stay in either Olivia or Eddie's room or both. They assure me that their support will be without limits. This is well intentioned but I know that I can't lean on them forever. They lead busy and fulfilled lives. They don't spend their days sleeping in deckchairs on the pebble beach. We have spoken almost daily. I can't believe how lucky I am to still have such energetic parents. Michael *only* really has me. And the twins.

My parents tell me that I can't go on lying to the twins. What if Michael doesn't recognise them when they come home in January? Danielle phones me from her mobile. She suspects that Michael's illness started at least a year ago, if not more. He has been covering up his mistakes and we have been making up excuses for him without realising it. She's probably right. His deterioration seems too fast. But we have been told that his early onset dementia is particularly aggressive. The diagnosis is utterly devasting.

The MRI scan is at 3 pm at The Royal Free Hospital. I am dreading it more than Michael. Despite his reaction to the NHS letter, bizarrely, he sees the appointment as an activity, something to do, an outing. I see it as an inconvenience, a nuisance, a chore. I am also depressed, anxious, moody, stressed, exhausted and lonely. I can't wait to see my parents. I text my closest friends and tell them that we need to talk; I don't say what it's about though. They're all mystified and wonder why I have been avoiding them.

Michael is offered a sedative. I remember wishing that I had taken one when I was in the cylinder a couple of years ago. We're told that the MRI scan will take half an hour. He should keep his eyes closed. If he has a panic attack (I tell the radiologist that that's my area of expertise) the process will have to start all over again. Not only is this stressful but it is very expensive for the NHS. We are told how the magnetic fields work and how they focus on radio waves to detect hydrogen atoms in tissues within the body. I have no idea what this means. But I do understand this part; that they also identify conditions such as strokes or brain atrophy; this is what they're looking for by way of reconfirming the diagnosis. We *have* the diagnosis. It's not going to change. This is just the icing on the cake, the tip of the iceberg, the nail in the coffin... The MRI scanning machine is belligerently noisy; it's louder than a pneumatic drill. It's clearly upsetting Michael, even though he has earplugs and headphones on. I can see his legs twitching and his feet moving from side-to-side. He is told to stay still. I sit next to him; hold his hand; squeeze it and comfort him. He can't really hear what I'm saying but he knows that I am there. I'm there for him but he's not really here for me. I know it's not his fault. Sometimes I forget this. I am only human, and an imperfect one at that.

When it's over, I remind Michael that my parents are coming to stay with us. In my opinion, it's not a moment too soon. I am desperate. He has always had a good relationship with them though in truth, I think my parents would have preferred a southerner. I am not sure why. He calls them mum and dad not Sheila and Henry. We pop into the M & S next to the hospital and buy semi-skimmed milk, a few apples, a loaf of brown seeded bread and a Victoria sponge cake. My mother won't partake of the cake. My father will. Michael carries the shopping bag and we walk back home. We don't own a car at the moment– we rarely used it when we did – but Michael has been barred from driving since the formal diagnosis. Not that he cares about this. But I care. We had talked about buying a small car for the twins to practise on. I think it's important to be able to drive. This is probably going to have to wait, like everything else at the moment. I feel as though my whole life is on hold.

Once home, my parents bustle around. My mother has bought a bag full of food and my father has bought a couple of bottles of wine from our corner shop. The orange price-tag is still on the bottles. He has totally overpaid. But he can afford to, at least. As we walk into our house, they warmly greet us. I put the M & S food bag onto the kitchen table and immediately hug both my parents, one after the other. I don't want to let go of them. *Sophie, Sophie, Sophie.* I'm Mrs Boswell at school; mummy to the twins and nameless to Michael. It sounds strange to hear my name; it almost feels as though it belongs to someone else now. My father kisses the top of my head, just as he did when I was a child, and embraces me. I try not to flinch as he squeezes my tender wounds. It's as if I am eleven years old and it's my first day at my secondary school. He has shrunk a bit but he's still well over six foot tall. He has a lovely thick head of soft snow-white hair which I think makes him look distinguished. He's not unlike David Attenborough, only younger. My mother is still pretty. She has high cheekbones and bright blue eyes. She's vain and takes good care of her appearance. She has silvery grey hair in a bob. She doesn't look her age: mid-seventies. Despite all those walks on the sea front, her skin has fared pretty well.

I wonder if mine will too. I'm a total mix of my parents. I love having them to stay. I haven't *lived* with them for years but we have had frequent holidays in their spacious house in Hove. The twins love it by the sea. I close my eyes and picture one of our summer holidays in Brighton and Hove. The past feels so unlikely now; it's as if it were a complete fabrication.

My father (Henry) takes Michael into the sitting room where they open up a bottle of Aussie Shiraz and chomp down salty Kettle crisps. My mother gives my father a slightly disapproving look. I tell her to give him a break and remind her how lucky she is to be married to him. And that she shouldn't take him for granted. Just because Michael has dementia doesn't mean that Henry won't develop it too. I know this sounds harsh. She makes us both a pot of tea and pours boiling water into a spare jug. She thanks me for buying the semi-skimmed milk. We usually only have skimmed. We sit down at the kitchen table and talk. I tell her about the MRI scan and how unpleasant it was for Michael. She's managed to get to her age and has never had one. Lucky her. They know that I'm fast approaching the busiest week of the school term. I can't take any more time off. They will take Michael to the Memory Clinic for his activities and also to all of his appointments. My parents are bordering on saints. They're fond of Michael but they're doing it for me.

When the weekend comes, the four of us sit down and talk about how we're going to tell the twins. Even Michael agrees that we should do it in stages. They tell us that they will book Christmas luncheon at the Grand Hotel in Brighton for the six of us. The twins must be home by then. I agree.

I have very little experience in breaking bad news to my own relatives so I Google this. The advice isn't particularly helpful. I am not sure what I expected to find on the internet that wasn't already common sense. I take a deep breath; open up my laptop and Facetime Olivia and Eddie. They look happy and well. They're sitting in an Australian friend's family kitchen-diner; it's so bright that it almost looks like a show home. I ask them to find a quiet room. We need to have a private conversation. I don't tell them that there's nothing to worry about. There is everything to worry about.

There is no easy way to tell one's children that their forty-nine-year-old father has a particularly aggressive form of early onset dementia. And that it's affecting his frontal lobe, which means that he will become aggressive. They immediately want to come home. They don't even hesitate. Their grandparents offer to pay for the flights. We all agree to meet them at the airport. We will have to get up at about 4 am. At least the traffic will be minimal: every cloud and all that.

Chapter 8
Fran

My children are on the long-haul flight from Sydney to London Heathrow; stopping over at Hong Kong for one night. They will land at 5 am unless they're delayed. As the twins will soon be reoccupying their rooms, my parents will have to relocate. I help them find quite a spacious apartment through Airbnb. It's not expensive and they can stay there for a week. After that they will return to Sussex and start preparing for Christmas. The owner of the flat is a psychiatrist. He's away in Germany for a series of lectures. I pay our cleaner – who only comes once a fortnight – to wash and change the sheets; hoover up; tidy up and generally make the house feel fresh. I also place an Ocado order for Saturday afternoon. My life has become a series of lists. Michael's life has become a series of appointments.

At school, we celebrate a raucous evening performing the pantomime in front of pupils and a considerable number of their parents. Although the panto is an annual event, this year it is funnier than in previous years. It is an opportunity for our students to laugh at us and for us to let them do so. For me, it a chance to escape the new reality that is my life: total responsibility.

Fran and Freddie, neither of whom participated in the School Revue this year, have been very preoccupied. I invite the nervous couple into my office. Fran is looking huge and extremely uncomfortable. Technically she is due in early January, but her waters could break at any time from here on in. Fran looks as though she is ready to rupture. She tells me that she's expecting twins (which I already know) and asks my advice. I take a deep breath and tell her to get lots of sleep; to stick to a routine; to read Gina Ford's book – *A Contented House with Twins* – and to enlist as much free help as possible, and not just go along with the army of paid help her mother has already engaged. They may be helpful but they won't be her friends. I advise her to stay in touch with her antenatal group. She listens and even makes notes on her iPhone. Freddie simply looks petrified at the thought of being a father. He is only sixteen and won't be seventeen until the summer. Neither Fran nor Freddie is in any rush to leave my office. They remark on how peaceful it is and what a pleasant contrast it is to the Year 11 classroom and the Sixth Form common room respectively. I don't disagree. I let them stay whilst I respond to the plethora of kind comments about the staff's performance in *Cinderella*.

I am mid-flow when Fran lets out a loud yelp. It has started. Freddie is clueless and thinks she has simply wet herself. I immediately call an ambulance and am now grateful that my office is on the ground floor. I reassure her that everything will be fine. It is not unusual for waters to break before labour. I tell her mine did though the truth is that I had a planned caesarean. There's no point telling Fran the truth now.

Once again, I find myself being the first port of call with the paramedics. There are some benefits of having a school in town though this one won't be making it onto our website. The two paramedics – both of whom look very experienced – are light-hearted, chatty and positive. I don't know how they do their jobs. They tell me that they've just come from a stabbing in Euston and before that they were giving CPR to an old man who had collapsed in his retirement home on the Finchley Road. Fran is plonked straight onto the wheelie stretcher. Freddie looks as though he should be on one too. His face looks like a rice pudding with no jam.

I immediately call Fran's mother and Freddie's mother. We're off to UCLH, again. Fran is most insistent that I stay with her in the ambulance. When we arrive, I once again marvel at this state-of-the-art hospital. I'm told it has two birthing pools. I don't think Fran will be using either of them. There is a sense of urgency as we all pile out of the ambulance. The contractions have started and Fran is looking paler than usual. She is clearly in expert hands and is whizzed off to the appropriate ward whilst I hang around with Freddie until we are told where to go. Fran and Freddie's mothers arrive very quickly. They are armed with mobile phone chargers, iPads, camcorders and cameras.

I send Freddie off to be with Fran and suggest he buys her some flowers from the hospital shop. I give him £10. I explain that it's not appropriate for me to be there too but that I will be in the waiting room slurping a café latte, savouring the few minutes that I have to myself. He relaxes a little and totters off in the direction of the maternity ward. He's left his backpack with me. I phone Principal Peter and update him. I want him to go ahead with the end of term assembly and not delay it on my behalf, not that he would. I promise to keep him in the loop. He may even have something to say other than Merry Christmas.

I phone my mother's mobile and tell her what's happened. She's at the Memory Clinic with Michael. It's in Willesden. It's just a few stops going north from Swiss Cottage on the Jubilee Line. My father is going to meet them for lunch afterwards. He's in Willesden library, reading the newspapers and journals in there. He got fed up with reading Freud, Carl Jung and Jean Baker Miller in the B & B flat. I forget to ask about the appointment.

Things move rather faster than I expected. Fran gives birth to two perfectly formed beautiful babies: one boy and one girl. The boy weighs in at 5lbs 4 ounces (2381g) and the girl weighs in at 6 lbs 6 ounces (2891g). They're incredibly cute but they're swiftly put into special care. It's just a precaution. Immediately Dr Enderby and Mrs Adebayo (Freddie's mother) burst into happy tears. I am the first non-family member to be included in the celebration. I feel intense happiness. The twins are perfect – just like mine were – and I feel a great sense of hope for all present.

I phone up Louisa, our receptionist back at school. She's very good about answering the phone within six rings. Fran and Freddie are the proud parents of twins: Sophie and Peter. I am so touched by the names that I dissolve into tears over the phone. I gather from Louisa's version of events that Principal Peter is emotional too. He's such a hulking figure – always towering over everyone within his sight – but on this occasion, he speaks softly and quietly. The tension in the school hall is palpable. Most of them watched the ambulance leave through their classroom windows. But when he announces the news, the pupils and staff break into a spontaneous round of applause. He also wishes them a Merry Christmas.

Chapter 9
The Festive Season

We are a family of four again. A proper little nuclear family. Despite cutting their excursion short, the twins are pleased to be home. It is a huge relief to have them here. Eddie takes Michael off to the swimming pool at Swiss Cottage (on the Finchley Road) and Olivia and I go for a bracing walk on Hampstead Heath. We take the spare stale bread with us and feed the ducks. Half the pond is frozen so most of them are waddling around on the little stretch of sand and stones. It's surprisingly relaxing and cathartic. We are surrounded by cheerful toddlers wearing bright red and blue wellies. Olivia is eighteen but she will always be my daughter. We talk non-stop. We have always been close. I tell her *almost* everything. I am not ready to tell her about the assault. I am not even sure she will believe me; it was so out of character. Olivia's eyes are watery. I'm not sure if it's our conversation or the cold weather that has brought this on. I think it's both.

We walk towards the ponds. It's so cold that we eventually abandon the heath and head for a café near Highgate Cemetery. We drink hot chocolate and share a toasted ham and cheese sandwich. She asks me how long daddy has been sick and why none of us noticed it before. I repeat what the doctor has said to me: word for word. She is young and hopeful. There *must* be a cure. *What about going to America?* I look at her again and think how beautiful she is. We start walking back across the heath towards the Royal Free; it's such an ugly, grey monstrosity of a building but I can forgive it its exterior because of the wonderful miracles that are performed within its prison-like walls. We are a short walk from home and I wonder what drama has prevailed at the swimming pool.

Olivia and I are frozen again. We turn the radiators up and huddle under a soft blanket on the sitting room sofa. She raises it to her nostrils – just as I did with her pink hoodie whilst she was away – and says it smells of Grandma and Grandpa: perfume and aftershave. Fragrant not overpowering. Like them. She takes out her iPhone and shows me numerous pictures of Australia; she's taken hundreds but says she doesn't want to bore me. She can never do this. I admire her photographs. They're mostly of beautiful people in beautiful places. The sky is so blue it looks as though it has been photoshopped. But I know that all of her pictures are unadulterated. Like her.

Eddie and Michael return about half an hour later. They're both in desperate need of a haircut. I am already planning their next outing. They've had lunch at the café that overlooks swimming pool, one level up. I am relieved. Sometimes I yearn to have live-in help but mostly I don't. I think that day might be coming soon though. The four of us exchange stories. The atmosphere is congenial. But after a few minutes, Michael yawns ostentatiously and says he is shattered. He takes himself off to the bedroom for a nap. We are all quite relieved. I have barely had a moment with both Olivia and Eddie together. Someone else has always been there: one of their friends, a neighbour, a friend of mine. Someone. I need to talk to them properly. I ask Eddie how he found Michael. He confesses that the outing was hard work though daddy remains a very strong swimmer. I don't think he will lose this skill for a long time; at least I hope not. Swimming can become a weekly activity, can't it? But Eddie is less enthusiastic. Michael struggled to use the padlock on the locker and for some inexplicable reason, he refused to accept help. The actual swimming part was fine. But afterwards, he didn't want to have a shower in front of other people because he thought they would laugh at his hairy chest; he's never been paranoid before. And his chest isn't all that hairy anyway. Eddie looks a bit fed up. I ruffle his long, shaggy hair and thank him for looking after his dad. He asks me what we're going to do. Even mothers don't have all the answers.

The landline rings. I know it's my parents as no one else calls us on it anymore. Eddie picks it up and chats for ages. Olivia is desperate to interject but he uses his long arms to distance the phone from her outstretched ones. It's a game that they play. There is no malice in it. Eventually, after about forty-five minutes, Olivia speaks to her grandparents and I get my turn too. I take the portable phone to the sitting room so that I can be alone. Michael is still sleeping. He has started to turn day into night and night into day; this isn't good for the rest of us, least of all me.

My mother's call is reassuring. We should all head down to the Sussex coast on the 23rd December, before the Christmas rush. She reminds me to use our Family Railcard and book seats with a table. We are not to bring any food. They don't want to receive presents; they neither want nor need anything! My mother asks me what I want: the impossible, I say.

Chapter 10
Christmas Eve and Christmas Day

Global warming is a distant memory in Sussex this year. It is freezing. The sea looks an unwelcoming greenish greyish dark brown. It isn't really a colour at all. There is no hint of blue in it: it's a stark contrast to the dazzling May Bank Holiday visitors enjoyed earlier in the year. We didn't go though. The twins had their A Levels; Michael was working flat-out and I was too. I even held additional English A Level Literature revision sessions on the Bank Holiday Monday. We were all committed. I start to think that it wasn't worth it.

Despite the cold weather, the six of us are all out in force. We have been brought up with the phrase: there's no such thing as bad weather. Only bad clothes. Or something like that. The promenade is substantial in its width so we can even walk six abreast. But after a few minutes, we break off into pairs. We walk into Brighton. The festive decorations and lights are up in abundance here; this is in contrast with Hove where they're barely noticeable. My parents insist on popping into the Grand Hotel to use the euphemism and also check that our Christmas luncheon booking is confirmed. My parents don't like sitting in either a draught or near the kitchen door. Sheila and Henry are united on this. When we leave the hotel, Michael stares up at its beautiful white Renaissance-style façade. He is amazed how quickly it has been rebuilt after the bomb. He asks me if Margaret Thatcher is alive. I tell him she isn't. But I know that we are talking at cross-purposes. Eddie and Olivia regard the incident as history; for me, it's just the past. I remember it well.

I suggest we wander into the Lanes. My father, Michael and Eddie all go into the barber's for a haircut. I ask dad to make sure that Michael is given a professional shave. Mum, Olivia and I wander around the clothes shops. Everything seems much easier in Brighton. My daughter refuses to go into Will's – she says it's no longer hip and fashionable – and pulls me into a second-hand clothes' store instead. She chooses a pair of long brown boots and a brown suede skirt. She tries them on and my mother and I both offer to pay for them. She looks lovely in everything. No matter what.

When we emerge, the "boys" all look like shorn sheep, even my father. I suppose their hair will grow back. They wrap themselves up in their long scarves and complain that their ears are cold. We decide to have a cup of tea but struggle to get a table anywhere. We refuse to go to Starbucks (or rather, the twins do) and I don't admit to being a regular whilst at home. Eventually, we return to the Grand Hotel. Michael asks why we haven't been there before; it's lovely.

We borrow the newspapers off the rack and share them between the six of us. I insist on ordering the afternoon tea. After all, it is Christmas Eve. We are all cold and hungry. Even my mother, who doesn't usually order her own cake, consumes everything in sight. Michael very much enjoys this "new experience" and says it's the first time he has tasted scones. Can I make them for him at home? At least I am not on my own and Michael's nasty temper has held off thus far. He is happier here in Brighton. I think we all are.

We return to my parents' house in Hove and do what we want. No one is obliged to do anything. "Shingles" is magnificent. It is a double-fronted, white washed Regency building which is perfectly symmetrical. Eddie, whose social conscience is getting ready for university, says it could be converted into four flats. I elbow him to be quiet and whisper that one day he might be grateful to escape here, especially when I am back at work. Unlike our poky little mews house, "Shingles" is spacious and has magnificent high ceilings. There is a lovely hall with black and white squares stretching to the central staircase which is carpeted in tasteful pale blue and green stripes. There are two sitting rooms on the left off the corridor and a modern kitchen-diner on the right. The windows are generous and there's a lovely window seat in both curved bays. Upstairs, there are five large bedrooms. My parents' room faces both front and back. They have an en suite bathroom which is bigger than our bedroom back in Belsize Village. There are two further bedrooms on the right and another room in the attic which has its own bathroom. It has the same black and white squares on its floor as the hall. Olivia decides to take the room at the top. I tell Eddie to choose next but in reality, there's only one other room he can take as ours has a double bed in it and the other one doesn't.

None of us wants to eat supper. We are full of scones, cream and jam. My father switches on the television. He says there are too many repeats but we eventually find something we can all watch. The sitting room is a beautiful mix of antiques and modern sofas; they just blend in effortlessly. And the sofas are so comfortable. Everyone can relax. I feel so calm or worn-out that I fall asleep. When I wake up it's dark, except for the lights on the enormous Christmas tree. There are several well-wrapped presents beneath it. There are two for the twins and one for us. I have bought my parents "an experience" since they didn't want anything tangible. I didn't really believe my mother when she said she didn't want *anything*. No one has dared to wake me up or move me. I'm alone in their elegant but comfortable sitting room. The television has been switched off. Someone has kindly put a rug over me. It's so quiet. I can just about hear the waves crashing against the breakwaters. Sometimes the wind and the gales are so forceful that the stones are hurled onto the promenade. I'm hoping that it will snow. I wouldn't mind being holed up here forever.

Chapter 11
The White Christmas

It is finally Christmas Day. People of all faiths and none are celebrating it in their own ways. For some, it's just a day off. For others, it's their only chance to reunite with their families. For me, it's a chance to be my mother's daughter again. We are a family of early-risers. My mother switches the radio on; it's permanently tuned into Radio 4, like mine at home, or Radio 2. Christmas music blares out. I hope that the DJ on Radio 2 is old enough to remember John Lennon. But I know that Happy Christmas (War is Over) will make me cry. It always does. And at the moment, I feel emotionally labile. I still haven't had time to get in touch with my old counsellor; it's on my "things to do list" like everything else. We all drink large mugs of tea and sit around the base of the Christmas tree. I wonder how my father has managed to get it into the house. Eddie mutters under his breath that someone has obviously been paid to do it, even the decorations. They look too professional. I admonish him for his socialist tone and remind him where we are and why we are here. He apologises. He blames his father. I think this rather unfair but what do I know?

Olivia rushes to the window and sees the first few flakes of snow falling gently onto the garden. She shrieks with joy, as if she were a child again. The falling snow mingles with the drifting wind. We press our faces against the window seats and enjoy the blizzard from the warm confines of the house. It is a mesmerizing sight. My father breaks the spell by suggesting that we open our presents now – while we're still sober – and head off to the Grand Hotel for drinks followed by lunch. He insists that we wear smart clothes and not silly Christmas jumpers. Michael protests, saying he's too cold to wear a jacket. We all wear jumpers and jackets, just to appease him. We are instructed to wear layers. Michael takes no notice. My mother lends me one of her coats as I stupidly didn't bring a warm one with me. The coat is too long for me and I am too young for it. I can't protest, otherwise I might freeze to death.

We walk for twenty minutes or so, admiring the crashing waves and the foam-filled sea. Eddie and Olivia throw snowballs at each other. I'm glad that they have regained their sense of fun, even if it's just for one day. They look younger when they're in Brighton. I link arms with Michael. We haven't done this for a while. He is protective of me and we walk in unison together, even though this means that I have to take elongated steps just to keep up with him. I am just relieved that Michael is being Michael and not a demented stranger.

After we imbibe drinks at the bar and guzzle down unnecessary crisps and pretzels, my father insists that we take our seats in the dining room. He hates being late for anything. We are the first people in there. We are always the first everywhere we go. I watch him discreetly fold a twenty-pound note in his hand and inconspicuously transfer this to the Head Waiter's. I have underestimated my father. The Head Waiter is dressed in a very smart uniform with epaulettes on his shoulders. He nods at my father, with a reassuring smile, and brings over a complimentary glass of champagne for all six of us. Michael loves champagne. He always has. But the joy on his face is almost surreal; it's as if he's sipping it for the first time. He still loves it. Dementia has its compensations, I guess.

We enjoy the food. It's not sophisticated but it's generous and we don't have to do the washing up. The crackers are a bonus. Mine has a silver keyring in it; Eddie's has cufflinks and Olivia's has a miniature silver cruet set. My mother and Michael both have silver dice in theirs. We put them on one side and say that we're definitely taking them home. The dining room is full now and despite the sub-zero temperature outside, it's far too hot in the hotel. We peel off our jackets and remove our jerseys as well. Michael isn't wearing anything underneath his so he has to swiftly put it back on. A few of the guests, who aren't yet inebriated, scowl at him and then scowl at me. How could I let my husband go out like this?

That aside, the lunch goes rather well. There are no arguments, at least. We walk up to the Brighton Marina and all the way back to the house. My parents suddenly look their age and withdraw to their beautiful bedroom. They're exhausted. It was too far and too cold. I don't know what we were all thinking, if we were, that is. Ordinarily they would have taken a taxi home. I am not sure how long we should stay with them. Michael, Olivia, Eddie and I sit in front of the television. We start to watch *Love Actually*. I had forgotten that it is a film full of pathos and wish we were watching something more enjoyable. It's completely lost on Michael. He can barely follow the plot. He keeps asking who's who. Both Eddie and Olivia are remarkably patient with their father. They don't mind repeating themselves and do so endlessly. I can no longer bear it and decide to retreat. I run a bath and lock the door.

I finally feel quite relaxed again and get into the crisp white sheets. There is no duvet. We have blankets and a pale blue eiderdown instead. I put my head on the luxurious feather pillow and hope that I fall asleep before Michael returns. It's about five past eleven before he reappears. Eddie has escorted him to our bedroom and ushered him in. I am wide awake but pretend to be fast asleep. He starts removing all his clothes in quick succession until he's only wearing his socks. He puts on a pair of trousers and a jumper as opposed to his pyjamas. He must be so confused. I can only just make out his silhouette as the landing light it still on. He leaves the room and relieves himself in the family bathroom. I hear the loo flush. I think it's a reflex action. He forgets to brush his teeth and returns to our bedroom without closing the door. I can't sleep with the door open. I debate in my head whether it's worth getting up but this will shatter the illusion that I have been trying so hard to maintain.

Not satisfied that he might have already woken me up (though I am lying incredibly still, feigning sleep rather well), he clatters and bangs about. It seems deliberate. He starts moving the substantial armchair from one end of the room to the other. It's just all too much. I tell him that he's selfish and self-centred. I say it's not all about him. I am overtired and bad tempered but I can't stop myself from telling the truth. Of course, I regret this. He reproaches me for pretending to be asleep and reprimands me for not packing his pyjamas. Nothing is his fault. Everything is mine. I ask him if he has finished telling me off. He turns away for a moment, as if to say that he has, but shocks me with a fierce back handed slap across my face. I let out a loud yell but the house is so huge that no one else can hear me. The wind is howling between our window panes and the waves are crashing against each other as if in harmony with his temper. I feel as though I am a character in a novel. I want to tear this page out.

The snow continues to fall along with the decline of our marriage.

In the morning, Michael fails to apologise. It is worse than that. He has no recollection of what he has done. I look in the mirror and can see that my face is puffy and swollen on one side. My right eye is tinged with a blackish bluish bruise, about the size of a golf ball. I am not sure whether to run to my father and fold myself into his arms or cry to my mother, who will tell me to put him into a residential care home. I decide that I am not ready for the imperious tone of my host and hostess.

Michael and I have had more than thirty years of happiness together. I'm not going to inform on him now. I cover up the bruise with carefully applied makeup. I almost look normal. I vow to wear my hair down and keep a large cashmere scarf wrapped around my neck, as if I am cold all day. My husband is changing and so am I. I never used to lie to my parents, or my children, and now I fear that I will be doing both until the day that he dies.

Chapter 12
Boxing Day

It is Boxing Day. Olivia and Eddie want to walk into Brighton again and meet up with some friends. Apparently, it's the place to be this year. I say this is fine and don't consult Michael. He doesn't deserve to have an opinion after last night's misconduct. I still love him but I love him a little less today.

My mother senses my weariness and suggests we visit her friends in Rottingdean; it's about six miles from the house. Henry and Michael can find something to do here. My response is a little overenthusiastic. I think we should walk or take an Uber but mother won't hear of it. She tells me to stop being so middle-class and overanxious. We get into her silver BMW convertible with its dark red leather interior. It's a lovely car. She drives straight to the main road which has been generously gritted. Mother glances at me as if to say *I told you* so but stops herself. She has seen my bruises and my swollen face. She puts her hand on my face and turns it towards hers. *So that's how it is. Brute.* It's difficult to permanently hide beneath my hair and scarf. Mother swiftly turns the car around, skidding a little, and heads back into Hove and beyond. She drives too fast for me to leap out.

She tells me that she has been looking into care homes in the local area. This is news to me. Half of Brighton and Hove is geriatric, she says. I remind her that Michael isn't ancient. He is nearly fifty, not nearly ninety. My mother doesn't give up. She has done her research. Residential care homes are more spacious here and they're less expensive than London. I try to dissuade her but she's unstoppable in this vein. I suppose this is mother's love. I am her only child.

When we arrive at Sunny Cliff Grove, I remark on the impressive entrance; it *almost* resembles a hotel with its double-fronted appearance and empty flagpole. There's a small but well decorated Christmas tree opposite the reception desk; the surface of which is curved and made out of a light solid oak. The young blonde receptionist is dressed as an elf. She's all smiles. She points to the large paisley visitors' book and pen attached to a cord; even the pen can't escape. My mother signs in for both of us. I stand there like a small child. I get the impression that she has been to this place more than once. We are shown to the waiting room where there is a sprinkling of other visitors, all of whom are appear to be related to the "inmates" who they call guests or residents. The room is a perfect square and apart from the chairs, has virtually nothing in it except for a copy of last week's *Daily Mail* and a pile of brochures about the care home. We sit beneath the window. I look out and my mother looks in. My view is of a small front garden; it's covered in a thick layer of snow. There are no footprints on it. I'm sure it's the same at the back. As I said, they are "inmates" not guests. I feel disloyal to Michael and resent being brought here under false pretences, even if my mother means well by it. It is too soon.

My mother picks up one of the glossy brochures in a vain attempt to capture my interest. Most of the residents (as I *should* call them) are either old or in gigantic wheelchairs with head and neck supports. No one looks under seventy, let alone fifty. I am not even sure that this place has a licence for people under sixty-five. Mother takes no notice of my grousing. She tells me that some of them have their own bathrooms and they all have en suite lavatories. Wonderful, I say. We don't even have that at home. I ask her why we are here. I tell her that I can manage. I am not in denial. I am adjusting, that's all. It's a learning curve. But she is persuasive and persistent. This is the future. I insist that it's the "long-term future" and not the immediate future. We agree to disagree on this matter. She loves me and she wants to protect me. It's for my own good.

In contrast to the smiley elf-cum-receptionist, we are greeted by an officious looking woman with shoulder length straight greyish-brown hair. She looks slightly younger than my mother but old enough to be mine. Her name badge says Mary Anderson. Such a lovely name, I think. "Mrs Ash? And Mrs Boswell?" I haven't heard anyone say "Mrs Ash" for some time. My mother insists that the woman calls her **Sheila** and I insist that the woman calls me **Sophie**. My mother jabs me very hard in the arm. It hurts almost as much as a tetanus injection. And she scolds me rather publicly for being rude. It is mortifying. Why is it that adult children always regress in the presence of their parents? I am on the verge of stomping off in a huff.

I am informed that there is a whole floor for people with early onset dementia. I ask to see that first but Mary is in charge. Not me. Mother mutters under her breath that M A R Y is *not* one of my little pupils. I bite the side of my cheek to stop myself from answering her back. Mary strides ahead, next to my mother, and I follow on behind. The woman is very tall. I would say she's almost as tall as Michael. I can hardly keep up with her. We start with the reception areas and proceed to the main dining room. They're both clean and tastefully furnished. The chairs are all mauve, as are the walls. There is also a feature wall of cherry blossoms at the far end. It's tasteful if a bit contrived. A few of the residents are trying to eat a meal (possibly breakfast) and there's a rather strong smell of porridge. It's not unpleasant. The home doesn't smell of disinfectant or urine. To be fair, the staff look very attentive and I note that the ratio between them and the residents is high, even though it is Boxing Day. But as I watch Mary punch in the keycode next to the staircase door, I realise that all the residents are wearing jogging trousers with elasticated waists. There's nothing decorous about an adult wearing a gigantic nappy. I find this depressing and hope that Michael is years away from this indignity.

As we walk up the carpeted staircase, I worry that this place is simply too quiet. When we reach the first floor, Mary announces that this is the designated floor for people with early onset dementia in addition to young people (that means between fifty and sixty) who are suffering from other neurological issues. She throws open several doors en route. Each of the bedroom doors is painted a different colour in the style of an external front door. The walls on either side of each door is wall papered with imitation brickwork. Everyone's room has a photograph of its occupant along with his or her name. Some of the signs also have hand-written notes beneath them saying things like: *You can talk to me about music, bingo or cards.* Or: *I like gardening and flowers but I don't like crosswords.* I wonder whether that means you can't talk to them about anything else. I wonder what Michael's door sign would say. I can hardly bring myself to think about it.

Some of the rooms are occupied with the residents and their visitors. As we stride past, I see an elegant lady with snow white hair having her nails done. The manicurist looks kind and it is clear that she is trying to have a conversation with the lady though it is only one way. I don't want to stare so I just smile and we carry on walking from one end of the corridor to the other. Mary tells us that the lady used to be a High Court Judge. Dementia does not discriminate.

There's a festive spirit in the home and it really doesn't seem too bad though the thought of sectioning Michael and abandoning him here is clearly out of the question. There must be more suitable places than this. I need to do my own research, when the time comes. As we walk down the corridor, it is clear that for every six rooms there is one blue door marked bathroom and a darker blue door marked lavatory, even though each of the residents has an en suite. All the doors have images as well as words on them. We stop for a moment whilst Mary chats to another member of staff. I can't hear a word they're saying but it looks as though it is important.

We have a few seconds to observe. I look down at Mary's feet and see that she is wearing soft white plimsoles which match her starch white uniform. None of the other staff are dressed like this. They're all in normal or festive clothes with care-home aprons. She reminds me of Nurse Ratched in *One Flew Over the Cuckoo's Nest*. I suddenly feel like running. She has finished talking to the orderly and is staring straight at me. It is as if she can read my mind. Nurse Ratched (Mary) places her fingers around my upper arm with a vicelike grip. She propels me into the only vacant room on the corridor. It even has a large sign above the door saying "Vacant for Occupancy" in clear black bold letters. She tells me again that the home has a number of people with my husband's condition. I feel slighted as that's our word; it's almost as if she has stolen it from me. For a brief moment I try to resist her firm grasp. I wonder whether she treats her patients like way. I find her intimidating. I certainly don't manhandle my pupils like this. I would be sacked on the spot. My mother senses the tension between us and motions us both to sit down. Apparently, I am overwhelmed and oversensitive. I can't even be bothered to respond to her commentary. Mary and Mother choose the only two chairs in the room so I'm left with the bed; it has a pink plastic mattress protector over it which squeaks when I sit on it. The door to the en suite lavatory is wide open. The loo has a rail on either side of the seat. There are no pictures on the magnolia walls and no mirror. The ceilings are mercifully high but the windows look as though they don't open.

I tell both matriarchs that I am not ready to put Michael into a home. Think of the expense. It's thousands of pounds, every month. We simply can't afford it. I would rather pay for an occasional carer and send MY husband to the Day Centre in West Hampstead. Besides, Michael will never forgive me and neither will Eddie or Olivia. They're young adults. Shouldn't they be allowed an opinion about their father's future? Nurse Ratched (Mary) and my mother (Sheila Who Must Be Obeyed) tell me otherwise. My mother completely takes over. She informs the woman-in-white that my husband is violent. She tells her he's twice my size and that I can't possibly defend myself when he's in a rage. I refuse to recognise the man that is being described. I lie and say that last night was the first time Michael has hit me in twenty years but she knows that I am lying. Mother's intuition. Hasn't it occurred to me that Olivia could be next? I admit that it hasn't, and start to take the tour rather more seriously after that. I ask Mary how they "manage" violent patients. She tells me that everything is "well managed" in this place and that I have nothing to fear on that count. My mother and I exchange glances. I think she finally understands my reservations.

Before we leave, my thirst for knowledge still needs quenching. The "home" is so quiet that it feels like a place to die as opposed to a place to live. I want to know what the activities are and where they are held. Mary marches us off to a small lounge at the end of the corridor; it has a large flat screen television and a noticeboard with a printed schedule. There's one activity every morning and another in the afternoon. Each session lasts no more than forty-five minutes.

There are about six elderly people sitting on mauve chairs watching the television screen. Oddly, there's no sound. The carer in the room tells us that they're all enjoying "film night" even though it's still morning. No wonder they're confused in here. We sit down again though I am conscious that we may be disturbing the residents; these seem to be the ones without visitors. A woman in grey jogging trousers and a frilly flowery dress tries to talk to us. She thinks we have come to visit her. We go through the pretence to keep her happy. It is truly pathetic.

I get the impression that Mary has better things to do with her time as she fetches another member of staff to relieve her; his name is Angel. He's from the Philippines and fortunately he has a sunny disposition. He's the total opposite of Mary. I ask him about the activities, besides watching the television. Michael and I don't watch many programmes but when we do, they come with subtitles as the only Danish word we have learned over the years is *"tak"*. Angel proudly escorts us to the Arts and Crafts Room which is next to the lounge that we have been sitting in. There's a large blackboard on the wall. I haven't seen one of these since I was at school myself and even then, they were a rarity. There are several plastic bottles of poster paint on a table which is generously covered with a red plastic cloth. The paintbrushes are huge. It looks like a kindergarten. My mother and I exchange glances once again. We do not need to speak. Angel continues to tells us about the home's "activities" which include gardening (but not in the snow); singing; exercise in the gym (which is full of hoists and crutches) and cookery without knives or sharp objects. The highlight of the week is Saturday's bingo night.

Before we leave, I have a sudden urge to make footprints in the back garden as well as the front. I ask Angel to show us the outdoor areas. The care home is so overheated that he's only wearing a short-sleeved shirt (it has the home's logo and name emblazoned on the pocket). He tries very hard to put me off, as does my mother, but I stand firm on this one. We walk back through the reception and take a different and rather narrow corridor towards a door marked exit. As soon as he opens it, there's blast of cold air that smacks us in the faces like wet fish. I venture outside but my mother and Angel don't. As I stump about in the snow, I notice that there are cigarette butts near the fence. I ask Angel about this. He admits that the residents do have a smoking area and some will even smoke in a blizzard. It never occurred to me that residents would be allowed to smoke. At least they have rights.

We return to the car which is all iced up again. I tell my mother to get in and start the engine. I will wipe the screens, back and front. I am no longer the ten-year-old child two steps behind my mother and Mary. I can breathe the fresh air again and be myself. We slam the BMW doors shut and chat about the home as if it were a daytrip to a National Trust property.

We return to "Shingles" which is nearly as big as the care home. The twins are still out and I'm guessing that they won't be back for ages. Michael is in the kitchen slicing up bread and stuffing overly thick slices into the toaster. He is easily frustrated and thrusts his hand down onto granite work surface. My father is reading the newspaper in the sitting room listening to Schubert. It's very loud. He is totally oblivious to Michael's temper tantrums.

I am still recovering from the cold but offer to help Michael with the toaster. He is in a foul mood. He tells me to leave him alone. He once again reprimands me for interfering and emasculating him. He must be allowed to do *something* for himself. He raises his hand towards me but sees my mother in the hall. They look at each other like two seagulls fighting over a discarded portion of chips. The male seagull has to be content with his toast on this occasion. I leave the kitchen unscathed, this time.

Chapter 13
New Year's Eve

Although we have grossly outstayed our welcome, my nuclear family has decided to encroach on Sheila and Henry's hospitality until the 2nd January. I love my parents but I miss seeing people of my own age: my friends. I have been ignoring their texts or fobbing them off with lame excuses about being too tired or too busy. I am only harming myself. They have a right to know what's going on. I promise to confide in someone. Maybe Emma? Maybe Rosie? Probably both. They doubtless share all their news anyway; it must be par for the course when you work as closely together as they do.

I return to school on the 5th. I am starting to think about having a sabbatical but my mother thinks I will regret this. I wonder whether I will ever be a grown-up in her eyes. And besides, there too many little piranhas swimming around the school pond. Once I leave, I will never be allowed back in.

It is already New Year's Eve and it's Michael's birthday on the 1st January. He is genuinely depressed about being washed-up at fifty. The twins have made arrangements to meet friends at a beach bar near the Palace Pier; it sounds horrible to me. Too loud and too trendy. My parents, Michael and I, decide to have dinner at Otello's in Hove; it's a short walk from their house and at least the atmosphere there will be lively. We don't even need to make polite conversation as the waiters will do that for us. I am conscious that we should reciprocate in some way and give Michael a wad of cash to put in his wallet. I want him to pay for the restaurant bill later. I want to restore some of his dignity. But I ruin this by telling him not to lose it so he loses his temper instead. I apologise for being a teacher on holiday; at least this makes him laugh. The bruise on my face is a barely traceable yellowish green now – much easier to conceal – so I really don't want to receive another one, especially before the beginning of term. I need to be more careful around my altered husband. I keep telling myself that he can't help it or at least I hope he can't. But his deterioration is horribly swift. It's almost surreal.

Before we go out, I lie down on the bed with the pretty blue eiderdown and think about all the things that I haven't done. There are too many to put on my list. I haven't re-read *Macbeth* or *Lord of the Flies* but reassure myself that I have taught them so many times I could teach them in my sleep. I haven't looked at my emails; I haven't prepared the induction day for the new teacher, Samantha Fox. I haven't updated or printed out *any* of my worksheets. I haven't even planned my first week back. I begin to feel all panicky and anxious again. I retrieve the laptop from my little suitcase; its battery is flat so I plug the charger into the device and leave it to do its magic. I won't be able to do anything until Michael's birthday and probably not even then. I'm beginning to feel completely overwhelmed. And that's just my work. What about the twins? What about Michael? What will he do when I'm back at work? How will he fill the whole day? Will he remember to eat lunch? Go to his appointments? Go to the day-care centre that we have found for him? I can feel my blood pressure rising. I feel sick. And tired. And stressed. And I don't feel like putting on "a nice dress" and pretending to be happy. I don't even care if it's New Year's Eve.

I'm enjoying wallowing in my own self-pity when my father comes into the room. He wants to talk to me about money. I really don't want to have this conversation. I tell him I don't want their money. If Michael ends up in care we will be means tested. We are only allowed to keep £23,000. This may sound like a decent amount of money, but we have been trying to save up for years. Neither Michael nor I want our children to emerge from university with a tonne of debt dragging them down like a dead albatross. If my parents subsidise us, they will have nothing for themselves and the government will take everything we do have anyway. I feel like giving up. What is the point? My father sits down on the bed next to me. He has a plan. He's discussed it with Sheila. In fact, they have spoken of little else since we have been staying with them here in Hove. They will pay for the children's university tuition fees and help them get through the next few years. I will have to worry about Michael. I think this sounds fair. I feel so relieved that I sink into my father's soft cashmere jumper and cry. He kisses me on the forehead and puts his arms gently around me. I never want him to let go.

Our table is booked for 9 pm No one wants to spend five hours in a stuffy Italian restaurant, even if it's lively, and so a late meal is agreed. My mother suggests we make a bit of an effort with our clothes though it is still bitterly cold outside. We have to wrap up. The twins are still out. I ask Michael to come up to our room and change. He has been wearing the same clothes for two days; these also double up as his pyjamas. He won't borrow my father's nightclothes under any circumstances. Reluctantly, like some recalcitrant schoolboy, he plonks himself down heavily on the armchair which he moved the other night. I open the cupboard and take out a pair of black jeans and a blue shirt and a V neck jumper. I also carefully place a clean pair of boxer shorts and socks on top of his other clothes. I watch him as he struggles to remove one item and replace it with another. I can really see the decline in his motor skills. I dread to think what his brain scan is going to reveal.

Otello's is quite a large family Italian restaurant in Hove. It's clearly a popular venue for New Year's Eve as we are sitting cheek-by-jowl with neighbouring customers at their tables on both sides. Michael finds the restaurant claustro-phobic. It's also much too hot. It feels even hotter than the care home. We order from the main menu and hope that we won't have to wait until midnight for our food. Luckily, it comes very quickly and we are spared this anguish. Michael tries to befriend the people on the adjacent table, thinking that they're friends of ours. We have never seen them before. But Michael is convinced that they both know him but that they are deliberately ignoring him. He has become deeply paranoid. I whisper that we don't know these people but he shouts at me instead, saying that he can't hear me. The restaurant is too noisy.

We decide to get on with the business of eating. My parents and I make polite conversation and I wonder what they think of the twins finding work experience near them. Michael is offended that he's not included in this tête-à-tête. I'm fearful that he will erupt. His recent spate of anger has no boundaries. I try to comfort him, and make him feel loved by putting my hand on his leg; this proves to be a futile gesture. Michael criticises us *all* for excluding him from the conver-sation with the people on the table next to us (the strangers) and also for not consulting him about the twins (guilty as charged). He lashes out (verbally) at the youngish woman on the next table, telling her that she is horrible too. At least he doesn't touch her. I am horrified. We all are.

My father pays the bill and gives the waiter an overgener-ous tip. We leave the restaurant. My parents are shaking their heads with anger and disbelief. This is their local. They will have to return there at some point. The pavements are full of ice so I start walking in the middle of the partially grit-ted road. Everyone follows me. But it's here that my father decides to rebuke his son-in-law. He tells him that he could at least be civil; grateful even; pleasant and polite. He doesn't need to talk about pensions or Brexit. No one expects him to appear on University Challenge. He just has to behave him-self. My mother and I try to intervene. We both know that the man whom my father is talking to isn't really my husband anymore. Fragments of him remain but much of him is disappearing almost daily. It is totally unnerving. Michael is bad-tempered, volatile and depressed. His first-class brain is atrophying faster than the melting snow.

Even Michael, in his altered state, does not know how to react as my father is a match for him both in height and intelligence. He used to look on my father as *his* father. As I said before, he calls him dad when he remembers. Once again, Michael looks totally bewildered. He plunges his big hands into his coat pockets and fishes out his woollen gloves. Michael doesn't answer my father back this time. We carry on walking. No one is talking. I wonder whether we would have had a more enjoyable New Year's Eve in London.

When we enter "Shingles" again, I try to lift the mood by asking Michael what he wants to do on his birthday. He doesn't want one. My father, who is still seething from his spoilt dinner, says that *sometimes death is not the worst option*. When we go up to our room, this phrase buzzes in my head like a grating earworm. I start to wonder whether an early death would save him from a great deal of suffering. And it would save us from financial ruin. But I can't even think that.

I try to behave as though we have returned from a normal evening out. I get into my towelling robe and wander over to the family bathroom. Someone has left the window open so it's like being outside inside. I turn the taps on and add bubble bath. I want to sink into oblivion. I can't bear to be with this form of Michael. He is whimpering on the bed, feeling sorry for himself. He refuses to apologise because he refuses to admit he is at fault. He says he can't remember anything. I don't know whether to believe him or not. He has changed. He seems to revel in his nastiness knowing full well that one day he will be exonerated on the grounds of insanity. He has become so unpleasant. I know I should feel sorry for him but I also know that he doesn't want my pity.

He is hard to love at the moment. I mourn the loss of my perfect partner.

He tries to have a conversation with me when I am already in the bath. We have lived together for more than twenty years and known each other for over thirty. We have never been inhibited in front of one another. But it feels so different now. Michael doesn't feel like my husband anymore. I don't want a stranger sharing the bathroom with me.

I ask him politely to leave me alone. I have nothing more to say to him. I'm tired and cold, a little depressed and totally overwhelmed. I just want a few minutes to myself. Is this a crime? I close my eyes and let myself submerge beneath the warm bubbly water; it's ecstasy. I don't want to come up to the surface, in case he's still lurking over the bath. My peace is short-lived. I can feel his ominous presence over the water's edge.

A large, broad-shouldered man, with stubble on his face, puts his clothed arm into the water and reaches in. I open my eyes beneath the surface – immediately raising my head above the water – and sit up in a state of shock. His large hand covers my mouth, preventing me from screaming.

A few moments later, he lets go and pins himself to the door. It is as if he has suddenly woken up and realised his misdemeanour. He clasps his head in his hands and cries. It is a pitiful sight.

We cry in unison. We are partners again.

Chapter 14
Back to School

I can't accept my parents' offer to look after Michael. I don't think they're safe. I know that I am not either. I promise them that I will take steps to protect myself. Michael will *never* touch me again, not abusively. I won't let his illness turn me into a helpless victim. I am doubtful that we will ever be intimate again.

Instead of Michael staying in Hove, Eddie and Olivia do instead. They have been offered work at the Beach Bar and the Brighton Theatre Royal respectively. I am relieved that Olivia will be working at the theatre but my father isn't at all pleased. He won't have her walking the three miles back to Hove in the dark and has insisted on collecting her every evening. Or she must take an Uber. She thinks he's overprotective but agrees to abide by his rules. Anything is better than coming back to London with their so-called father.

I am desperate to return to work. I pretend that I start on the 4th, as opposed to the 5th, just to escape from Michael. I'm also ludicrously behind with all my admin and preparation. I have never been so unprepared for the onslaught of a new term. I have arranged for Michael to visit a day-care centre in the Swiss Cottage area. He doesn't even need to get on a bus. I've put money in his wallet (since the cash I gave him in Brighton has disappeared) and made sure that his Oyster card, should he need it, has £20 on it. There's food in the fridge and a loaf of sliced bread on the table. I can't wait to get out of the house.

I cycle furiously through the half-empty slightly icy streets of London. The temperature feels relatively mild. The freezing weather has ceased for the time being. When I arrive, I drag my bicycle into the hallway. Hardly anyone will be here today so I can leave it where I like. I prop it up against the large iron radiator and don't bother to use the padlock. The reception area is empty as Louisa doesn't come back until tomorrow. I wander down the corridor to see if anyone else is in. Principal Peter is reading the *Times* at his desk. We exchange pleasantries. We're quite close, in a professional sort of way, and I think it's time to tell him the truth. I don't ask for a sabbatical as not only do I think he won't grant me this but I don't even want it anymore. I don't want to be Michael's carer. It isn't Michael whom I would be caring for anyway. He's all Hyde and no Jekyll these days. The person I really want to confide in is Abbas but that will have to wait until tomorrow.

I sit at my desk and swivel round to the window sill; it's covered in Christmas cards left over from the end of last term. I scoop them up and put the whole lot in a drawer. I don't want to throw them away though I know that I eventually I will. I wander off to the staff room. No one is around. There's a surprising amount of post in my pigeonhole; it's mostly literature magazines and freebies from marketing companies. There's also a lovely thankyou card from Fran and Freddie. At least they're happy. I wonder what this forthcoming year will bring.

It's amazing how much work I can get done when there are no students around. Or staff, for that matter. I prepare the induction day for Samantha. She will have a full tour of the school; a shared lesson with me initially; a meeting with the English department; lunch with Harry-the-Harrovian followed up by some real teaching. It's a gentle start to a ferocious term. I also print out a week's worth of lessons. I can print straight from my computer to the photocopier, as long as I don't use colour. And I don't. It costs a small fortune and isn't worth it anyway. We have to be more scrupulous with our funds. Our charitable status may be withdrawn. Everything is in a state of flux, including my marriage.

Before I leave work, I wonder whether I should contact a divorce lawyer. Michael may no longer be of sound mind. I phone my mother to see what she thinks. I tell her that there's something called Judicial Separation. Should I go for this instead of a full-blown divorce? My mother is a retired lecturer in Linguistics. She doesn't know anything about the law, let alone family law. The weather has eased though. The snow has melted in Hove.

I text Michael. I say I will be home soon. Love Sophie xxx. I don't love him anymore and I am not sure why I add the x's. Habit, I suppose. He doesn't reply. He has barely used his mobile since we were in Croatia. I wonder if he can. I cycle slowly. So much so, that people beep at me and rather elderly woman, with a wicker shopping basket at the front of her bicycle, overtakes me. This has never happened to me before. It's obvious to me, even if it's not obvious to everyone else, that I have no desire to go home. I don't know what state the house will be in when I get there; Michael may be in a foul mood; it's possible that he will try and take a swipe at me; the front door may be open; the place will definitely be in a mess; he may be dressed; he may be in a state of undress. I have no idea. And I don't want to find out.

Chapter 15
January and the Spring Term

Once again, I am at school bright and early. It is safer than being at home but I remain torn between the two. I keep reminding myself that it's the dementia that makes Michael so unpleasant; it's not *him*. And it is not his fault. I'm trying very hard to hang onto these thoughts. I have arranged for *him* to be collected by an Uber and taken onto his first activity at the Day Centre in West Hampstead. He will be given lunch there. After that, another Uber (I have requested the same driver) will pick him up and take him onto the Royal Free Hospital for a follow up appointment with Mr R Patel, the consultant neurologist. This is at 5 pm I will meet him at the hospital. I have repeated these instructions three times and also written them down. I can live with the verbal abuse. I know that he hates being patronised, particularly by me.

I am living in two parallel worlds. Neither of them is straightforward.

My first proper day back is enjoyable! We have a long and lively whole school assembly; this is led by Principal Peter. It's all centred on new resolutions. It is accompanied by PowerPoint slides including a list of his *own*: eat less chocolate; give up vaping; swim more often and be kinder to pupils! The slides of him stuffing a large Cadbury's bar into his mouth whilst sitting on the edge of the swimming pool (paunch on view) instantly increase his under-18 fan club. My resolutions are different from his. Kindness is at the top of my list.

My parallel teaching lesson with Samantha (the new teacher of English) goes rather well. We moved around the Year 11 classroom like compasses: one of us always north and the other always south. I think the pupils benefited from our double act because they asked if we could do it again. Aside from my own teaching schedule, I also have to monitor my students, particularly those considered "vulnerable". I want to speak to Jake but I definitely need a second person with me as the subject of his gender fluidity is such a delicate one. I decide to invite his Form Teacher and the Head of Year 9 to join me. Not everything can be resolved by emails.

Abbas comes to see me. He asks me about my Christmas; it seems like years ago. I focus on the twins' return and my parents' good health. He presses me to talk about Michael. I turn the conversation back to his wife, Leila. Various pupils walk past us, smirking and gesturing as they do so. They probably think we're having an affair.

Whilst back in my office, I take the opportunity of contacting the counsellor (Lara) who helped me after 7/7. She told me straight from the start that she couldn't eradicate the memory of being on the bombed tube carriage but she could help me come to terms with it. Even when Michael was my "lovely husband", he was always a bit scathing about my sessions; he thought they were pure indulgence. Plaster casts and physiotherapy were one thing but counselling was quite another. He used to be stoic; ironically it was one of the traits I admired him for. Until recently, and particularly when we argued (as all normal couples do) he would suggest that I wasted my money as I'm still not back on the tube. He knows it is my Achilles' heel. I used to tease him about not being able to ride a bicycle; that's his. But I can't unsay anything now. I just hope he forgets our arguments and remembers our love for each other. Somehow, I don't think his memory is selective in that way.

At four o'clock, most people head off home. I uncharacteristically need to go too. I switch everything off in my office and shut the door. I make no pretence of pretending to work late. I am too old for that charade. I head off to our house first so that I can leave my bicycle there before making the short walk to the Royal Free. I dump my backpack and put my water bottle back into the fridge. The house is just as I left it this morning. I assume that Michael has had a good day and been to the Day Centre. He hasn't left his usual trail of untidiness.

When I arrive at the hospital, I ask the receptionist to point me in the direction of the Neurology Department. She literally points her finger at the signage: 6 South. I assume this means it's on the sixth floor. Miraculously, Michael is already there. He looks reasonably smart except that he is wearing two right shoes. I make a mental note to myself to label all his shoes with L's and R's. He proudly tells me that he got here all by himself. I am genuinely impressed. He has a better sense of direction now than many others. I wonder how long this will last. Michael has obviously been taking his pills. He isn't at all nervous; on the contrary, he is quite cheerful. I am apprehensive. We are like the weather people on a weather vane: one in and one out.

We sit on the plastic grey chairs (there are two) outside Dr Patel's door; this is also grey but not a fashionable grey. Just grey. He's running late. Michael asks me about my day and whether I have any anecdotes. We actually talk. I think I have done him a terrible disservice and want to help him get some sort of work. But he's despondent when I mention this. He has lost his confidence and his self-esteem. I wonder if this is my fault. I suggest voluntary work at the bookshop or our local charity shop. He agrees to give this a go if they give him a go. I feel as though we are making progress.

The grey door opens. Dr Patel steps out of his office and immediately fills up the corridor. He's not at all what I am expecting. The ebullient consultant is both high and wide. And he's as bald as a coot. He is dressed head to toe in various shades of grey. He has a broad face and moustache. Dr Patel looks like a marauding but affable walrus. We sit down in his office; it's the size of a galley kitchen and the same shape. There's a narrow consulting bed on the right-hand side; a desk in the middle with a computer on it and two chairs opposite his one. All the chairs are the same plastic grey. There are no plants. No photographs. No mementoes. The walls are stark white. Clinical. He notices me undressing the room. He shares it with at least three other colleagues, hence the lack of personalisation. He is aware of it.

As we make small talk, he clicks on the mouse and a picture of Michael's MRI brain scan appears. There are two clear images of brains: the one on the left is a "normal" one and the one on the right is Michael's. The most obvious difference is that Michael's brain is significantly smaller than the one on the left. The consultant talks, almost too enthusiastically, about its shrinkage. He is particularly interested in the frontal lobe; he explains that although we may all desire to tell someone he or she is ugly or irritating, we learn self-restraint. The frontal lobe suppresses unacceptable social behaviour. He goes on to explain that people with damage to their frontal lobe, such as Michael, lose their inhibitions and their behaviour changes. The proteins built up in the brain (not a good thing) harm the brain cells. I am really trying to concentrate on what the consultant is saying. I know that Michael won't remember much of it. I would like to "phone a friend" or "ask the audience" at this point. Michael calmly and clearly asks how long he has to live. The consultant jumps to his feet (he is full of energy and enthusiasm), strokes his ludicrous moustache, and pats my husband on the back. He says he has no idea. Michael won't take no for an answer. He badgers the walrus until he submits.

On the way back to our house, we think of all the things someone can do in eight years. But I know that Michael won't enjoy eight healthy years; the last few will be excruciatingly painful. I am overwhelmed with feelings of guilt and sorrow. Instead of going straight home, I take Michael into the bakery on Haverstock Hill. He has always been rather partial to his cake. I see that scones are available so I order two of those; one with raisins and one plain. I can't remember which one he liked more when we enjoyed tea at the Grand Hotel in Brighton. We sit down and I slice the scone open with the sharp knife provided. Michael drops a large blob of cream onto the scone followed by a large dollop of jam. He shoves the whole thing into his mouth and tries to speak at the same time. He helps himself to my scone too. The woman at the counter smirks at me and I smirk back. I realise that there is no spite in it.

When we get home, Michael asks me when he's going to the Day Centre and whether he will have lunch when he gets there. I think he has probably eaten enough for now but I placate him with a cup of tea and two of his favourite biscuits. I also give him a large apple to munch so that he doesn't interrupt me when I phone my parents and the twins. I need to tell them the truth.

As I press the buttons, I look at my husband; he's not really there anymore. I miss him. He has put on weight but it suits him. He remains a good-looking man.

I wanted to grow old with Michael but I don't want to grow old with this version of him. How can I love someone who has changed beyond recognition?

Chapter 16
The Twins (Fran and Freddie's)

We're only into the third day of the third week of term and Fran is going to return to school as a full-time pupil the following Monday. She will be just in time for the official mocks. I have persuaded her to visit Year 11 and the Sixth Form with her twins, Sophie and Peter. I can't wait to see them again. I make an announcement in the Sixth Form common room. Freddie has given me his consent to do this but all the same, he looks two shades pinker afterwards. I also visit the two Year 11 form rooms and tell them the good news. All the girls are very excited. Most of the boys aren't. Freddie has been a model student since the arrival of the baby. I find his transformation remarkable. He has even changed the way he dresses. The Goth phase has been replaced by a rather preppie appearance: jeans; a stripy buttoned-down shirt and hoodie with an American university emblazoned on the back. He is a good-looking young man. I decide to check on his progress. The spreadsheets recording this are updated on a two-week cycle. Freddie is keeping up. His grades for effort are much higher than those for achievement but at least he is trying. I think he will be all right.

Fran comes into school wearing a purple and pink outfit. She's all flowers and soft edges. There's no trace of the Goth there either. I had half expected the babies to be dressed in black baby-grows. I wonder if they're still avid churchgoers. Everyone in the reception descends into treacle when they see the twins in their matching pink and blue outfits.

They look so comfortable and cuddly in their smart new double-buggy. I ask if I can pick them up. I promise not to drop them! Fran looks amazed that the Deputy Head uses the "can" word. They're lovely babies. Beautiful, in fact. And they smell of Johnson's baby oil, a smell that takes me back to my own twins. As I put baby Sophie onto my shoulder, she burps. I'm asked how I managed to do that so quickly. Practice. But I have forgotten about the milky residue that babies leave and there is a little deposit on my jacket shoulder. I hand baby Sophie back to Fran and take little Peter out, along with a white muslin. He feels about the same weight as his sister. A whole cluster of female teachers have found their way to the reception. Everyone wants a turn with the twins.

Once the excitement has died down, I talk to Liam about the GCSE and A Level mocks; these are imminent. He has everything under control. I express my concern that if we use last year's actual GCSE and A Level papers, the vast majority of our students will download the answers off the AQA website. He suggests we conflate two papers but I am worried that this will cause all manner of confusion amongst the staff. Most of them have already set and printed their exams; they're lounging about in their in-trays. We reach an impasse on this and I wonder what he will say in the staff meeting. We are supposed to be discussing invigilation and the provision of extra time for those that need it. It's all very boring.

We congregate in the panelled Randolph Room at 1 pm Liam proposes the "hybrid examination". It is very unpopular. We should do it next year instead. I suspect there would have been more protesting if it were not for the huge tray of sandwiches laid on especially for the occasion. I feel guilty for raising the subject. I suggest that we organise things differently next year. It's too late now. Common sense must prevail. Peter Principal agrees with me. We don't even talk about the other agenda items. The staff can't leave quickly enough.

Liam is furious. He demands an immediate meeting with me in his office. It's a masculine place and is unusually cluttered. There are piles of papers on every surface. At best it is organised chaos. His office is *his* territory. We are very different: he's the "LEAVE" and I am the "REMAIN" in this school. We are both a bit stubborn. Neither of us sits down. We are equally important or unimportant in the scheme of things. We are not each other's bosses. He has no authority over me and I have no authority over him. Liam straightens his stripy black and blue tie and pulls it right up to his top shirt button. He looks as though he is going to throttle himself. I have never seen him so angry. His suited arms start to flay around like fuming flames in a fire. One of them comes very close to my face. I immediately withdraw in a defensive position and cower in the corner of the room. I know that this is totally irrational. Liam is not Michael.

I apologise outright. But I stay cowering in the corner of the room like a tiny little mouse, begging its tormentor for its life. I keep saying that I am sorry. As I turn around, I can see the shocked expression on his face. He apologises too. We are both at fault. He instigates the discussion that I don't have time for today. He wants to cross-examine me about Michael's illness. I have too many lessons to teach and too much to do. Today was going to be a good day; it started so positively with the baby twins' visit. He tells me that he's not an Academic Deputy for nothing, and immediately puts Benedict (*the smug eejit*, as he calls him) on "emergency cover". The poor man has been assigned my Year 9 class.

In a softer and gentler tone, Liam mentions Michael and the "condition" word again. We are both sitting down now. A small Year 7 boy appears at the door. He obviously needs to talk to Liam. He's sent away in a horribly aggressive manner. I can't even look at him. I know it's all my fault. I explain that until now, I have managed to compartmentalise my life. I don't want any favours. I can manage. Liam disagrees. He's noticed that my mocks haven't been printed out yet;

that I was late for a meeting last week and that I have been making and taking too many random telephone calls in my office. Every time he walks past, the phone is glued to my ear. I didn't realise he was spying on me. He says he wants to help. He is much more agreeable than I had given him credit. Sleet slants sideways, slashing the window panes in its path. Nature's protest, I say.

Chapter 17
Friends Reunited

I am quite relieved that it is the weekend. I can't quite work out whether I would rather be at school or at home these days; everything has become tainted with the strain of trying to keep my head above water. I am neither waving nor drowning. I am neither ship nor shore. I am becoming adrift, just like Michael. I miss Olivia and Eddie. I ask Michael if he fancies a trip to Hove. We could catch a train from Victoria and be there by lunch time. He doesn't want to go. He says he *hates* Sussex in the rain and he *hates* my parents. Besides, he has to complete a risk assessment for a client; it's urgent, apparently.

Michael hasn't worked for months. There is no client. I am not sure whether to correct him or not. Is there any harm in him thinking that he is still gainfully employed? We still haven't had a response from our local charity shop, or the bookshop. No one wants to employ my husband, not even on a voluntary basis. Michael starts opening up all the kitchen drawers and rummages around my old exam papers; I tend to keep these for private tutoring. Not that I have done any lately. He can't find the "pension document" or the "spreadsheet". He sounds confused. I suggest we go for a walk to our local café; read the newspapers and meet up with friends. We haven't seen anyone for ages. Most of them have no idea what's going on. I must see them. I am resolved to confide in my local friends; we used to be such a tight-knit circle. I start composing a text message to Emma and Rosie; they live locally and their children are a similar age to ours. I have left it too long. Michael refuses to budge from the kitchen drawers. He is a man on a mission. I suggest we do our own thing. I am not his keeper and he is not mine.

Luckily, both Emma and Rosie are very keen to meet up in Ronnie's in Belsize Village. As we sit down amongst other people's enthusiastic golden retrievers and genial Cockapoos, I feel resentful that my life is so much worse than everyone else's. This is a recent phenomenon. Until now, I have been lucky. Emma and Rosie are not my "best friends" and, although I am fond of them, they wouldn't be my first choice as confidants. They know almost everyone that I know. Neither of them is discreet. Emma orders. None of us drinks anything "normal". It costs a small fortune but she offers to pay. I say I will pay next time. I have never been a freeloader.

At first, we talk about our children's respective achievements and plans. Emma's son, David, has been offered a place to study engineering at Bristol University. I can't help thinking about its status as a dementia-friendly city. And Rosie's daughter has opted for Physiotherapy at Bournemouth University. I update them about Olivia and Eddie. We are all committed to Facebook so none of us is actually out of the loop. Our children barely use it. Instagram and Tick Tock are much more in vogue than FB. Politeness prevails, even amongst good friends. But it doesn't take long for the atmosphere to change from frivolity to gravity. I know that I have to come clean. I start at the beginning. There's a buzz in the café. Neighbours and friends-of-friends keep coming up to our table. It has been ages. I know. My friends seem to know everyone. I ask if we can go to Emma or Rosie's house; the café atmosphere isn't conducive to the conversation that I know we need to have but haven't. Why not mine? I'm the closest. I realise that they have no understanding of my situation. How can they? I have been so foolish in trying to keep things to myself. The GP's advice is ringing in my ears: it's a difficult journey. Confide in your friends. Michael has probably emptied all the drawers by now. I have visions of the house resembling a full-blown burglary. I don't want to go home. And I don't want them in my home either.

Rosie's having her house redecorated so we make our way to Emma's. She is the furthest away from here but has the loveliest home. Her husband is successful banker and pleasant with it. He has no need to be obnoxious as he has nothing to complain about. He has the perfect job, the perfect wife, the perfect child and the perfect house. Life couldn't be much better. The only thing that could possibly ruin it for him would be a Labour government.

The house is one of those beautiful tall white villas facing Primrose Hill. They always apologise for living in it. They purchased it during the housing crash in the early 1990s. Even then, it must have cost at least a million and they were too young to have earned much of that themselves. I am not jealous. I love being in Emma and Rupert's house. As soon as we enter, there is a sense of casual grandeur. The hall way is generous in both its length and width. There's a beautiful crystal chandelier hanging from the ceiling; it has tiny blue flecks of glass hanging in between translucent ones. It has the effect of stalactites and stalagmites which catch the sun as it glints through the persistent rain. We walk straight into the huge Shaker-style kitchen. There's almost nothing on the surfaces. I am not sure how anyone can be this tidy and cook. None of us needs another coffee but we indulge anyway. I kick my shoes off and make myself comfortable on the squishy blue sofa at the back of the kitchen. Emma and Rosie join me and the three of us talk. I finally surrender myself to life's new reality and share every last detail with them. We all need tissues. Of course, there is a great deal of sympathy. I learn all about their wretched octogenarian relatives who have suffered from dementia or Alzheimer's or Pick's disease or frankly, the whole lot put together. They mean well. Emma suggests dinner – the six of us – and she will host it.

I am a bit reticent about this and wonder whether Michael will be treated as a freak or a friend. I think I should accept; after all, if not now, definitely not later. He's deteriorating so fast. Besides, the offer is genuine. I have good friends.

I'm just about spent – both emotionally and physically – when my mobile buzzes. Neither Emma nor Rosie have even glanced at theirs. They're so restrained. And I say so. But I can't ignore mine, much as they goad me into so doing. I never know what catastrophe Michael has got himself into. I can't pretend that everything is normal because everything is abnormal. And I hate it. I apologise and take the call. I really don't have a choice.

My grumpy neighbour, Matt, is calling me. I didn't think we were on speaking terms anymore. Michael is at *his* house. He has locked himself out of *ours*. I ask him if he can "entertain" my husband for an hour. He makes a big hoo-hah out of this but reluctantly agrees. Emma offers to drive me back to Daleham Mews; it's a kind gesture which I immediately accept. She drops me off right outside our tiny little house; the whole thing would probably fit into her enormous kitchen. She can't stay. She has too many things to do. I expect they're agreeable and she says that they are. I am a little jealous but mostly on the verge of despair. It is no one's fault.

Chapter 18
A Juggling Act

Most working parents are very good at multitasking and delegating or driving themselves insane trying to do everything that is expected of us. We are half way through the GCSE and A Level mock-examinations; these are being held in our school hall; it's called the Long Hall, for obvious reasons. It has windows on both sides of a long rectangle and a boxed-in glass cubicle for the Examinations Officer. We oversee and supervise the mocks between ourselves (the staff, that is) but we pay professional invigilators for the public examinations. AQA and Edexcel, the two examination boards that we use, both conduct spot checks on key centres. We are particularly keen to remain one and don't want to lose our current status.

The Long Hall presents its own challenges, partly because it's on the fifth floor and partly because we're in central London. In winter, we are plagued by the sirens from desperate ambulances and frantic police cars. The heating is inadequate and our students are encouraged to wear extra layers. In summer, it is the opposite. Not only is the room stuffy and stifling, but we are invariably assaulted by the charming chimes of the ice-cream vans. The students' responses are so Pavlovian that it takes all their self-restraint not to rush down the five flights of stairs and give chase. Principal Peter has asked Liam to start most of the examinations this year; it is his "right" as the Academic Deputy Head. He has, however, invited me alongside him, by way of appearing to work better together in front of the other staff. Everything is done to replicate what we will do in the summer, when it all counts. Students line up outside the hall; they switch off their mobiles and hand them in; only plastic pencil cases or zip-lock bags are permitted and now even watches are systematically removed. Last year we confiscated two ultraviolet pens; these were being used to expose invisible ink on so-called blank paper. These pens are not to be confused with Wizcom reading pens which help pupils with dyslexia.

Today it's the GCSE maths, Paper 1 (the non-calculator paper). It's a ninety-minute examination. We realise that there is a fair bit of scope for cheating but students who have been found so doing, have been threatened with suspension at best and exclusion at worst. I pace up and down the room like a foot-soldier. Liam prefers to hang around the back rows. This is the first year that we have installed CCTV cameras so that if we do have an incident, we can conduct a thorough investigation. I am uncomfortable about this as the cameras have been camouflaged as smoke detectors. It's all probably highly irregular.

In the past, we have distributed plastic water bottles to all the students sitting their exams. We do this regardless of the weather outside. This year, however, students are expected to bring in their own metal water bottles. We are trying to do our bit for the environment. As I walk up and down the aisles, I am surprised to see so many plastic ones. I start to think that our Eco Council Reps are a bunch of sanctimonious hypocrites. I glance over a couple of the students' shoulders and look at their scrawl. Fran's strong suit clearly isn't maths. There's what looks like quite an easy question asking for the following triangles to be named. The first example says "equilateral" but the others are all blank. She has put: Bob, John, Mia and Dave! I let out a quiet chuckle but immediately change this into a cough. But strangely, Fran is the *only* person who seems to be struggling. Everyone else has his or her head down and is completing each page with alarming speed. Even the students who are entitled to extra time don't look as though they're going to need it.

I walk over to Liam and he is concerned that I have left the front of the hall vulnerable. I suppose my suspicions can wait. I have no evidence and at least no one is coughing; there is no excessive nose-blowing; no ultraviolet pens in view and no calculators, even on wristwatches. Everything looks totally normal. After about an hour, I am relieved by Benedict (whose shirt is still untucked). We whisper conspiratorially which is probably a bit annoying though the students barely notice. I leave him to it.

I return to my office on the ground floor. I have one free period. I make a detour to the staff room and find Abbas reading the instruction manual for our new coffee machine. Peter has donated it. I gather he received two for Christmas. I have banned myself from touching it, given how reckless I was with the Nespresso appliance. Finally, I have Abbas to myself. Despite his cuddly appearance, I realise that he would have made a very good barrister. He is utterly charming and sweet but within thirty minutes, has extracted my darkest secrets. I don't want to hear his advice though. He thinks I should report Michael's violence to Social Services. I can't and I won't.

After break, I teach some of the younger pupils (7 and 8) who don't have mocks or exams; this is relief from the tension elsewhere in the school. I also take the opportunity to send out a reminder email to all the parents of the forthcoming 11 Plus examinees. The 11 Plus is on Friday. Year 11 are delighted, as they will have a three-day weekend. Their parents are apoplectic, as they will have a four-day week.

I finally realise that my mobile has been switched off since the maths GCSE. There are seven missed calls from Michael's old actuarial firm, Dayton Hardwick & Chase. I think I know what's happened. I hurry back to my office and close the door. It transpires that my husband has returned to his former place of employment and picked an argument with the receptionist who has refused to let him go any further. She wants me, or someone else, to collect him as he's refusing to leave. I look at my A4 planner to see whether there's a gap anywhere in today's schedule. There isn't. My day is jam-packed. The English GCSE mock is this afternoon – which I am supposed to start alongside Liam – and I should be getting things ready for the 11 Plus Consortium day this Friday. There is so much to do. And by 6 pm this evening, I will also have a pile of examinations to mark.

I apologise to Principal Peter. I apologise to Liam. I say sorry to the staff that have to cover for me at such notice. I promise to return later and catch up. I will stay until midnight if necessary. I call Matt (the grumpy neighbour) to see if he can help out so that I don't have to babysit Michael. Amazingly he agrees. I wonder if he is lonely. When I arrive at Dayton Hardwick & Chase, Michael is eating biscuits and drinking water in the lavish and modern reception. He is not reading despite the plethora of magazines and newspapers on the large glass table in front of him. He looks untidy, unkempt and unlike his old self. I feel an overwhelming sense of sadness when I greet him. Less than a year ago, he was booted and suited, confident and strident. Now he is a lost soul, wandering around London with no purpose and no direction. He makes a bit of a fuss when I try to escort him out of his old territory. I don't blame him. I wonder whether to visit his old boss and ask him to find something Michael could do. But I don't.

We take two buses to get home. It is not easy. His Oyster card has no money left on it. Everything is a hassle. I have been meaning to apply for a Freedom Pass for him, on the grounds of his new "disability". I add this to my things-to-list when we get home. I ring Matt's doorbell and he immediately gathers up his things, including two bottles of beer from the fridge, and joins Michael on the sofa. I have completely underestimated Matt. He is so kind and sympathetic. He isn't the judgemental irritable man that I had him pegged to be. I will lose the parenthesis (grumpy) from here on in!

Satisfied that Michael is in safe hands, I return to school. This whole travesty has taken up four hours. It is not the first time and it won't be the last. I pop to the school's swanky canteen to pick up something to eat. It is officially closed but the door is unlocked. The only food on view is a steel bowl of green and red apples. Everything else is inaccessible. Even the fridge is padlocked. There is a lingering smell of lasagne or pasta (which was evidently on today's menu); this makes me even more ravenous. I don't have time to go to the Sainsbury's Local. I can't survive off one Diet Coke for the duration of what will be a very long day. I gingerly take one red and one green apple from the bowl; at least there is an even amount of fruit left.

I telephone Matt, rather than my husband, to get a progress report. I have *permission* to work late so I do. They're going to watch a film. I can hear Michael chortling in the background. I don't need to know what they're watching; they're not children. The English Language papers are delivered to my office; there's a huge pile of them. I am only marking questions 1, 2. 3 and 4. Harry-the-Harrovian is marking question 5 which is worth as much as all the others put together. I print off the mark scheme directly from the AQA website and go through the paper meticulously, ensuring that I have added in all the variants. The bells eventually stop ringing. I have completely lost track of the time but at least I have finished marking. I enter the marks onto the spreadsheet and tidy up my office.

I am just about to leave when two emails pop up onto my screen. Firstly, why haven't I updated our Twitter feed? And secondly, there's a problem with the GCSE mock maths' results. I address the Twitter problem first and post various pictures and messages that should have been uploaded earlier in the week. I re-read the email about the maths' results. The department have been efficient in marking the papers, for which I congratulate them, but soon realise that the whole process has been a farce. Virtually the whole of Year 11 has achieved 99% or even 100%. Very few of our pupils are capable of achieving these scores. Fran is the only person who has failed. This is ridiculous.

Liam is still in his office. Principal Peter is still in his. The whole of the maths department is in theirs. We meet in Liam's though there aren't enough chairs in there for all of us. It's now 9 pm but it feels much later. It is pitch dark outside. We sit in a cramped circle and take it in turns to analyse the answer papers. We know that 99% of the students have cheated. The question is: how?

Liam turns his screen monitor around so that we can all see it. He plays back the CCTV footage of Year 11 entering the Long Hall. They all look remarkably calm and collected. Once the students are seated, he pauses the monitor so that we can really look at their hands, arms and any visible flesh. Nothing suspicious. I feel a bit embarrassed when the footage shows Benedict and I having a private conversation which lasts much longer than I realised. We forward the footage a little further on until we all realise the scam: the water bottles! We zoom in on one of our weakest Year 11 boys. His name is Jamie. He has never achieved more than about 35% in maths and no more than 55% in any other subject since he was in Year 7. He appears to be holding his water bottle with his left hand whilst copying the ingredients with his right hand. We zoom in on other pupils too. They're all at it. Everyone with a plastic water bottle has all the answers inscribed on the inside of the label; it's ingenious. Fran is the *only* person who has refrained from cheating; perhaps she feels indebted to us or maybe she was absent when this trick was conceived.

The maths department decide to set another mock; this time it will date back at least three years and the students will not be told about it until an hour before the exam. Principal Peter, Liam and the entire maths department head for the pub. I head home.

Chapter 19
The 11 Plus

The 11 Plus is a stressful day for everyone. The schedule is much more complex than prospective parents can possibly imagine. It's a masterclass in admission and omission.

The building (though smart) is fundamentally too small to accommodate all the existing pupils alongside all the hopeful ones. Unlike some schools, we don't have spare blocks or classrooms; in fact, we don't have *any* spare space. Instead, we have the whole of London at our disposal. Entire year groups are sent out on unnecessary but educational outings. We have got this down to a fine art. Years 8 and 9 will visit the Globe Theatre on the South Bank; there's a suitably physical workshop centred on *Romeo and Juliet* followed up by a condensed version of the tragedy afterwards. This is ideal. Year 9 are studying the play this year and Year 8 will be in the future. Year 10 will be sketching and painting some of the famous paintings at the Wallace Collection with Annie-the-Art teacher (and a few other colleagues) until lunch time. The only pupils in the school will be Year 7 and the Sixth Form; each of them will be ambassadors. Prefect-style badges are distributed to the younger children; these are immediately pinned to the lapels on their smart blazers. Sashes in the school's colours are dispersed to the Sixth Form; there is a little resistance to these but eventually everyone puts one on.

Principal Peter and I are the designated parent ambassadors; it will be our job to sell the school once again, and also to reassure parents that their children are in good hands.

We don't wear sashes but we do have name badges. We will keep repeating the mantra that it's essential that the school matches the pupil and vice versa. No one wants to be a square peg in a round hole. Besides, we don't wish to appear desperate.

Parents are invited to stay for forty-five minutes (for light refreshments) and should return at 1 pm when the ordeal is over. The Year 6 (11 Plus examinees) will be tested on maths, English, verbal reasoning and non-verbal reasoning. They will receive a goody bag at the end which will include a Bond Street School bookmark; a tote bag with our school crest on it; a pen; a bar of chocolate and a fridge magnet. They will be given mini Magnum ice-creams in between the maths and English examination. Any more than this and we will be accused of corruption.

Once the innocent lambs are escorted upstairs to the Long Hall, Liam explains the rules. He is far less officious with them than he is with our own pupils. After a period of silence, there is a soundless scribble and the tests are clearly underway. Harry-the-Harrovian and I will oversee the marking whilst the rest of the department make their contribution. We accept most pupils so the whole process is something of a sham; however, we do place quite a lot of importance on the interview and the meet/greet with parents. We don't want to encourage any difficult ones. Last year, we erroneously gave the children a choice of composition titles which included: "The Best Day of My Life". Marking them was the "worst day" of my life: how many surprise parties have these children really been to? This year, we have set much more interesting titles such as: *What's your favourite museum and why? Co-educational schools are better than single-sex ones. Discuss. If I could be Prime Minister for a year. Write a campaign to save our environment* and *The Perfect Home*.

Once the day is over, the English department congregates in one of the classrooms and the maths department assembles in another. The department that marks the fastest takes the other one out for a drink. We know it's preposterous. Caffeine and crisps on tap, in addition to the leftovers from the 11 Plus refreshments (we aren't too proud to accept them) and we start. We begin with the verbal reasoning as the maths department start with the nonverbal reasoning. It is not subjective but we are all tired and we know we make mistakes; this is why we double mark everything. After about an hour, we have a five-minute comfort break. I decide not to check my mobile. It's not that I don't care. I promise myself that I will be a better wife tomorrow. We start marking the compositions. We separate them into three piles: offer, maybe and reject. The last pile is always the smallest. Some of the children have beautiful handwriting. Some can barely write at all. A few bright sparks write with flair and discuss the environment; enforcing laws to protect our oceans, mostly along those lines; whilst others write in lists, forcing adjectives into their sentences, just because they have learned them. My particular favourite this year is "incredulous" which must be on a tutor's list, as at least a quarter of the cohort has used it whether it makes sense to or not.

We are progressing well; however, I am a little disturbed by one of the entries and stop to re-read it; I know that this slows me down. But it seems important. The departmental race isn't. The girl who has written the essay has tiny handwriting; it's almost apologising for being on the page. The title is: *The Perfect Home*. She has drawn a picture of a house next to the title. She won't get any marks for this. As I read each paragraph, I can't hide my discomfort. The girl (whom I shall call X) writes that a perfect home would be one with a sister or a brother so that she could have less attention. She could sleep the whole night through; have a lock on her door; not have to do "certain" things in exchange for pocket money. It gets worse. I decide to read the child's closing paragraph to the rest of the department. It sounds like a case study from the Child Protection Course that I did last year.

I put the paper on one side and write "REFER TO PETER" on the top.

We are only about halfway through our marking when the smug maths department come tumbling into our classroom. They have finished. They're going to the pub. We continue until 10 pm Bond Street is buzzing. It's Friday night for everyone else. I had almost forgotten. It could be any day of the week during the exam season. I cycle home, relieved that the roads are emptier than the pubs.

When I enter our house, there's a strong smell of gas. I walk straight into the kitchen and switch the lights on. There's a small saucepan with two eggs in it; they've been boiled to death. The water has totally evaporated and the hob is still on. There is no sign of Michael but he has left his usual trail behind: cereal on the work surfaces; two slices of bread in the toaster; the Flora is on the kitchen table (without its lid) and the telephone is off the hook. Michael's mobile (which he never uses anymore anyway) is also on the table. I rush up the stairs and check each room methodically. I call Matt; my friends Emma and Rosie; their husbands; Olivia and Eddie; my parents and finally the police. I dread to think what has happened. No one knows here he is. He hasn't been arrested. I suppose that's something.

I am so weary and worn out that I just want to curl up and go to bed. I can't lie down for fear of passing out, even though I am the world's worst sleeper. I have got to find Michael. I don't really like wandering around at night on my own, even in our area. I change into warmer, more comfortable clothes, and put on my trainers. I take £20 with me and one debit card. I leave everything else behind, except for my mobile and house keys. I write Michael a large hand-written note saying that I am looking for him but will come back at various intervals. I am almost sleepwalking. I don't even have a route planned. Various people approach me and ask me if I need help. I don't accept. I don't know who these people are. I keep going until I realise that it's 2 am and I am almost back at work. The traffic lights look as though they're dancing in some sort of haze; the rain starts bucketing down, right on cue, and I am drenched. My mobile is down to 10% so I decide to switch if off to preserve the battery until I really need it.

I don't know how I keep going. I am drunk with fatigue. My steps are becoming shorter and shorter until I collapse into the alcove of the flagship store, John Lewis, opposite Cavendish Square. I don't even know why I am here. I have been to all the places that I think Michael might have gone to. After a few minutes, a homeless man gestures for me to leave. I am in his space. His rolled up sleeping bag is tucked neatly under his arm. Ex-army, perhaps? I realise that I am sitting on his cardboard. I am not too tired to say sorry; it's something we British people say without thinking. It all seems totally futile. I make my way to the entrance of Bond Street School. Even if I had the keys on me, I don't think I would go in. I sit on the steps and try to think where Michael might go. There is just one place left.

Chapter 20
Missing

At 10 am I wake up, fully dressed and grimy, on the bed. The curtains are open and the lights are on. I cannot remember getting home. I feel totally disorientated. Is this an insight into dementia? If so, it is terrifying. I vow to be more sympathetic to Michael. I come downstairs to find both my parents and the twins sitting at the table; they're all talking about me. They drove down earlier this morning. I say you can stop saying "she" and "mummy" because I am here now. I sound annoyed and resentful when I say this. I hate myself a bit more every day. My mother sends me straight back upstairs. My odour lingers behind me; it's a combination of dried sweat (quite an achievement in the cold weather) and damp clothes. I run a bath, chuck my laundry into the washing machine and submerge myself in the water; I haven't done this since Michael nearly drowned me. I wash my hair; dress in warm comfortable clothes and return to the kitchen. I am not wearing any makeup and my hair is still damp. I remind my parents to put a visitor's permit in their car; it's Saturday and the parking restrictions aren't lifted until lunch time. I haven't totally lost the plot.

Olivia looks horrified at my natural state. I probably have more lines that she realised. I look pale and gaunt. It doesn't suit me. A mug of tea is placed in my hand and I drink it in silence. Everyone else is making plans. My son, Eddie, is the note-taker. He has always had remarkably neat handwriting. Missing posters will be printed off and plastered to lampposts and trees from here and beyond, all friends and contacts will be informed and asked to help find Michael, one of us will contact all the hospitals within a designated radius, his disappearance will be formally reported to the police again and we will use all modern methods of media to see if that helps. Eddie wants to know why I haven't tagged his father. I explain that not only is there Life360 on his mobile (which I know he no longer uses) but his anorak has a GPS tracker sewn into the pocket and he is or was wearing an identity bracelet. We should be able to find him. But, of course. it is not that simple. Michael isn't wearing the anorak of choice and the identity bracelet is in the bathroom next to washbasin. We are back to square one. We all have our specific areas of research. Mine starts with the police station. Emma has offered to meet me there, once the ordeal is over.

The business of reporting a missing person takes hours. He is "wandering" as opposed to "missing" though I fear it is tantamount to the same thing. I explain that his dementia makes him vulnerable and am about to launch into a description of his illness when the policewoman interrupts me. She asks me for the Herbert Protocol form. I have never heard of it. I have no recollection of either of our GPs telling us to complete one. I start to question my own memory. I ask the officer to enlighten me. The Herbert Protocol form (*safe and found*) contains vital information which can help the police immediately start searching for the "wandering" person. If I had completed this form, and kept numerous copies, I would be able to instantly avail the police of all the information that they require. The policewoman hands me the nine-page document to complete now; better late than never, she says. She can see that I am visibly upset and puts her hand on my shoulder by way of reassurance. A little tear falls onto the first page which says "confidential when complete".

The second page is straightforward and simply requires facts like Mr Gradgrind from *Hard Times*: name, date of birth, address, etc. The third page centres on the diagnosis;

the medical condition, any phobias, what he might be scared of, what the consequences are if the medicine isn't taken and the person's walking ability. I am able to answer all of these questions though I am not sure if Michael's phobia of rats is what they're after. I suppose it would make him vulnerable on the streets of any major city in the United Kingdom. The fourth page is of real interest to me as I explain to the police-woman that I think it is possible that Michael has tried to return to his childhood home or his parents' grave. I also have to list his old school; his late parents' address (which is in Staffordshire) and his former place of work (he's not there this time). I ask if a search party can be sent to Stoke-on-Trent. I'm told to take one step at a time.

I'm also asked to list Michael's favourite activities; restaurants and cafés; preferred hobbies and any special interests. He doesn't have many hobbies though he enjoys swimming. He loved his job, reading the newspapers and spending time with the twins. He played the occasional game of golf and enjoyed walking. He can't ride a bicycle. I'm getting a little frustrated with some of the questions on the form but the policewoman is patient and says it all helps. She brings me a mug of tea with sugar in it. I can't drink it. I'm bemused by the question on page five; it wants to know his favourite cake. I write down chocolate though he also likes tiramisu. I add scones to the list for good measure but I am not sure if they count. My phone buzzes several times. My father has checked all the hospitals (by phone) and Michael definitely isn't in any of them. He has been thorough. My mother has phoned all of our friends and his contacts (not that there were all that many); this has been time-consuming but equally fruitless. Olivia and Eddie have printed off hundreds of "Missing" posters. Olivia sends me a picture of the poster via WhatsApp: it looks like a wanted poster for murder. I complete the form and hand it to the policewoman (Sally) who will photocopy it and return it to me in a few minutes. She will leave me to respond to my messages. Just before she leaves the room, Sally asks me if I am happily married and sexually active.

Emma arrives just as the photocopied Herbert Protocol forms are returned to me. I am so grateful for her company. I explain that my whole family are involved in Michael's search. She's wearing a soft white puffer coat that almost reaches her ankles. Emma is classically beautiful and would look glamorous in a binbag. She gives me a hug which lasts for a long time. Sally, who is about sixty, looks as though she wants to join in. I see that she isn't wearing a wedding band or any rings, in fact. I'm not sure if members of the police force are allowed to when they're on duty. I decide it would be impolite to ask.

I send a text to the "immediate family group" giving them an update and asking for one in return. Messages flood in. Emma has brought her car – the one with the red leather seats – so we get in and drive to Michael's late parents' home in the vague hope that he might have been there or is still hanging around. The drive to Bradeley, Stoke-on-Trent, is going to take us about three hours; it's over 150 miles but most of it is via motorways. The weather is still awful – though at least it's dry – so I'm hopeful that most people won't want to go out for the day. I feel so guilt-ridden for wasting Emma's Saturday. She lightens the atmosphere saying that car needs some exercise; this is supposed to alleviate my conscience. We chat from Luton to Northampton but by the time we reach Loughborough I am all talked out. We only stop once. When we arrive at Bradeley, I can see from Emma's expression that it's a far cry from Primrose Hill. Michael once took me to Staffordshire on the anniversary of his parents' death. We spent hours in their local pub: The Bradeley on Stratheden Road. Emma parks her car outside the large estate-style pub which is on the main road behind Smallthorne. I am not familiar with the area as we haven't been back for years. It's warm and full of atmosphere. It looks and feels like a good English pub should: not a restaurant-cum-gastropub with which I am more familiar. We order soft drinks and food at the bar. We're given a number on a stick and place this on the table for two. We take turns to use the loo. I pop into the Gents just in case Michael is in there. He isn't. I walk around the pub; check the snooker table; the huge beer garden (where there are several children playing "it") and can't see him. We eat lunch: baked potatoes with tuna and cheese. It's comfort-food which we need.

We revive a little and I pluck up the courage to ask the bar staff and the landlord whether they have seen Michael. I show them the "Missing" poster which is on my WhatsApp. I don't have a hardcopy, unfortunately. The landlord, Bill, asks me to email him the poster. He will print it off and ask his son, who is also behind the bar, to put them up in all the key places. Bill is old enough to remember the fatal car accident that killed Michael's parents. Most of the older locals do too. He hasn't been in the pub but they will be ready to pounce on him if he does. I am overwhelmed by people's kindness and sympathy. Bill refuses to take any money from us, saying that lunch is on the house. We drop a few pound coins into the charity box instead.

We walk for a few minutes, straight down the Stratheden Road until we find Michael's former family home. It's a three-bedroom bungalow with a pretty front garden and a generous driveway. There's a rail leading up to the door; I think it's new as the previous owners were a young family. They must have moved on. An elderly lady answers the door but keeps the latch on. She looks frail and I am concerned that we have frightened her. I explain who we are ask her if we may come in. She's a little nervous but acquiesces to our request.

We sit down in her overheated but otherwise comfortable lounge. As we talk, I admire her ornaments and her photographs. There's one of her late husband dressed in full military uniform. And a few of her daughter and grandchildren baking and gardening. We talk for about an hour. As we sit there, I can see a man wandering in the grassy field behind the back garden. I rush to the window and try to open it but it's locked and the key is nowhere to be found. I say I think it could be him; it's hard to tell because I don't recognise the coat and he just looks like a speck. But the man is tall and has dark hair like Michael's. I ask the old lady to open up the back door. Her fingers are bent with arthritis and I can see that holding and turning keys is difficult for her. I offer to open the door and do so quickly, shutting it behind me so that the heat doesn't escape. It's still very cold and I wonder how a homeless person can survive in it, especially in the countryside. I can see the man, stumbling across the grass behind the house. It's not an allotment and it's not a field. Just grass. I imagine that Michael played here when he was a boy. He often said he had more freedom than children have these days. I quicken my pace until I reach him. A scruffy old man wearing a greyish coat turns to look at me. He is so frightened that he cowers in my presence. He runs like a hare across the icy ground until he is a speck once more. There's nothing we can do. It may be pointless but I am convinced that Michael is somewhere in this region.

Emma doesn't want to drive back in the dark, at least not the whole way, so we decide to visit the graveyard and then call it quits. We drive to Stoke Cemetery, which the locals call Hartshill. It is open twenty-four hours a day, seven days a week. We wander around, searching for Michael's late parents' gravestones; they were buried side by side. It's virtually impossible. There are so many, both old and new. Some are shrouded in beautiful red poppies. Others are buried in long grass and dandelions. It is, however, a well-maintained place of rest. We continue to methodically work our way down the rows until we reach Mary and Edward Boswell. Someone has placed a bunch of flowers between the two of them. I wonder if Michael has been here. We keep looking, determined to find something to reward us for our tenacity. We walk through the woodland garden of remembrance, hoping upon hope that we will find my elusive husband.

We see a body, lying face down on the earth, carefully hidden between three leylandii trees. The body is not wearing a coat. It has dark brown corduroy trousers, a grubby white shirt, a caramel jersey and a cashmere Burberry scarf. I recognise the scarf; I gave it to Michael on our tenth anniversary. The body is groaning and breathing but it isn't speaking or making any sense. Emma crouches down next to it and calls an ambulance: possibly unconscious but definitely breathing. Conceivably an overdose. The man is – she looks at me for reassurance – fifty. He has early onset dementia. Hearing these three words never gets any better.

Chapter 21
Found

Whilst we are in the ambulance, I telephone my mother. The word "found" is repeated to the others, all of whom have regrouped in our mews house. They offer to drive up this evening but I say it's too late now; it's almost dark. Get a good night's sleep and come up tomorrow, with the twins. And please bring me my washbag and a change of clothes. And some for Michael too. I've got to be optimistic that he will come out alive. Olivia and Eddie are desperate with worry. My parents are overwrought. This is not how they imagined their retirement. They all demand details but I can't elaborate. We are in the ambulance. Emma is following in her car. She won't take "no" for an answer, even though I told her I could manage. Besides, Rupert is out with work colleagues so he won't miss her. The Royal Stoke University Hospital is part of the larger group called the University Hospitals of the North Midlands. It isn't far. Our flashing blue lights are vanquished by the sheer velocity of the helicopter that lands precisely on its helipad. I wonder whether both patients will survive the night.

The ambulance enters the hospital via the Lower Ground Floor, adjacent to the main entrance of the building. Michael is rapidly treated from every angle. The speed at which the doctors, nurses and paramedics work is synonymous with the changeover of tyres at the Grand Prix. It is remarkable. Emma turns up, looking frantic, and says she will book us rooms at a local hotel. Anything to help. I can't thank her enough. I am so hysterical that I forget how tired I am. I try following Michael and his stretcher into the theatre but I'm stopped by the doors which are key-padded like the ones in the care home. I am instructed to wait in the hospital's canteen. Buy a coffee. Read a newspaper. I have so much adrenalin pumping round my body that I am not sure how to jettison it. A coffee is the last drink I want or need. I find a payphone, as I'm worried that my mobile won't last more than a few minutes, and phone home again; this time, I speak to my father, Henry. He repeats the phrase: *death is not always the worst option. Sophie, think of all the aggravation you will save, not to mention the money.* He is thinking of me, of course. I say there are other options: an in-house carer, day centres, residential homes and respite care. He interjects: *For you or for him? Have you looked in the mirror lately? How can you stay in your job? What about the twins? At this rate, they won't have either of their parents by their twenty-first birthday.* I can't pretend that my husband's untimely death doesn't cross my mind; it might be easier for him and for me. But I don't allow myself to entertain these distressing thoughts for more than a minute. This is one miserable year out of a wealth of happy ones. I need to maintain a sense of perspective.

I can't remain on the phone because the cord doesn't stretch far enough for me to sit down. The adrenalin dump has worn off. I am feeling weak and wobbly. There's one spare chair at a table already occupied by a family. No one speaks. I'm too exhausted to be polite so I don't say anything either. I look at my mobile instead. I send Emma another text and she replies, sending me the name of the hotel she has found us along with the room numbers: 44 and 45. I wander down to the A & E reception; it's horribly busy with inebriated people who have been out on the town. There's an array of superficial injuries ranging from bloody noses to swollen ankles. No one in this room is going to die today.

Michael is immediately taken to surgery. The doctors suspect him of overdosing on aspirin and beer. His breath smells and he is unconscious but definitely breathing, albeit rapidly and erratically. I still can't gauge how he managed to get to Stoke-on-Trent. I have obviously underestimated him. I ask one of the nurses if I can see him but they firmly suggest that I wait until tomorrow. In fact, it's not a suggestion. Michael is having a "gastric lavage" – that's having your stomach pumped to you and me. It is pretty unusual these days, apparently. He is still unconscious; just as well, otherwise I don't see how they would have successfully intubated him. A senior nurse takes it upon herself to explain this unpleasant procedure as if I were about to sit my GCSE in the subject. Michael will be placed on his left side, with his head lowered. A plastic tube, that is lubricated, will be inserted through the nose or mouth into the stomach. Once the tube is correctly in place, the suction procedure begins; the stomach is literally washed out with warm water until the fluids are clear. I assume that he will feel groggy and uncomfortable after this procedure. He may also wake up angry and resentful. After all, this was probably his last chance to determine his future without intervention from others. I have taken away his independence; even the decision to take his own life. I want to understand more. I need to understand more. I feel desperately sad.

Suicide attempts invite a whole raft of visitors such as social workers; psychiatrists, counsellors, psychotherapists and mental health workers, not to mention the doctors. Many years ago, one of my pupils tried to commit suicide with a friend in the school lavatories – they had a pact – so I am already familiar with the aftermath but only when it has successfully failed. Once I realise that there is nothing more I can do, or am permitted to do, and that the doctors and nurses won't let me slump into a chair next to Michael, I can go to the hotel without a guilty conscience. It's nothing fancy. Emma has found us two small doubles at the Travelodge; it's only about two miles away. And it has a car park so she doesn't have to pay the exorbitant Pay and Display charges at the hospital.

We have rooms opposite each other. They're tastefully furnished and clean. I thank her again, and apologise for ruining her weekend. She won't hear another word of it. She has proved to be a true friend. I run a bath, even though I had one this morning, and leave the television on for company. I don't have a radio here and haven't worked out how to use the one embedded in the headboard. I don't have a nightie or a change of clothes with me – I didn't really plan to stay the night – so I drape everything neatly over the desk chair and try out the bed. It is soft and springy. I lie between the well-ironed sheets and imagine how many thousands of people have slept here before me; the very thought fills me with horror, but much to my surprise, I sleep.

In the morning, we eat a light breakfast in the small modern dining room. It's a buffet but the choice is limited to toast, Cornflakes, Bran Flakes and Special K with berries. There are some yoghurts as well. I opt for the Cornflakes. Emma has toast. We both drink copious amounts of tea. I tell Emma that as my family will be here soon, she doesn't have to stay. It's not that I am ungrateful. I am *so* indebted. But I can't return the favour. Not for another eight years or so. She finally gives in graciously and drops me back at the hospital before driving on to London. I realise afterwards that she has paid the hotel bill.

I report to the reception. I'm sent up to Level 2 where I find Michael conscious and awake though silent apart from his laboured breathing. I am not particularly squeamish but seeing him attached to so many tubes and drips is disconcerting. The Glaswegian consultant, Dr Angela Shaw, is just about to check on him (she liaises with the Junior Doctor who is by his bed and reading the charts). His heart rate is a little high, as is his blood pressure, but that aside, he has been lucky. He has escaped kidney damage and the harm to his liver is marginal. He will have an MRI scan at some point this week. And no, he can't have that in London. He's her patient now. I hand the consultant a copy of the Herbert

Protocol form, since I have spares in my handbag, but she only gives it a cursory glance. She is fully aware of Michael's illness; she has accessed his records. Everyone has.

As I wait in the wings, two cheerful nurses, most probably at the beginning of their long shift, attempt to give Michael a bed bath. He resists their good intentions by shoving the sponge to one side and kicking his legs beneath the sheets. I suppose this is a good sign as he is back to his old-new grumpy self. Either way, it is preferable to his comatose state. His speech is inaudible but it's obvious to all of us that he has not given his consent for this. Michael is a proud man. He has never much liked being prodded and poked by anyone other than me. Dr Shaw, who can't be more than forty-five, instructs the nurse to ignore the patient's objections; this is a routine wash and it is "absolutely necessary" if infections are to be avoided. Her accent is clipped and harsh. Everything sounds like an order. An intravenous drip is reattached by the Junior doctor and the catheter is changed by the senior nurse. I am glad that Michael is barely aware of this as I know how much he would hate the indignity.

As predicted, a psychiatrist arrives to establish Michael's state of mind. I think it's a little too soon as his throat must be sore and I'm sure he's feeling groggy but what do I know? He has barely spoken a word all morning. I wonder if the doctors are considering sectioning him under the Mental Health Act. The psychiatrist has a sympathetic bedside manner; is relaxed but professional; methodical but sympathetic. He has snowy white hair with a parting almost carved into his sculp. His line of questioning is not altogether different from our GP's only this time, they're predisposed towards his mental health. After establishing Michael's limited cognitive abilities, Dr Jackson-Hale asks his new patient to sit up in bed. The nurse presses a button to enable this to happen. He looks less like an invalid and more like himself now though he could do with a haircut and a shave. He is unkempt and unclean, despite the nurse's efforts. The backless surgical gown does nothing for him. Besides, it hasn't been changed since the "gastric lavage" as there are spots and stains on both sides.

Dr Jackson-Hale tilts his head to the side, and looks Michael straight in the eyes. He speaks to him directly, as if he is all there. *Do you feel that your life is worth living? Do you want to escape from your life? If you could do anything, what would it be?* He pauses between each question and repeats them as often as necessary. He is extraordinarily persistent. The first two questions are clearly focused on his mental health but I don't anticipate Michael's answer to the third one: he wants to be an astronaut. I'm confused now but for a brief moment, especially after he asks for a glass of Ribena, I realise what has happened. I fail to see how Michael could be relatively normal one month and totally disorientated in the next. I wonder whether his medication should be reviewed. The questions start to come thick and fast. Michael cannot cope with the pace or the content. It is cruel and humiliating though it is not designed to be either. Dr Jackson-Hale asks him the season; the month of the year; the name of our prime minister before Boris Johnson. He cannot answer any of these. Finally, he is asked how old he is; he doesn't know. But it's worse than that. He is looking forward to casting his first vote. I know that Michael can be quite lucid – despite his dementia – and wonder how much damage the drugs are doing to his demented brain.

The doctors consult with each other, in that conspiratorial way that they do, and smile politely at me. I tell them that the whole entourage (my family) are descending on the hospital in an hour or two, so if there are any more tests, could they do them now? They look at me with incredulity. A young nurse pads over to his bedside and takes Michael's blood pressure. He winces when the armband is tightened and breathes a sigh of relief when it's loosened. He is too shattered to speak anymore. I expect his throat is sore and ask the nurse whether she could give him something soothing for it. I can buy him some throat sweets from the pharmacy. I thank her for this advice. She looks down at the bag of urine attached to the catheter and changes it without further comment.

I switch on my mobile; it immediately vibrates and uploads the messages: my family have arrived and they are waiting for me in the same café that I was in last night. We are all a little fraught. Olivia and Eddie want to go straight to the ward. I try to prepare them but nothing I say will do that. We can't all enter the ward together; it wouldn't be fair on the other patients. There are only three of them. They're all men, even though the ward is sign-posted as "mixed". Sheila, Henry and I wait behind the door, and just peer through its long glass panel. The twins descend on their father like falling petals: all kisses and hugs. He acknowledges them by nodding but he looks bewildered by their incessant talking. I can see Eddie's face from where I am standing; he's so like his father used to be. I just hope the condition is not hereditary. We still haven't found out.

Olivia and Eddie sit patiently by the bed, holding their father's large hands in theirs. He doesn't resist their attention the way he did the nurse's but he doesn't reciprocate either. I wonder if he knows who they are. They stay with their father for at least half an hour. They would have stayed all morning had the nurse not intervened. They throw themselves into my arms, just as they did when they were half my size, and I repeat what the nurses said to me earlier: there will be good days and bad days; this was the latter. Things will improve. I'm about to say that they can't get worse but I know that this isn't true. I still can't establish how Michael managed to make his way to Stoke-on-Trent without any assistance. The doctors advise us that childhood memories are the last to go.

We end the conversation graciously, thanking all the staff for their valiant efforts. My parents, the twins and I take an Uber to the Travelodge and decide that we need to have the conversation that no one wants to hear.

Chapter 22
The Conversation

We leave the hospital with mixed feelings. Michael, though a little thinner, looks surprisingly well. He has received a professional shave, haircut and had his first proper bath for days. Superficially, the children have their father back. I appear to have my husband back. He is almost attractive again. We gather our little bags and sign all the relevant forms so that he can be formally discharged into my care; this is only the beginning though. We have a series of appointments to attend back in London. And we also need to have a conversation about the future.

My parents have agreed to spend two nights in London so that I can return to work until we find a solution. Michael, the twins and I travel from Stoke-on-Trent by train; my parents drive straight to the Premier Inn, Belsize Park. It has a car park but it is not owned by the hotel so they have to pay an additional charge for the privilege. The hotel is a five-minute walk from our house and it has its own restaurant; it's near the shops and plenty of local coffee shops in addition to an Everyman cinema. It if were not for Michael, they could almost make a minibreak out of their stay.

By 2 pm we are home and Michael's good humour has worn off. He is attempting to make himself a cup of tea. I watch him fill up the kettle; I think, this is all right. He can do this. The procedure must be embedded in his long-term memory. But he has forgotten where we keep the mugs – even though they have always been in the same cupboard above the dishwasher – he takes out a tumbler instead. The kettle is boiled and the water is poured into the glass; I wonder if it will crack. He has forgotten about the teabag. I take a moment to decide whether to intervene. At school, we occasionally use the *pose, pause, pounce* and *bounce* strategy. I try this out on Michael. *Would you like to use your favourite mug?* (The Keep Calm & Carry On one) – this is the pose: the difficult question. I am not being patronising. I know this is tough for Michael. I give him approximately ten seconds to respond; this is the pause. I have had to re-educate myself not to answer my pupils' questions before they have a chance of so doing. The ten seconds are up: no response. He is thinking. It is time for the "pounce"; this is when the teacher insists on no hands going up; it's time to pick on someone. I choose my husband. I decide to help him. I take out two teabags and two mugs, thinking erroneously that we might sit down together and talk.

The frontotemporal dementia does the "bounce". It hurls the glass of boiling water at my feet; it smashes into smithereens. Droplets of what feels like oil splatter into my face. I scream with the shock and excruciating pain. I throw water over my face but it is still agonising; the scorching water fees like acid. The pain is all consuming. My response is desperate. I tell him that he can go into a care home. It is not too soon. Our marriage is definitely over. Michael is not remotely remorseful. Instead, he stomps off in a huff, telling me that he doesn't understand why he is here or why he is no longer a carpenter. I don't laugh. This time, I report the incident to Social Services. I need their help.

I berate myself for sounding off; it was cruel and unkind. I find a tea towel and run it under the cold tap. I press it against my blistered skin and soothe the pain. I apologise. He apologises. I press my scorched face into his cotton shirt and weep for what we have lost: our future together.

Neither of us sleeps. Olivia invites me into her room and I reluctantly take up the offer. I still haven't returned to school and still haven't talked. My parents need to return to Hove as they have their own appointments to attend. Time is running out. In the morning, after breakfast, Eddie takes Michael to the Day Centre in West Hampstead. We need him to be taken care of; out of the way; anywhere but here. They walk there, as it's not far, and Michael is always fidgety and restless. Eddie has a calming effect on his father; there is less anger when he's next to him. I pack up a snack for my *third* adult child; it's two of his favourite chocolate biscuits wrapped up in foil. And some blueberries though this superfood is probably too late to have an impact on him. He doesn't need a packed lunch; the Day Centre will provide this, thankfully.

When Eddie returns, we meet at the Premier Inn Hotel as I can't bear to have "the conversation" at home. My face is a bit blotchy and there are a couple of mottled blisters forming near my chin. I have swallowed painkillers but they're not strong enough. I might phone Daniella (our friendly GP) and ask for something stronger but I know that my needs will not be met until Michael's are; this is how it is living with dementia. I wish she could inject me with morphine, anything to reduce the discomfort of being me. Henry, Sheila and Olivia are already assembled in the hotel's restaurant. It is clear that Olivia has already briefed my parents about the glass incident. Unusually for them, they don't open the conversation with a comment about my appearance. As we wait for Eddie, I look at my school emails; there are 513. This is a new record. Somehow, nothing seems important to me anymore. I have to return to work after this meeting: how can I? I am in no fit state to teach, let alone conduct interviews with ten and eleven-year-olds hoping to be offered a future in our school. My parents seem more concerned about my career than they are about my face. They know that I have made sacrifices to be in this position.

By the time Eddie has arrived, I have already reported last night's incident to Social Services, albeit half-heartedly.

They are sympathetic but business-like. Uncomfortable questions are asked of me including any other experiences of my husband's violent behaviour. I feel utterly disloyal but with some nudging from my "support group", I come clean. I feel dirty. There is nothing cathartic about informing on the person that you love. We finally have the conversation – the elephant in the room that is called dementia. My children are understandably anxious that they may inherit the condition. I explain that although having a test would give them a definitive answer, the consultant neurologist thought it was a one in a five million chance; in other words, this form of dementia is not genetic. My parents are visibly relieved. We don't have dementia in our family. We have cancer and Parkinson's disease instead. My mother asks the waiter for a piece of paper and pen; he returns with a stack of hotel stationery for which he is both thanked and tipped. My parents have always been generous in that way.

My mother makes list of five care homes in the London and Sussex areas. We systematically telephone them to see if they have a spare bed. My children take some persuasion and insist on viewing the homes before we commit; I know this is essential. There are *homes* and there are *homes*. We only phone the ones with good ratings. Some of the images on Google are disturbing; particularly the ones with "smoking gardens" and cigarette butts strewn across the lawns. At least your father will be safe. I keep repeating this although I know that it sounds like an excuse to get rid of him. I am not entirely in control of my mind; it isn't disintegrating like Michael's but it's at breaking point. I don't know how I really feel anymore.

I confess that I cannot go on; it is not that I don't love their father. It is because I *do* love him that he must be accommodated elsewhere. Besides, I no longer feel safe in my own home; that has to account for something. It takes a bruise, a swollen face or a scald for someone to ask me how I am these days. It's all about him. It's all about the dementia; that horrible illness that is a malicious thief. The robber returns each night to steal a little more of the man that was once Michael Boswell: the brilliant mathematician; the successful actuary; the loving and affectionate father and tender husband.

Dementia is a bastard that deserves to be assassinated.

Chapter 23
The Interviews

I am finally back at work. Principal Peter, the big loveable Canadian, has been exceptionally sympathetic. He will give me a sabbatical *if* I need one: a week, a month or even a year. It's my choice. I couldn't have a more generous boss. We sit in his minimalist office. He has acquired a desk calendar, at least. It has a cartoon for each day of the week. Principal Peter hands me the schedule for the 11 Plus interviews. We have fifty places but 155 pupils to interview. The vast majority of these children are considering at least four schools. We are rarely their first choice; this makes life difficult for us. We always have to take a gamble and over-offer, just in case we don't fill up our places. One year, we didn't anticipate the volume of acceptances. We had to convert four lavatories into a small classroom in the summer holidays. It has forever been known as Waterloo. The battle was mainly centred on getting planning permission at such short notice. The Governing body want a meeting before we send out our offer letters; they were not impressed by the over-spend last year.

My first interviewee is a girl called Eloise Fiona Whitely. She is a tiny little thing – looks no more than eight – but her voice is loud and confident. She wears her purple and grey uniform well. I can easily imagine her on a poster for Uniform 4 Kids. Most of our young candidates are a little nervous, which is why we start with the object that they have brought in; however, Eloise is so poised and self-assured that this doesn't seem necessary. We chat about her current school, her favourite subjects, her menagerie (which comprises a dog, fish and a reptile, amongst others) and her many ambitions. I ask her about what she does on a typical weekend; her answer is swift and a bit rehearsed but it's an impressive response. She plays football at Regent's Park on Saturday mornings (I really wasn't expecting this), takes her dog out for a walk afterwards, visits her *maternal* (her word, not mine) grandparents in Maida Vale every other Saturday and enjoys kickboxing on Sunday mornings. I had visions of her prancing about in a pink tutu and ballet shoes. She reminds me that we haven't discussed her chosen object; I have never forgotten to raise this before. I know my mind is preoccupied. To my utter amazement and dismay, this innocent looking child removes a white rat from her school backpack. It is definitely not a mouse as its tail is too long. I fear rats even more than Michael does. We should be having this interview in the photocopier room! I am fixated on my room 101. I can't take my eyes off it in case it leaps out of her dainty little hands and into my lap. It is a "girl" and she is called Miranda; this seems like a big name for a little creature. I stifle a laugh though it's really a cry for help. It takes every modicum of my strength to keep the interview going; after all, I don't want to offend Eloise. I say Miranda is adorable and cute; it's just what she wants to hear. For some reason that I cannot fathom, I tell her that my daughter's middle name is Miranda. I quickly wrap up the interview.

The second candidate is a mischievous looking boy called Freddie. He is impeccably dressed in Jasper Conran clothes. He has the face of an angel; now I need to establish whether he has the character to match it. I ask him about his object; it isn't what I am expecting. It's his "voice" which he says he brings with him all the time. Quite a comedian. But is he going to be on a permanent ego trip? I want to find out more. I mistakenly assume that he is going to sing me a song – judging by the way he is turned out, something from the

1970s perhaps? He can't sing. His forte is putting on accents. I think this sounds fun. I know that I should reign myself in and be professional. The children aren't here to entertain me. But life is too short. Michael is living proof of that. Little does this boy know that I am rather good at this game too. We start with the Welsh accent; his is better than mine which often deteriorates into a Pakistani accent (no offence meant). His Russian accent is very authentic and his Italian inflection is simply delightful though the words "spaghetti" and "cappuccino" make me want to eat and drink. He is a loveable rogue. I want to adopt this boy. We finish "the game" and I start interviewing him properly. I have a reputation to protect. We talk about Bond Street School's close proximity to the West End theatres; this is not lost on him. He wants to be an actor or a comedian. I think he might have what it takes and say so. Flattery costs nothing.

Girls and boys come in and out of my office all morning. Most of them are polite and enthusiastic. I see a multitude of objects: baked cakes, diving medals, knitted blankets, bug houses, photographs of pets and a range of instruments including a harp! I have one more child to see before an enforced lunch break. I notice that his parents, who are sitting outside my office, are both extraordinarily good looking. The father is dressed in an expensive suit; a white shirt and a bright red tie. His upper body is very slim whilst his lower body is muscular. The man's wife is a bottle blonde and wearing a rather short red dress and matching stilettoes; she looks as though she's going to a cocktail party rather than a school. The child is wearing a uniform that I immediately recognise. The blazer is navy with a double white stripe; the tie is similar and the grey trousers are tailored. Even his shoes look more expensive than my suit. I trot out the same questions that I have meted out to the rest of the children. His favourite subject is science (so I tell him about our STEM lab which of course he has seen) and his least favourite subject is English. I try not to overreact. He is only a child. His ambition is to be a professional footballer, like his father. I immediately question his parents' judgement. We are a school in town with no playing fields. I suspect his mother fancies the idea of shopping in Gucci before collecting him in her Ferrari. Whilst we're talking about his object (an impressive Lego model of the Emirates Stadium) I furtively Google the boy's surname. His father has only just retired from playing for Arsenal. He is thirty-five.

Whilst Abbas, Principal Peter, Annie and I are eating lunch in the canteen, we are joined by Liam. He is overexcited about something. He mentions the name of a band that neither Abbas nor I have heard of; the lead singer was in our reception. He has just interviewed the daughter. Peter Principal indulges him; Annie enjoys partaking of her cheese and tomato baguette (her diet is over) and I tell my colleagues about Eloise and her white rat. I decide to save the story about the Arsenal player's son for another time.

In the afternoon, I have to teach; after all, that's really why I am here. My A Level set makes it all worth it. They have all done their essays centred on the doppelgänger in *Frankenstein*. Jeremy asks me why so many people think the creature is called Frankenstein; I tell *him* that he's just written a whole essay on the subject! We are about halfway through the Poetry Anthology, which we are all enjoying, and I set an essay on "relationships". After double English, I teach Year 11. I regret to inform them that I can't return their mocks until next week; this goes down like a lead balloon. I don't set them any homework. I will probably have to do my marking between midnight and 2 am I should have taught maths...

I have intentionally kept my mobile off until now. My parents are still in London; I know they can handle a crisis, should one arise. But temptation gets the better of me and I take a look anyway. There's some good news. One of the care homes – the one in Buckinghamshire – has two "beds" (rooms) available. My heart leaps and sinks in unison. I return to my office to call the care home; its number is the most recent call. I speak to the receptionist first; she places me on hold for a lengthy period of time. Her name is Arti. I put my mobile onto loudspeaker as the lobby music is over-powering in my ear. Whilst I am waiting, I Google *Greenbank Lodge*; it is not my first choice. It's not really close enough but I consider myself more of a beggar than a chooser right now. I know it achieved a "good" for its inspection and it has never dropped below this grading. It is definitely worth a look. I book an appointment for noon on Saturday. I think we should all go. We can pretend we're going on a family outing.

At 5.30 pm most of my colleagues have left. There are a sprinkling of pupils using our computer room. It's already dark outside. I fetch my bicycle from the disabled loo and switch the head light and back light on, ready to make a quick exit. I take all the unmarked essays with me in the vain hope that I might mark them when everyone else is asleep. I know this is unrealistic. I ring Olivia before I leave, just to check in. I'm literally poised on my bicycle in Bond Street, about to cross over Oxford Street. It's buzzing with shop-pers as the sales are in full swing. I could do with some retail therapy of my own and I would love to take the twins shop-ping. I know that other's people's lives are not always what they seem but to me, today, everyone else's life appears to be more normal than mine, whatever that is. My cycle route follows the buses; it's unpleasant but flat which appeals to my lazy self. I have never been this tired for such a prolonged period, not even after the twins were born.

I pull up to the front door and press my head against the window; for a brief moment, I can see a happy trio sitting at the table, playing Monopoly. It looks so perfect I want to take a snapshot of it. I wonder if Michael can remember the rules; they must be embedded into his brain, given the number of times we used to play when the children were young. The scene looks so perfect that I don't want to intrude. I linger for a while. I take off my helmet, cycling gloves and yellow fluorescent jacket. I switch off the headlamp and the back-light. I fear that as soon as I enter the house, the magical scene will vanish.

I'm touched to find that the twins are making supper for the four of us: spaghetti Bolognese and a salad. Good hearty food. It's just what I need in the depths of winter. I rush upstairs to change and return to the hob within a couple of minutes. I take over stirring the sauce so that the others can continue playing the board game. The twins are so patient with their father. Even as I stand here, the pair of them end-lessly repeat the rules. He is particularly confused by the Chance and Community Chest cards. Michael has a pile of unsorted money and three random properties: The Electric Company; Mayfair and Liverpool Street Station. He also has a Get Out of Jail Free card. The twins already have a set each: the orange set and the yellow set. No one has bought Regent's Street, Oxford Street or Bond Street. Eddie throws a six which takes him to The Electric Company. I think this is the perfect time for a break. I don't want a commotion.

The spell is broken. Michael doesn't want supper. He isn't hungry. I suspect he has been snacking on biscuits as there are crumbs all over the kitchen work surface. Besides, Eddie *owes* him money. It's four times the number on the die. He reads the card very slowly and deliberately. Four times six. I don't want Michael to be humiliated in front of his own children. I know they're kind and patient, but do they really have to witness his dementia-induced mathematical inepti-tude? I am not sure they realise that he no longer has a con-cept of numbers. *I know it. Don't tell me. I can do it.* But Eddie just blurts out the amount and tells him which denomina-tions to give him: a £20 and four single £1s. He leans over the table and helps himself to the money. He doesn't mean to be insensitive. I think he is hungry. I want everyone to sit down at the table. The salad is prepared. I dish up the spaghetti into four bowls and add parmesan on everyone's except Olivia's as she has never liked it. I put a jug of ice-cold water on the table and a bottle of red wine with four glasses. No one moves. I repeat myself, just as the twins keep repeating the rules countless times. Michael is looking at the die as if it is a strange object that has fallen out of the sky.

His frustration and anger are vented. The doctors warned us about the role-reversal but it doesn't make it easier. It is painful for young adults to watch their father's rapid decline. It is unnatural. The board flies up; the money wafts down. The property cards are dispersed and mostly land on the floor. He takes the Get Out of Jail Free card and holds it up to my face. *You're not putting me in a jail. I am not a criminal. I would never treat you like this.* I deny treating him badly. Everything is centred on him these days. I barely have a life; the twins can't live theirs; my parents are constantly round to help and even my friends are too. I haven't even told him about the care home yet. How can he know?

It only takes a few minutes for that perfect snapshot – the one I wish I had taken – to dissolve into total misery.

Michael goes upstairs and pisses in the sink. It is all too much to bear.

Chapter 24
Burning the Midnight Oil

I have often wondered whether it has been worth the sacrifice of living in a small house in a smart area. Right now, I would do anything to have an extra room, even a broom cupboard. I know it's all temporary. The twins will go to university in the autumn. I don't know where Michael will be but it's unlikely to be here. At least he is asleep; in that state, I hope, he can find peace. I am downstairs, sitting in the kitchen, attempting to mark the plethora of essays in front of me. I arrange them in three piles: Sixth Form; Year 11 and "others". I like to mark with music. I fiddle about with my iPod and press the earplugs hard into my ears. I am hermetically sealed in my own little world of Faure and *Frankenstein*, Mozart and *Macbeth*, Schubert and *Simon Armitage*. It is almost spiritual. In between essays, I make myself cups of tea; empty the dishwasher; tidy up the pile of magazines strewn across the floor. Anything to avoid continuous marking. I also put away all remnants of the disastrous Monopoly game. At 4 am I am finished. I am not sure whether I should creep back up to bed; if I do, I will only get two hours of rest. I won't sleep. I am already feeling a little light-headed and sick. I decide to bed down on the sofa. My head rests on the cushion that says "Thirty years on the couch together." I turn it upside down.

When I wake up at 6 am the house is still quiet. I need fresh clothes. The darkness cloaks my figure as I creep into the bedroom. I am almost successful, clutching a bundle, when Michael thinks I am a burglar. He is out of the bed so quickly that I realise that he hasn't been asleep. *It's me. Don't touch me.* He knows me and yet he doesn't know me. I am too exhausted to put up much resistance. The disturbance wakes up Olivia; her room is closer to ours. Eddie can sleep through anything. She rushes up to our door, trying to wedge it open with her bare feet. I don't want her to come in. She doesn't have to witness this. But Olivia and I are very close. She is as protective of me as I am of her. *Stop it, Daddy. Stop it.* I think the word "Daddy" brings him to his senses. He is paralysed with shame. I am paralysed with fear. Olivia grabs my wrist and yanks me out of the room, away from her motionless father. My bundle of clothes falls to the floor. He holds his head in his hands and howls; it is the sound of a wounded animal. I can't leave him like this but I can't think straight. I am too worn out. *It's not you, Michael. It's the dementia. None of this is your fault.* But I fear my husband in this altered state more than I fear the underground. He has no control over his temper. He is explosive and volatile. The kind and gentle man whom I loved for many years is no longer in his body; he has all but disappeared. The howl becomes a cry. We all cry. I can't believe Eddie is still asleep. I don't want to scuttle off to work, knowing that Michael is so distraught. It is hopeless.

I have no choice. My family has to come first. I telephone Principal Peter on his mobile and explain that I can't come into school. He offers to send a courier to pick up the marked essays and exam papers; as I said, he is a generous man. I need to set cover for the few lessons that I am scheduled to teach today. I feel as though I am developing flu. My head is cloudy and throbbing. I'm on the verge of some sort of breakdown. My to-do list has never been so long. I am trying to squeeze in appointments for and about Michael, some of which are now urgent: medical assessments; trips to the Memory Clinic, blood tests, home-help, financial assistance, his entitlement to his pension, albeit early, and so on. It is never-ending. Half-term can't come soon enough. Olivia makes me a Lemsip; I hate the taste of the undissolved powdery bits but force it down. I don't have time to develop full-blown flu. Michael is offended that he hasn't been offered a yellow concoction. Everything offends him these days. We are treated to yet another rant about being excluded from the family. I can't do anything right. I am failing as a mother and failing as a wife; this is what dementia does. It affects the whole family not just the individual. There are 45,000 people suffering from early onset dementia. I don't want to be a member of this exclusive club.

My parents telephone the landline at 8 am; Olivia picks up the phone. Her voice quivers a little. Instead of driving straight back to Sussex, Sheila and Henry offer to come over instead. We are less than a ten-minute walk from their hotel. As soon as they're through the door, they're both in control: meting out advice and giving us instructions. I would rather be at work, away from this middle-class version of a Mike Leigh film.

My father, who used to be close to Michael, takes him on one side to talk to him. Or rather, give him a good talking-to. It is becoming something of a habit. I know it's pointless. *Keep your northern brutish ways away from my beautiful daughter, do you hear? You were never good enough for her.* This is untrue. Michael was always good enough for me. Henry says too much, most of which my husband won't remember anyway. But it's hurtful and unnecessary. Saturday can't come soon enough. My mother wants me to bring the appointment forward. She is the voice of common sense. And she reminds me that the Social Worker must complete the assessment so that Michael can go into the home as soon as possible. I know she is right. What about respite care? It's an option. Sheila (mother) offers to drive us down there. Despite Monopoly-gate, we agree that Eddie is best suited to looking after Michael today. He can escort him to the Day Centre and collect him at 3 pm when it closes. He enjoys it. It's where he "works" now and it has become part of his new routine.

Henry and Sheila have decided. They will inspect Greenbank Care Home in Buckinghamshire with us. We will be the revamped Fab Four.

Chapter 25
Greenbank Care Home

The drive to Greenbank Care Home in Buckinghamshire takes under an hour. The large two-storey red brick building looks quite attractive as it is flanked by trees, grass and huge plant pots. Despite the winter, gardeners have ensured that there is plenty of flora and fauna on display. It makes for a good first impression. As we approach the entrance, a youngish man in a catatonic state, is wheeled out onto the drive. His mouth is open and he is drooling. It is sad to see. His wheelchair has a neck support but his head remains tilted to one side. None of us knows what to say so we just smile and say *hello* both to the young man and to the person pushing the wheelchair. We walk straight through to the entrance; it looks like a hotel lobby. The only difference is that there is a small kitchen to the right of the reception; everything in it is meticulously labelled: the cakes (50 pence), fresh fruit (50 pence), tea and coffee (25 pence) and bottles of water (£1). There are four chairs pushed neatly under a pine table and a small dishwasher under the sink. As in keeping with everything else, there is a laminated sign saying: *Guests and Visitors: You are all welcome!* I leave my parents and Olivia at the table. My father is both hungry and thirsty. He takes a piece of cake from the dish and carefully replaces the plastic domed top. It's carrot cake. Very sickly. It is taxed by my mother and Olivia. The calories don't count when they're on someone else's plate. The poor man only eats about two mouthfuls. He places £2 in the saucer and helps

163

himself to a cup of tea and makes one for Sheila and Olivia as well. I know I won't have time to drink one even though I am parched. It's like the Sahara in here.

Whilst they are eating and drinking, I introduce myself to Arti; I can see her name badge, so I'm pretty sure she's the same woman I spoke to from my office. At first, she thinks I am looking at the home for my parents. I am indignant on their behalf. I remind her that my husband has early onset dementia. We want to have a good look round, before he does, to make sure it is suitable. The woman nods her head and asks me to sign everyone into the visitors' book. Last time, my mother signed us both in. Arti escorts me to the small pine table, where my family are sitting patiently, and hands us two brochures. Amy will be with us shortly; she will be conducting the tour. We leaf through the glossy brochures; they are full of glamorous photographs of the furniture. It strikes me as peculiar that the only pictures of people are of the staff. Everyone here is a manager of something. I turn to the back page to look at the prices; they're astronomical. I already have power of attorney; unfortunately, it was a necessary evil as Michael can no longer be trusted with our money. But the thought of spending nearly £1000 a week on my fifty-year old husband, is jaw dropping. We have university fees to pay. I need to contact Social Services again. There may be a way of getting the Council to pay for continuous care. But I won't hold my breath.

Amy is one of the duty General Managers (according to her badge). She introduces herself to me, and then to the others, saying all our names out loud in order to remember them. She's a little bit younger than me – mid-forties – and is dressed in smart casual clothes. We walk through a double-door, straight onto the first corridor; it's for the patients without dementia, as they are at less risk of wandering off. The theme is the seaside; it seems a bit out-of-place in Buckinghamshire. Even Sunny Cliffe in Hove didn't look like this. At least Mary Nurse Ratched isn't here in any shape or form. Amy shows us some of the rooms which are occupied by residents; they're mostly eating lunch in the dining room which we will see shortly. All the doors are propped open; I think this is a good sign. Each room has a large single bed; a bedside table with a lampshade on it, a vanity unit/desk with a chair, a wardrobe and an en suite bathroom. They all have flat-screen televisions mounted on the wall; insofar as I can tell, all of them are permanently on. None of them are being watched. There are heaps of soft toys on almost every bed and armchair; it's almost as if a kindergarten is about to visit.

We are taken to a show room next; this is at the end of the corridor instead of the beginning, which I find a bit odd, but Amy says it's above the laundry room which is why no one sleeps in it. The room is pristine. The bed is made up with a light blue duvet, dark blue sheet and matching pillows. The walls are white but there are several seaside pictures, all framed, of famous resorts including our favourite: Brighton. There's even a little bowl with polished stones in it. Whilst we are all in the room, I notice that Amy waits in the corridor with her clipboard wedged under her arm. She reminds me of an estate agent. We ask to see the dining room; the activities room; the lounge and also the corridor designated for residents with dementia. I don't think she wants us to see it. The Dementia Unit is the mad woman in the attic.

The dining room is surprisingly pleasant. Even though it's winter, and the home, like the other one, is totally overheated, the top windows are all open, allowing some much-needed fresh air in. The tables are all round; this is necessary because half of the residents are in wheelchairs, thus giving them easy access. The tables are covered in heavy-duty white linen; napkins are neatly folded into glasses and fresh flowers are carefully arranged in tiny glass vases. It gives the residents the impression that they're staying in an upmarket hotel. It's all very pleasant. It's not the place that is the problem. It's the people. Once again, almost everyone is very elderly or infirm. Michael is only fifty. There must be at least thirty residents eating their lunch in this room. There is a carefully balanced menu printed and framed on a noticeboard. The residents look perfectly content. No one will starve here. The old residents smile at Olivia; I think they're pleased to see a young and pretty face. But I can see that she feels a little uncomfortable with all the attention. Amy senses that we have been in the dining room too long. She ushers my parents out first. She glides out of the room straight into the recreation room; it's a long narrow room, with large windows all down one side. At least it's bright and airy. There's a giant Scrabble board on wheels. The residents play as a group. Words such as "lacey" are linked with "cob" and "snipe". The words aren't childish. As we are leaving, a small group of elderly people start assembling for the quiz on classical music. At least Greenbank is true to its words; the residents here are stimulated. Those that want to be, that is.

I am already talking myself out of sending Michael here. He is too young. And too lucid. I know he can be difficult and is frequently disorientated but he is not ready for this. My parents know me too well, and tell me to remain focused. Olivia is finding the visit an ordeal. I admit that we all are. We have to go upstairs for the dementia "unit". Nothing is called a wing as it's not a prison, despite all the locks, keypads and CCTV cameras. Amy asks my parents if they would prefer to take the lift. We all walk up the stairs and follow Amy along a wide corridor; this one has a linoleum floor; it is more practical than a carpet, but less homely. The walls are plastered in framed pictures of old crooners. The only one I recognise is Frank Sinatra. Most of the bedroom doors are closed; perhaps the care home is trying to preserve people's dignity. Each door has a key on the outside (which I didn't notice downstairs) and I wonder whether the residents are locked in at night. I am desperate to ask questions but Amy has verbal diarrhoea. I have already made up my mind that Michael isn't going to come here so I am only half-listening.

One of bedroom doors is slightly ajar. As the rest of my family continue following the Duty Manager, I hold back to fiddle about with my shoelace; it's a ruse, of course. I just want to see a real room as opposed to a "show room". A very thin elderly lady is lying in a bed with metal sides; there is no chance of her falling out. She is "watching" Peppa Pig. She also has mountains of soft toys on her bed and on the tops of the cupboards. I stop to look at the door sign; it has a black and white picture of "Lilly" with a group of other women, all in their twenties. It is almost impossible to see the old woman in the young woman. I wonder whether she has had a family; a career; a life. Her "memory box" is mounted on her door; it contains a necklace, a piece of lace, a cat collar and a wedding ring. I decide she must be a widow.

I catch up with the others. I ask about bedtime and "the rules". My mother apologies on my behalf. *Sophie is a teacher. She can't help it. She lives by her rules.* I'm simply too tired to be obstreperous and I never lower myself to answer her back in front of Olivia. Amy refuses to give me a straight answer about bed times. She says there aren't any. I find this hard to believe and am appalled that the evening meal is served at 5.30 pm We walk past the hair salon; it's unisex though I can only see women in it. I ask about shaving, as this is something Michael finds difficult to do now, let alone in the future. She tells us that this is all taken care of under "personal care". Toenails are cut too. I am finding the "home" too hot. I am so sleep deprived that the combination of exhaustion and temperatures synonymous with Death Valley in Nevada, don't bring out the best in me. We end the tour in the main visitors' lounge; it is enormous, well-furnished and once again looks like a hotel. I am half-expecting to take afternoon tea here. I am desperate for some fresh air. My mother signs us all out.

We walk around the perimeter of the building; it has a

beautiful aspect with a golf course nearby. My father spots a little village pub in the distance so we walk towards it and decide to have a late lunch there. It's called The Goat and the Kid. The contrast between the warmth of the home and the coolness outside is welcome. Although it's not all that cold, even for January, the pub has an open log fire; there are heaters in the corners and there's a general buzz of happy weekenders eating chilli con carne and drinking pints. We find a table in the corner. My mother doesn't think Greenbank is preferable to Sunny Cliffe in Hove. My father is the most optimistic of the four of us. Once again, I find myself thinking that an in-house carer, even one for the day and one for the night, might be the lesser of two evils. Whilst we're in the pub, I Google some specialist agencies and fill in my contact details. If Michael isn't ready for the care home options, we need to make our home a more caring place.

Chapter 26
Agency Staff

It's almost half-term and despite everything, I have managed to come into work almost every day this month. February is much more depressing than January. The sales are over; it's significantly darker and colder; everyone is tired and no one wants to be here, except for me. It's my Escape Room. Principal Peter has decided that everyone would be cheered up by an impromptu Valentine's Day school disco. It will be held on Friday, 14th February, just before half-term. The Sixth Form have been tasked with selling the tickets; they will cost £5 and will include one drink (soft) and plenty of food. The school will subsidise the party. Teachers have a free pass. We need some sort of adult presence.

I congratulate Principal Peter on his inspired idea; after all, we haven't had a party since Halloween. Everyone is on their knees. My non-teaching friends still don't understand why we are shattered after only six weeks. For the first time since Michael's diagnosis, I am on top of my workload. This wouldn't be possible without our wonderful new live-in help. Her name is Kathleen and she's a retired nurse from Dublin, grateful for the opportunity. I pay her £400 a week which is £600 less than the care home. She has a sister in Kilburn whom she rarely sees so this is ideal for her. We can't be more than two or three miles from the main high street. She is tactful, robust and takes no nonsense from Michael. She is my Mary Poppins: practically perfect in every way. The cynic in me thinks she must have a flaw but I haven't found it yet. Obviously, Eddie and Olivia have had to move back to Sussex but they were ready to do this. They will be off travelling again soon. When Kathleen arrived, I let her choose between Eddie's room and Olivia's. She intuitively knew that I wanted her to choose Eddie's. Besides, I don't think she wanted to sleep next to our room. I am not sure whether it's because she wants to respect our privacy or whether she wants us to respect hers. A locksmith has fitted locks to all the bedroom doors, as she requested.

I am still at school, pretending that everything is normal. I hope that Fran and Freddie will be able to come to the disco. Their attendance has been remarkable; better than mine overall. And the baby twins are doing very well. Fran's mother has proved to be a doting grandma; no one expected this. I need to piggy-back other people's happiness at the moment. Most of the Sixth Form have bought tickets for the disco, as have Years 10 and 11. Years 7 to 9 are only allowed to come for the first two hours so they will only pay £1. All the profits will go to charity. The Sixth Form are somewhat over-familiar with me. I don't mind. It's a relationship built on a mutual trust and respect. They never forget that I am their Deputy Head. But I am asked whether I am bringing my husband to the disco. *God no*, I say, and then regret my reaction; it's so telling.

I cannot unsay what I have just said. Rumours fly around the school that I am getting a divorce. Even Abbas asks me if the rumour is true. I know that my marriage is dead in the water. It's a total sham. I don't know who Michael is any-more and he certainly doesn't respect me for who I am. I have one free lesson (out of eight) so I take the opportunity of telephoning Kathleen. She can't speak because she's in the Royal Academy with Michael. It is a few minutes away from school. I know that I sound churlish but I give clear instructions that Michael is not to be brought here. I make this very clear.

I am in mid-flow with my Year 11 class. We are studying

Seamus Heaney's poem, "Follower". It is not easy for me to teach. Eddie "stumbled" as a small child like Heaney did. Michael always picked up the pieces, just as Heaney's father did for him. Now the father is the follower. It is all too familiar. Some of my pupils show great emotional intelligence and say it's their favourite poem after "Winter Swans". I set the class a *pair and share* activity so that I can stand at the back and observe. I look out of the huge window, which faces Bond Street, and spot Michael and Kathleen. They are striding towards the front entrance of the school. He is playing follow-my-leader. I am unable to control my increasing heart rate.

Within minutes, the new receptionist pops up to the classroom. We still have five minutes remaining and I am a stickler for the bell. I don't want to hear what she's going to say. This is my space and I don't want Michael invading it. I thought I had made this explicit when I spoke to the agency and to Kathleen in person. The receptionist and I whisper to each other and I agree to meet Michael and "the woman" in the Randolph Room (if it's empty). Under no circumstances is he to come up to my office. I have no idea what sort of mood he will be in. He may be harmless but he can also be violent. I am unable to regain my poise and confidence. The lesson deteriorates and the pupils start chatting amongst themselves. I don't think they're talking about the poems anymore. I say hello to Michael and confront Kathleen. She is defensive and belligerent. She reminds me that he's my husband and he wanted to see me. I remind her that she's his carer and I'm paying her to look after him. The atmosphere is tense and unpleasant. I resent being undermined at work. There is no stopping Kathleen. She even lectures me about being a good wife whilst stuffing her face with chocolate biscuits. I reprimand her, as if she were a member of my staff. She firmly takes Michael's hand, as if he were her child, and ushers him out. He turns his head and says: *it's hard having two wives.* I am unable to concentrate for the remainder of the day. I telephone the agency and complain about Kathleen. I am in no rush to go home. In fact, I am dreading it. Now that I think of it, Kathleen reminds me of the overbearing maternity nurse we used immediately after the twins were born. There were complications. Nothing particularly unusual. She was bossy and imperious but we endured her because we felt life without her would be worse. We found out after she left. Kathleen reminds me of her. She has the same curly dyed orange hair and the same brazen personality.

In the evening, I return to find that Kathleen has made dinner: stir fried chicken, vegetables in chilli and lime and noodles. At least I haven't come home to a boiling rabbit. I am not sure if this is her way of saying sorry. Perhaps I have overreacted. I apologise and she does too. But the atmosphere is still tense. Our house is too small for an interloper. We really have to get on. As we eat, I start to think about Greenbank and all of its advantages. Michael *could* be happy there. He isn't happy here. After dinner, Kathleen loads the dishwasher. I ask Michael if he wants to watch something on television; we haven't seen anything for ages. He grabs all three of the remote controls: one is for the sound bar; one is the Sky remote and the other is just for the television. It is faintly ridiculous. He starts frantically pressing the buttons. I let him fumble around for a while. I am not trying to humiliate him. I am trying not to emasculate him.

I rarely have the opportunity to vegetate so I just take the remote-control back from my ham-fisted husband. I know it's not his fault and I do not pass judgement. *We cannot switch the television on because someone will be watching us;* this is probably not as ludicrous as it sounds. He is totally paranoid these days. I press a button and *MasterChef* comes on; it's about their fiftieth series. I haven't seen it for years but it hasn't changed. I try to have a conversation about the contestants and how difficult some of the dishes are but Michael is unresponsive. He is hungry again and asks me when we're having supper. I tell him that we have all eaten. We give up on the programme as neither of us can concentrate. Kathleen has gone to Kilburn to see her sister, Roisin. We agree to meet in the kitchen at 6.30 am in the morning!

Michael and I go upstairs. We have the house to ourselves. We both go to the bathroom as Kathleen has strongly suggested that we brush our teeth at the same time. He has been complaining of toothache lately. I still haven't been to the dentist. I am beginning to neglect myself. It's a bit too early to be in bed but after not watching television, I feel like reading. We are, or were, both avid readers. I am reading a collection of short stories at the moment; it is more manageable than a long novel right now. I offer to read out loud. The story is too complicated for Michael to follow but he doesn't mind listening. He lies on his back, on top of the duvet, whilst I nestle underneath it. I notice that he has a small burn on his wrist. I wonder how he got it. I read for ages, hoping that my soporific voice will send him to sleep. I can hardly focus on the pages as the print is getting smaller and more blurred as I try to continue. I need to go to the optician as well as the dentist. I'm forty-nine and probably need glasses.

I'm just about to settle down in Olivia's room when something triggers off a car alarm; it's a deafening sound. It stops for a brief moment and starts up again a minute later. Most people are probably eating dinner or watching television; it isn't late. I return to the bathroom to fetch some earplugs and squish them in as hard as I can; they're ineffective and I still can't drown out the noise. I toss and turn in bed for at least two hours. The alarm is stubborn and refuses to cut out. Michael is snoring. It's only 10 pm but I am so tired now that I am too exhausted to fall asleep. It doesn't make sense. I decide to get dressed in my navy joggers and navy hoodie. I fetch a hammer from the kitchen drawer and stuff it up my right sleeve and go outside. It has only ever been used to bash in picture hooks, not people's cars. No one is around. At first, I can't see the offending vehicle. I follow the noise all the way down the mews and out towards the village shops. At least I probably won't know the owner. I am so sleep deprived that it doesn't take much for me to lose control. It is as if there's a little voice in my head, goading me into committing my first crime. I let the hammer fall out of my sleeve and grasp it tightly. I tap the red back lights on both sides, and to my satisfaction, they instantly shatter. At least now there's a reason for the alarm; this is how I justify my irresponsible actions. I run back home, as if I were a jogger in the rain. Kathleen is letting herself in through our door. I hope she hasn't seen me.

My alarm wakes me at 6 am It is much too early and I am not at all rested. I am faintly amused at my *dream*. But I get a rude awakening when I spy my tracksuit draped over the chair, and the hammer placed at an angle on Olivia's dressing table. It takes a few seconds for me to realise that I have committed an offence. I can't explain it but I have an incredibly strong urge to tell someone; I suppose this is how criminals eventually get caught. I don't want to confide in Kathleen. I think she is more Alex Forrest than she is Mary Poppins. We talk for a few minutes and plan Michael's day. He enjoys the quizzes at the Day Centre so she will take him there. One of the care workers from Greenbank is going to come in the evening, to assess him, so I need to be back on time for that. It's important. I am not sure if I can tolerate Kathleen for much longer.

She comments on the "blessed car alarm". I don't respond. I can't be bothered to indulge her. Besides, she is no Priest and she isn't going to force a lousy confession out of me. I'll tell Abbas instead. Or Annie. Or Emma or Rosie. Anyone but Kathleen. I don't feel like cycling this morning. I walk down the cobbled mews until I reach the vandalised car. Several people are shaking their heads with contempt. I decide not to say anything. I don't want to look too interested or too disinterested. I am not sure how to behave. I still want to tell someone.

Chapter 27
Social Pariahs

Rosie sends me a text, offering to buy me a coffee at the Sotheby's café in Bond Street; it's a stone's throw from my school and she will be in the area today. We agree a time, subject to my *not* being dragged into a meeting or put on cover. My morning is full of tedious tasks and very little teaching; this gives me the freedom to go out. I am only answerable to Principal Peter (and the Governors who aren't coming in until after half-term). Although it's still cold and damp outside, I purposely leave my suit jacket on the back of my chair; this makes it looks as if I am somewhere in the building. I have to formally sign out though – in case there's a fire alarm or even a real fire – but the chances of that are miniscule. I walk down to Sotheby's. I always forget how luxurious and civilised it is in there. And there are no bells or noisy teenagers scrabbling up and down the stairwells. Rosie is already *in situ*, sipping a raspberry infused tea that smells as inviting as it looks. I order a café latte.

I express an interest in wandering around the sale rooms as I know that there's an Impressionist sale next Tuesday. We scamper up the carpeted stairs and observe the art as if we are potential buyers with millions to invest. The suited and booted custodians in the rooms – all of whom are probably Art History graduates from first-rate universities like Bristol or Exeter, greet us politely. They look bored stiff. They're too young to be confined to temperature-controlled rooms holding walkie-talkies. As we view the marvellous Monets and the

175

magnificent Manets, I update Rosie about the in-house carer. She doesn't much like the sound of her and suggests I buy a webcam or install a secret camera; she says you can't be too careful with "these sorts of people" but I am not entirely sure I understand what she means. She mentions her late grandmother, and an overzealous nurse, but I sense that she doesn't want to expand on this. I don't encourage her though she has got my attention. We end the rendezvous with a long stare at the beautiful Monet painting; it's one of his Giverny garden series. I would like to step into it and stay there. I enjoy our flights of fancy into the art world but afterwards find Rosie's comments about the webcam ricocheting around my head.

Back at school, everyone is gearing up for the Valentine's Day disco. It's tomorrow evening. Two hundred and fifty tickets have been sold. Stacks of food and soft drinks have already been delivered and stored in a locked room. We have a staff meeting at 4.15 pm It's mostly centred on the party and the security arrangements which we need to put in place. Apropos of this, Joe is also present at the meeting. I am quite pleased to see his ginger cat; in some ways, I prefer it to Joe. A conversation ensues about dog-people and cat-people; it's as trite as it sounds. Principal Peter asks the staff to raise their hands if they're coming tomorrow night; he can easily see who is volunteering his or her time and who has a life outside school. Abbas has a friend in catering who has kindly agreed to lend us his industrial sized chocolate fountain. Joe is concerned about the additional clearing up that this will create. I suppose he has a point. The meeting ends at about 5.45 pm which is a bit earlier than usual. Slap-bang into the middle of the rush hour. No one is celebrating.

I walk up to Oxford Street and catch a 13-bus straightaway. I click on the messages on my mobile; there are three from Kathleen and one from my friend, Emma. I read Kathleen's three messages first. They're concise professional updates, informing me about Michael's visit to the Day Centre; how he enjoyed the music quiz and finally, that he slipped over in the kitchen when he got home. No broken bones. I text her back, thanking her for the update, and say I will be home soon. I also tell her where the ice-packs are kept. I pop into the M & S in Swiss Cottage, to buy some salmon and fresh vegetables. I don't recall discussing supper with Kathleen. She is not contracted to for cook for us. Besides, I don't mind a bit of domestic therapy. I have forgotten to read Emma's message; it will have to wait. I try the landline; her mobile and my father's mobile. They all go to voicemail; they are probably at the cinema or the theatre. At least I hope they're having more fun than I am.

I'm just about to put my key in the lock when Matt (the neighbour) opens his door and comes out to speak to me. He has heard raised voices emanating from my house. I ask him to elaborate but he can't. He was watching *Peaky Blinders* at the time. I thank him for his concern. It is so dark that it feels like 9 pm though in reality it is only 7. I put the *shopping bag for life* onto immaculate work surface and start removing my purchases. Kathleen is wearing my pink and white "Best Mum" apron and my new red oven gloves; they both clash with her frizzy orange hair. I am reminded of an orangutan I saw in the Berlin zoo. There's a large cottage pie in the oven which has two minutes left on the oven clock. Her timing is immaculate. I wonder how she manages this. She takes it upon herself to fetch Michael from our bedroom so that I have time to "freshen up". It's not a phrase I particularly like. I decide to stay as I am. Michael and I sit down with the interloper. She's still wearing my apron; it was a birthday present from the twins. I ask Michael what he did at the Day Centre. Kathleen tells me that he enjoyed the quiz and his team came third (out of four). Michael is a bit subdued. I try to lift his spirits by telling him about the Valentine's Disco at my school. Kathleen thinks it would be a "grand" opportunity for us to spend some quality time together. I say it's really just for teenagers and that I am on duty all evening. I feel mean. I say "We'll see" though I don't really mean it.

I decide to leave her to do the clearing up. She might as well feel completely at home here. I sit on the sofa and read today's *Times*. Michael hovers around and I pat the cushion next to me, intimating that he should join me. I find his submissive behaviour rather strange since until now he has been so belligerent. I wonder whether Kathleen is dosing him up with sleep-inducing antidepressants. I vow to check this, insofar as I can. I ask Michael if he's all right. He *needs* to watch a film. It's a "work" thing. I am not sure I can ever get used to his new euphemisms. Kathleen couldn't make more noise with the cutlery if she tried to; this is when I regret the modern mania for open-plan living. We trawl through the film options on Sky. I say I don't mind what we watch though I am disappointed when he chooses *Shrek*. I can see Kathleen smirking. She will have a rest upstairs now that everything is "under control". I am beginning to resent having this patronising woman in my house. Michael cuddles up close to me and we find comfort with one another under a plush blanket; it has been too long. I wonder if this might be a good moment to abandon the film and go upstairs. But I am too subtle for him.

The film is much longer than I remembered. Eventually we retreat and start our evening routine. I don't know why but I feel fiercely protective of Michael tonight. I hand him a set of clean pressed pyjamas. He is reluctant to change in front of me which is the latest indication that he is a changed man. I run a bath with lots of bubbles and ask him if he wants to go in first. I can have the second bath or we can share it like we used to. It's big enough. I start getting undressed, folding my clothes up carefully, whilst he stands there staring at me. It is unnerving. I am an amoeba under his microscope. I try coaxing him into changing; after all, he has been in the Day Centre and there is evidence of his lunch and supper all down his sweatshirt. I step into the bath anyway. I feel bloated from the cottage pie that I didn't want and ate out of politeness. Michael refuses to take his clothes off but gets into the bath regardless. If he didn't have dementia, it would be like a sketch out of Monty Python. But he has, so it isn't.

Between us, we are too heavy for the amount of water in the tub; it overflows onto the tiled floor. We haven't locked the door and I momentarily forget that Kathleen is in Eddie's room. I screech at Michael but instead of getting out, he stretches his long-clothed legs, pushing his feet into my stomach. Hard. My lower back is pressed right up against the hot and cold taps. I yell noisily though I instantly wish that I hadn't. Michael's Fairy Godmother is in our bathroom. I shriek at her to get out but I might as well be a child. She is here for Micky (!) "the poor thing". She will attend to him. She cajoles him out of the bath; undressing him bit-by-bit and tenderly wrapping him up in my large beige bath sheet. Kathleen passes me the hand towel which is woefully in adequate and already damp. I run out of the room, feeling humiliated and embarrassed. I wonder why my husband is so acquiescent with her and yet so violent towards me. I am glad the twins aren't here to witness this debacle. But I am not too busy to miss them.

A few minutes later, Kathleen knocks on my bedroom door; it's an empty gesture. She has *seen* everything now. She presents me with a clean and respectable overgrown child wearing pyjamas, a blue dressing gown and slippers. He looks like an actor in *Peter Pan*. Michael walks into our room, muttering incoherently. We hug each other and I reassure him that everything is going to be all right. I close the door firmly and lock it. I briefly wonder again whether our marriage will be rekindled but he falls asleep with alarming speed. I envy him for that.

Although Michael snores relentlessly, I endure the din. I refuse to give Kathleen the satisfaction of knowing that I can no longer sleep with my own husband. I manage to doze off a few hours though I wake up long before the alarm. I tiptoe into the bathroom and lock the door. We have never gone in for locked doors; it's not second nature to me yet. I am reminded of last night's indignity and can't wait to go to work. I am mindful that we haven't discussed Michael's schedule yet. I do not want to see her smug obnoxious face this morning; instead, I send her a courteous text, reminding her that I will be back very late. She can take Michael bowling. I think he will enjoy it, even with *her*. I leave £30 on the kitchen table, just in case. I sneak out of the house, with my bicycle, and pedal furiously, venting my anger with each revolution.

The atmosphere at school is light-hearted and jolly. Annie-the-art-teacher has erected beautiful decorations of Andy Warhol style hearts and lips; they're all the way up the staircase and on every classroom door. She must have stayed late last night. I realise that for the first time in thirty years, I haven't bought Michael a Valentine's Day card. We have a long assembly, house meetings, a charity bake sale and about three lessons. No wonder the kids like our school. I find a few moments to telephone the agency that sent me Kathleen. I express my concern about their employee's behaviour though I don't mention Bath-gate. I am too mortified. I ask for some additional references and also the name of her previous employer. I follow up the telephone call with an email. As I send it, I receive a text from Kathleen. She is taking Michael bowling at 6 pm this evening and will make sure that he has supper whilst they're out. It will be like a "date". He was thrilled to receive the heart-shaped chocolates and the teddy-bear card that *she* bought. I know she is trying to provoke me so I just text her back: "Have fun" and add a smiley emoji. I will buy Michael a card later. And a box of chocolates. I'm sure he won't buy me either.

Most of our pupils get changed into smart-casual clothing. Some of the girls are wearing vast amounts of makeup whilst others go for the natural look. The boys are mostly wearing black leather jackets. I have forgotten to bring in a spare change of clothes. I blame Kathleen. I have a choice between cycling clothes and a dark suit. I decide to head to

Zara. I buy a black cocktail dress as at least I can wear it on another occasion. I try it on in the fitting room and wonder when that next occasion will be. We have barely been invited to anything these past few months. Word must have got around that we are the new social pariahs on the block.

Chapter 28
Half-Term

I stumble home at about 11 pm on Friday night; it's late and I feel guilty for leaving Michael with Kathleen for such a long day. At least it's the weekend and it is also half-term. I am not ready to go upstairs. I sit down at the kitchen table with my laptop and a cup of tea. I search for discreet hidden cameras that are idiot proof. I select and buy a tiny "nanny card" which can easily be inserted into a teddy bear or an ornament. It *has* to arrive before I leave for Sussex, otherwise I won't go. I have arranged to stay with my parents and the twins for two nights (Wednesday and Thursday inclusive). Kathleen will hold the fort, if I haven't sacked her by then. She's going to stay with her sister, Roisin, from Saturday until Tuesday; this will give me the time to fit the hidden camera and test it out. Maybe Rosie can help me with this; after all, it was her idea. I look around our open-plan kitchen-diner-cum-sitting room and start doing a recce. We have two bookshelves at the far end; both of these have ornaments on them, and stacks of books. There's also a small teddy bear, wearing a jumper with "I love Brighton" on it. It belongs to Olivia. Either way, there are no shortage of places for my subterfuge. Or I could just hide it in plain sight.

Michael's mobile is charging next to the bread bin. He hasn't used it for ages. I have a look at his Life360 which tracks his every move as it does mine. We are connected. He has been all over the place: The Day Centre, Waitrose, the tube station, the local village shops, Hampstead and finally to the Ten Pin Bowling Alley near Tavistock Square. It takes me a few seconds to realise that Kathleen has been using Michael's phone to track my whereabouts. I have underestimated her.

I walk up the stairs and go straight to the bathroom. It has never looked so clean. I open the cabinet to take out some Nurofen. Kathleen has reorganised my toiletries in height order and put the medicines in a zip-lock bag. I am surprised she has found the time to do this. I brush my teeth and retire to Olivia's bedroom; there's no point waking up Michael. There's a note with the receipts from today's activities on Olivia's bedside table. I can see that a hoover has been dragged over the carpet and the bed has been remade with hospital corners. I am reminded that Kathleen used to be a nurse. I am not sure how I am going to approach this intrusion; it's hard to reprimand someone who has cleaned the room and tidied up the mess. I lie in the bed reading through all my text messages. Emma is restarting her book club. Do I want to re-join? Do I even have the time? There's a message from my mother who wants me to bring down some warmer clothes for the twins (she is also looking forward to seeing me) and several from Olivia saying that she misses me. There's one from Eddie, updating me on his and Olivia's forthcoming travel plans. They've decided to work in a ski resort in France. At least it's not far away and the only cost will be the flights. I hope he's right about this.

It's now 1.35 am I think it's too late to send replies. I am feeling restless and the music from the school disco is still reverberating in my ears; it was far too loud. I start to pace up and down Olivia's room. I am like a lion in a cage with little to do and nowhere to go. I open the drawers; everything is too neat; too well folded; too colour-coded. This is not Olivia's handiwork. I feel a sense of outrage and indignation on my daughter's behalf. I am desperate to go into Eddie's room, to see what the interloper has been up to in there. I know I can't just go barging in. Pity Roisin lives in

Kilburn not Kildare. I fear that I won't have the time to conduct a thorough investigation. This is all very much out of
my comfort zone.

On Saturday morning, I wake up at 10.45 am with the
bedside lamp still on. Kathleen is occupying the kitchen,
allegedly making pancakes for Michael and herself. The first
interviewee is arriving in fifteen minutes. I am not dressed
and Kathleen is not out. I rush upstairs to the bedroom and
grab some clothes. I see that someone has invaded *my* wardrobe as well as Olivia's. She has made a small pile of garments
for charity; there's a question mark on my favourite pair of
ripped jeans. I can't believe the audacity of the woman. I put
on as many of the clothes from the "charity" pile as I can and
dump the remainder into the bottom of the tall cupboard. I
will decide who gets what and when. I tie my hair back into
a ponytail (it needs a wash and this will conceal that for a
while); put on some lipstick and rush back down the stairs
again. Michael is sitting at the table like a good boy, eating
up his pancakes. It's five to eleven and Kathleen is still faff-
ing around in my space. I thank her for her troubles; give her
the difference between the £30 I gave her and the £57 she
spent yesterday, and encourage her to make the most of her
free time. I am far from subtle and she is far from obliging.
We reach a state of impasse.

The doorbell rings and I know it must be Irena, the
young Polish woman from the agency. It's exactly eleven
o'clock. I rush to the door, stumbling over my own shoes,
and open it somewhat breathlessly. The woman is young,
pretty, blonde and Polish. She is inappropriately dressed for
an interview and isn't wearing a coat despite the incessant
rain. She comes straight into the open-plan living area and
asks for a towel. She confidently introduces herself first to
Michael and then to Kathleen whilst attempting to dry herself. "You are the Grandma, no?" This is enough to send the
Irish woman into a spin. "And you are the prostitute, yes?"
the retort is a poor imitation of Irena's Eastern European

accent. They hate each other on sight. Irena pulls up a chair next to Michael, and starts showing him photographs of her family: her mother, her father and her two younger sisters. They could all be models. Michael enjoys the attention from the attractive blonde. He tells her that he had a Polish client once, from a city starting with a K, but he can't remember its name. He can't recall anything much but there's a trace of a memory which he is desperately trying to retrieve from the locked filing cabinet in his brain. The conversation is a bit stilted but at least they're having one. I know that I still love Michael because I don't feel remotely jealous. I am glad that he is enjoying Irena's company. He deserves to have some happiness.

I interrupt Irena's flow and suggest we "walk and talk" as I show her around the house. It won't take long. It's hasn't got any bigger. As we reach Eddie's room, Kathleen emerges, clutching her overnight bag which is bursting at the seams like her. I stand to the side, waiting for her to move out of the way. I'm almost back on the Jubilee Line, letting the passengers off first. Even the thought makes me short of breath. Kathleen has lived with us long enough to know when I am stressed and suffering; she seems to take some pleasure out of it. Eventually she gives way and says she will miss Michael whilst she is "residing" in Kilburn. I wonder if she is genuinely fond of him. Maybe I shouldn't judge her so harshly. Her references were *all* excellent. I leave Irena in Eddie's room, and escort Kathleen back down the stairs and out of the house. I can't think of anything to say that won't provoke an argument so I just stand there, waiting for the pre-emptive strike. I don't know why I am so acquiescent in her presence. I suppose no one can be in charge all of the time; it's so exhausting. Kathleen, who is a few inches taller than me, looks me up and down, and places her booted foot over my bare one. She doesn't put her weight on it; it's just hovering there, letting me know that I am not her superior. I should move but I can't. I just wait for her to leave.

I watch the interloper walk down the mews and fade into a small blob. I am relieved that I won't see her until Tuesday night. I call Irena down and the three of us drink tea at the kitchen table. She takes hers black with one sugar. We talk about her experience and the number of hours that she is available. She can't do the nights as she lives with her fiancé; he's in construction and I get the impression that he is overbearing and possessive. He won't allow her to stay in anyone else's house. This is a huge setback. We exchange details and I tell her that I will be in touch on Monday morning. I ask Michael what he thinks of Irena. He looks me straight in the eyes and asks me if he has had sex with her. I immediately realise that he can't have what he wants. I need to rethink this. What's so terrible about someone who has OCD and organises your cupboards? I must be overreacting. I have seen too many nasty films. The next agency interviewee isn't coming until 3 pm

Despite the relentless rain, I persuade Michael to walk to Kenwood House with me; it is our local stately home. We can pretend to be a normal couple. We walk up Haverstock Hill and back down past the Royal Free Hospital. It takes us about thirty minutes to cut across the heath and enter the Kenwood estate. The ground is soggy and the bottoms of our jeans are muddy. Michael asks me how long we have lived in the country. He likes it here. He needs a period of adjustment. He keeps saying this word. It makes him sound articulate but he is anything but coherent. He is much more energetic than he was yesterday and he doesn't stop wittering on. I'm almost out of patience, and tired of being the person who is always responsible and sensible. We enter the house. I promise Michael that we will visit the café afterwards; this seems to be very important to him. At least he has remembered that there is one here. The custodian clicks her clicker. We have visited Kenwood hundreds of times, like most locals, so we don't want a guidebook for £6.99.

I find some solace in looking at the Rembrandt self-portrait in the Dining Room. Michael strikes up a conversation with the custodian whose security radio is too loud. My husband doesn't know much about art but he is a flamboyant critic today. He inadvertently gathers quite a crowd though most of them are mocking him. The words "early onset dementia" instantly silences their amusement. We aren't a normal couple anymore. Although I know how to circumvent the gift shop, we end up in it anyway. Michael keeps picking things up that we don't need and don't really want: a Kenwood House bone china mug; miniature pots of jam; a tin of fudge and a reduced priced Christmas bauble in the shape of a heart. It's the only tacky item on display. The woman behind the counter is watching Michael as if he were a kleptomaniac. Michael would never steal anything. He wouldn't even bring home a packet of post-it notes from the office without dropping £2 into the petty cash tin first. He is an upright man. Always has been. Despite his outlandish vocabulary and his occasional temper tantrums, I don't think an honest man becomes a dishonest man overnight. I resent the English Heritage Shop Manager. She obviously doesn't understand what it's like living with dementia 24/7. I can't explain this but I have an overwhelming desire to steal something. Just to spite her. I look around the gift shop, noting the discreet cameras poised in the corners of the corniced ceilings. I am not sure what to take. I don't want anything, of course. I don't need anything. But my mediating circumstances are that I am fed up of being in charge; sick of being responsible and tired of making all the decisions. Nothing is paired and shared in my marriage.

The rain is driving hard which brings the visitors indoors. We are huddled together in this tiny little shop. I can see that the Shop Manager is anxious. There may be other shoplifters here, besides Michael (who isn't one, of course). Her eyes are so closely secured onto my husband that I make the most of my window of opportunity. There's a little rotating display with inexpensive jewellery. Nothing costs more than £30. I have a quick look around the shop; it's absolutely heaving now. I take a pair of silver earrings and let them fall into my coat pocket. It is so easy. I choose a packet of postcards for £2.99 and queue up to pay for them, using my debit card as I only have a £20 note which she refuses to take. The Shop Manager puts the postcards into a small white paper bag, along with the receipt. I take Michael by the arm and talk about the delicious scones; jam and cream we will eat in the Kenwood café.

There's a very long queue which tests our patience. I am convinced that I am about to be arrested. Michael needs to go to the lavatory. It is so frustrating as we are almost at the front. I am holding the tray with our pots of tea, a pot of hot water and a plate with two scones, two miniature pots of jam and a dollop of whipped cream. I make Michael wait until I have paid with cash and reserved a table. He scuttles off to the Gents, which is back outside, and takes ages to return. I am about to send out a search party when he is escorted back in with a very elderly gentleman who hasn't lost his faculties like Michael. I feel it is so unfair. I run over to thank him and take my husband gently by the hand, bringing him back to our table. He is momentarily *The Tiger Who Came to Tea* as he demolishes the food and consumes the drink. There is nothing left in the pot.

We are both still rather wet and cold. My appetite certainly isn't satiated. I don't recall having eaten breakfast. Michael is always ravenous these days; perhaps his medication makes him like this. I don't know. I am no expert. And I don't want to be either. We are about to give up our much-wanted table to another couple when the Shop Manager points at us and nods her head at the Security Guard. He is armed with a walkie-talkie. I am feeling hot and panicky. My hands are a bit clammy. I'm convinced that I am about to have a heart attack. I am a thief. I hate myself. I don't even know why I did it. I must prepare my response. The Shop Manager rushes out of the café (and probably back to the shop; she can't afford to leave it unattended) and the Security

Manager walks very slowly up to our table. He hands me my debit card which I left inside the PIN machine.

I thank the man and decide that we should leave before my crime is discovered; besides, we have the second interviewee coming from the agency at 3 pm. I wonder whether we should take an Uber back but I make the decision for us both: we will walk. He likes the countryside.

We rush home for the 3 pm interviewee only to find that he has cancelled. I put my hands into my pockets and remove the soggy tissues, my keys and the stolen earrings. I don't want them now. I'm going to return them, next time I am in Kenwood.

Chapter 29
Bloody Sunday

I promised myself that I wouldn't work over half-term, especially as without Kathleen, I am Michael's only carer for the next few days. But Principal Peter has sent me an urgent directive in view of the lengthy Governors' meeting scheduled for Monday week. His email was sent at midnight. It's our first Education and Pastoral meeting this term and, in view of this, we need to update both our anti-bullying and healthy lifestyles policies; they all fall under my remit. He thinks we will be inspected within the year. This is the last thing I need right now. I start with the anti-bullying policy which was originally drawn up with the guidance issued by the DfE *Preventing and Tackling Bullying* (back in 2014). There is nothing wrong with our opening statement; I remember agonising over it last time. Until now, I have always approached our policies with detachment, even though I have two children of my own. But it feels different now.

As Michael softly sleeps, I take advantage of what is probably my only golden hour of the day. I read through the policies. The definition of bullying includes a wide variety of issues ranging from the emotional to the physical. I add a new bullet point to the list: children should not be bullied if and when they are undergoing gender reassignment. Fortunately, Joanna-cum-Jeremy has not been persecuted at all and neither have any of our other gender-fluid students. I Google another school's website, hoping to find their well-written policies on line. I find a "good" one and print it off so that I can easily see what I need to add to ours. I know it's cheating but there's no point reinventing the wheel.

It's 7.37 am now and I am on my third mug of tea though this time it's decaffeinated. I can hear movement upstairs. My golden hour is up. I leave the laptop on but stack my papers into a small pile on the kitchen work surface. I am going to give Michael my full attention today. I slip my bare feet back into my slippers and trudge up the stairs. Michael is standing at the top, half dressed. He looks like a demonic centaur. He has developed a bit of a paunch (for which I blame Kathleen) and his chest has sprouted a mass of knotted grey hairs. There is something animalistic about his appearance.

The house isn't warm – it never is – and I am worried that he will catch a cold or flu. I use the sweetest voice that I am capable of; it's usually reserved for babies and kittens. I suggest he puts on a tee shirt and a jumper or a shirt. I should have waited until I was on the small landing before I said this. I am not quite at the top of the stairs and he looks twice his normal size from where I am standing. I plead with him to return to our bedroom. I will help or I won't help. I will do whatever he wants; whatever makes him happy. My happiness isn't important right now. I might as well be speaking Arabic. He doesn't seem to understand a word I am saying. I am finding it hard to sustain this baby-kitten voice; it's not me. I am not being true to myself. I slowly manoeuvre my way up to the top of the staircase, the one before the landing which Michael is occupying with his whole bulky self. He is standing with his arms pressed against the wall on one side and the bannister on the other. He is the tank to my revolver. I change tactics. I will *be* Kathleen. I bet she is firm and authoritative when I am at work. I put on an Irish accent and I take on her mannerisms. He immediately shudders, hiding his face behind his hands. I say I am sorry. I am not Kathleen. I am not going to hurt you. Has she hurt you? Within seconds he is confident again, throwing his arms around and pushing me to one side. I switch from one persona to the other: the strong and formidable voice to the sweet and sympathetic one. Neither is effective. We screech at each other. He threatens me with dismissal. I am no longer welcome in his office. People don't behave in this way. They don't flaunt themselves in meetings wearing scanty clothing (I realise he means me). I repeat, many times, that this is our home; this is not an office; I am not his secretary; he cannot fire me; I am his wife; he is my husband. He bursts into tears but maintains his aggressive demeanour. It is distressing and confusing. I plead with him again but he is impassable. It's not even 8 am and I have already failed.

I return to the kitchen and sit down at my laptop. I am on the verge of having a panic attack. I calm myself down with a search on Google. I find the number for the Samaritans: 116 123. The website is reassuring; it says: *Call us any time, day or night*. I must remember this. I have left my mobile charging upstairs – in Olivia's room – so I hurry back into the sitting room area to pick up the landline. I'm half way through pressing the numbers when a large hand snatches the phone from me. *You're not allowed to make personal calls from the office. You aren't dressed for work. Why haven't you booked a meeting room for me?* I find it bizarre that he is so aggressive in his "office" as he had a reputation for being one of the kindest and most amenable bosses in his firm. But it's not him. It's the dementia, and I must remember this. It is hard for me not to take his accusations personally. They don't make sense and yet they sound like they do. Michael still has an extensive vocabulary. I explain once again that I am his wife. He doesn't recognise me this morning. He is banging the receiver into his chest. I wonder if he is using pain to find his true self. I urge him to return the phone to its base. I promise not to use it. We will go out for breakfast; or a walk; or a swim. Anything. He can decide. He's the boss. Maybe we should see a film? See some friends? Go down to Brighton to see the children? He doesn't have any children; why are we living in Liverpool? I have no idea what he is talking about.

It must be very frightening living in his topsy-turvy world but it's equally terrifying living in mine. I tell him to stop ranting and raving but this only exacerbates the argument between us. He grabs hold of my cotton nightie and tears a piece off as I struggle to move away from him.

The doorbell rings. Michael's reaction to the bell is Pavlovian. He stops and simply stands to attention, waiting for further instructions. It's Matt from next door. He has heard "raised voices" and wants to know if everything is all right. I tell him it is anything but all right. I am desperate for him to stay. I cannot hide my fear or distress. I ask him to distract Michael so that I can get dressed. He is keen to help. He shuts the front door and attaches the chain; I'm not sure why he does this. I don't interfere. I am just grateful to be rescued. Matt tries to approach my husband, man-to-man, and adopts a measured but commanding tone. I almost wish he could move in. I dash up the stairs, the ones that were impassable only a few minutes ago, and lock myself into my bedroom. I phone my parents whilst I have the opportunity. I explain that we have reached a crisis point; that I can't cope without Kathleen; that I am incapable as Michael's carer and I think he might try and kill me. My father is on the verge of calling the police but I say that Matt is here and that everything is all right. They want to come up to London to rescue me. I can hear shouting from the landing so I tell my father that I will call him back in a minute. I reiterate: don't call the police. I didn't mean what I said.

I catch sight of myself in the mirror. I look like the Wreck of the Hesperus: torn nightie, matted hair, no makeup and grey shadows under my eyes. I am the shipwreck torn apart by Michael's powerful and stormy waves. Matt has dragged Michael up the stairs like a recalcitrant teenager. I can hear them both swearing. I unlock the door and come out with one of Michael's tee shirts and a sweatshirt. Between us, we attempt to clothe the wild centaur which kicks and punches with all its strength. Its eyes burn into mine, seething with resentment and anger. It wants Kathleen. This is illogical. I thought he was terrified of her. The tee shirt is on but Matt uses the sweatshirt to bind the centaur's wrists together. He is still kicking him in the shins. I question this tactic, thinking of my bullying policy, but he insists that it's necessary. I realise that I haven't administered Michael's medication; perhaps this explains his volcanic eruption. I fetch the pills from the bathroom. Matt is still doing battle. He is precariously close to the top of the stairs. I try to put the white pill into the centaur's mouth and clamp it shut with both my hands. It chews the pill whilst screwing up its face; the taste must be repulsive. We are moving down the gears, back into neutral, when Matt retaliates, saying that Michael should be sectioned. The centaur reappears, raises his bound wrists and thumps Matt on the nose, causing him to lose his balance. It is a bloody Sunday.

Chapter 30
Intervention

Bloody Sunday has been the catalyst for yet more appointments which are now lined up for the duration of the week. Social Services are coming on Tuesday afternoon. There will be a full assessment involving the neurologist, a Social Worker with expertise in psychiatric patients and even our GP, Daniella, will be present. I spend most of Monday on the telephone. Michael is in no fit state to go to the Day Centre as he has refused to wash, shave or get dressed. I am trying to persuade him to take his medication but he is refusing to do that too. I am at my wit's end. I let him slump in front of the Panasonic babysitter, vegetating, whilst I confirm all the appointments for the week ahead. It doesn't look as though I will be able to get down to Sussex after all. I decide to send Kathleen a text, with an update, but I am not sure whether I want her to be present when the assessment is carried out.

The day passes without incident. I spend most of it on my computer, working, whilst Michael sits passively in front of the television. I make us supper and join him on the sofa to eat it; this is something I hate doing but I am too shattered to have an argument. It is nine o'clock and it's very dark outside so I suggest we go up to bed. Michael isn't tired. He has had no physical exercise all day. Neither have I. I suggest a walk. It can be quite pleasant when all the traffic has ceased. He asks me what we're doing today. I explain that the day is over. But we can go for a little walk, around the block. *He needs to get ready for work; there's an important meeting with the Polish client.* I remind him that he's not working anymore. I tell him he's on a sabbatical; it seems more tactful. Anyway, the office is closed. He has toothache and a headache. I leave a message on the dentist's answering machine asking for an emergency appointment. I am not hopeful. I spend an hour repeating myself whilst tidying up the house. Kathleen hasn't reorganised the kitchen cupboards yet; I almost wish she had.

It is now Tuesday morning: D-Day. It feels as if the whole world is descending on my little house. I cajole Michael into having a shower. He insists on doing this himself. Most of the water seeps under the door. He emerges from the bathroom looking slightly damper than when he entered it. He smells of sweat and urine. He comes into the bedroom, wrapped up in a towel. He is still wearing his boxer shorts which aren't remotely wet. I remind him that we have visitors coming and that he should make an effort to look respectable. Michael looks so unkempt that I am wondering whether to take him to my hairdressers. I lay out some clean clothes on our bed. *He doesn't want to wear someone else's clothes. Why are Matt's things in our wardrobe?* I text Matt. I thank him for not pressing charges and update him insofar as I can. Michael insists on having privacy; this reminds me, I still haven't installed the secret "nanny" card device.

I telephone my mother. She is going to pay for Eddie and Olivia's flights to Geneva Airport; they will catch a coach from there to the resort in Chamonix. My parents will take the twins into Brighton and treat them to some new clothes although they have insisted that I bring up their ski boots and ski wear when I come down on Wednesday. They won't take no for an answer. Whilst I am waiting for the health team to arrive, I take out the suitcases we used in Croatia. The luggage tags are still on them. For a brief moment, I allow myself to think about our holiday last summer; it feels as though it was someone else's. I no longer own that memory. How could things have been so normal then and so abnormal now? It is surreal. I know that Kathleen is returning today so I pack Eddie's case first. I lug it into Olivia's room so that it won't be in anyone's way. I find it easier to pack for Olivia. I lock the cases with a small padlock and put the key into my purse. Michael comes into the room. He thinks I am sending him away. He has a sixth sense. He is not reassured by the name tags; he says I could be pretending, just to trick him. He doesn't offer to take them downstairs – which he would have done in the past – so I drag them down myself, bumping them down the staircase which I notice still has Matt's blood on it.

Dr Patel arrives first. He in the same grey suit but this time is wearing a red tie. The Social Worker and our GP arrive minutes later. We gather in the kitchen and sit down at the table. I offer them tea and coffee but all three decline. Maybe later. Dr Patel puts his hand out to shake Michael's; he says he will do his best for the interview. No one reacts. The Social Worker asks the first question. It is a gentle beginning to an otherwise gruelling process. Michael is unable to say the name of our prime minister, he has no idea what is going on, he has heard of Brexit but he can't explain what it is, he doesn't know why he isn't working and he doesn't want to leave home. She wants to know if he can manage by himself, how he feels when I am at work, can he cook? He says he's "independent" and makes a "mean lasagne". This is news to me. I am astonished at how well he is doing. But the Social Worker is not fooled. She continues to press him. *How would you feel if you had a few days away from home? A mini holiday?* Dr Patel furnishes Michael with a little more information. He mentions tests and scans. *What is this? One Flew Over the Cuckoo's Nest?* This is Michael's response. He is not brain dead yet. I almost think it would be easier for him if he were less aware of his condition. Dr Patel is very tactful. He informs him that it's just for a few days. Our GP takes me to one side and tells me to pack a small bag for Michael. He will most probably be admitted for at least three nights, possibly more. She also asks me if I want to come over for dinner. We are lucky to have such an empathetic GP. I consider her a friend these days.

I go upstairs to pack, again; this time it's for my husband. I put a wash bag together; an electric toothbrush, toothpaste, his favourite bath towel and several changes of clothes. I don't bother with a novel as he hasn't read one for ages. Even when he does pick up a coffee table book, he turns the pages over so quickly that he can't possibly be taking much in. It is heart-breaking. I bring the bag downstairs and put it next to the front door. I'm about to return to the table when Kathleen comes bounding into the open-plan living space. She almost knocks me over. I introduce her to the "team" and she makes a sarcastic comment about my not offering them any hospitality. I look at Daniella and shrug my shoulders. I don't need to say anything to her. The interloper puts the kettle on but Dr Patel intervenes. He wants Michael to do the honours. I don't think this is necessary. We all know that he is incapable of it. But my husband leaps up with enthusiasm; it's something to do. He can prove himself. He doesn't have to be admitted or sectioned or whatever the word is these days. The interloper can't help herself. She hands him the teabags and teaspoons. She is doing her best to undermine the whole charade but she doesn't have to try. Michael stuffs all five teabags into one mug. She puts her body in between Dr Patel's and the mugs so that he can't get a straight view of the action. It's all academic now. We sit down with our hot concoctions and pretend to sip them. Michael is sitting back in the chair with his arms folded against his red jumper; it's clean, at least, though I notice that he isn't wearing anything underneath it. I ask Kathleen to fetch a shirt for Michael. She dutifully gets one (not the one I selected but a checked shirt from the drawer) and helps him to dress and undress. He is compliant and helps her by stretching out his arms. I still don't understand why is so acquiescent with her and so difficult with me. She seems to have a hold over him.

The Social Worker starts to interview Kathleen. Is she

capable of looking after Michael overnight? And for a series of days? Is she really prepared to have all that responsibility? Kathleen is lapping it all up now. She is worth more than the £400 that I pay her. One patient? She used to manage hundreds. Besides, she and Michael have a special rapport. This is what she tells the "team". I try to intervene a couple of times, explaining that Michael can be volatile and violent. She might not be safe with him, home alone. And I might not be either. She tells me to lock the door. I can hear an engine grinding outside and see a small ambulance parked on the cobbles. It's for Michael. It's just for twenty-four hours. It's routine.

Dr Patel, Daniella and the Social Worker escort a rather subdued Michael out of the house and into the ambulance. Kathleen runs after him. I push her out of the way and get in myself. She is not his wife. I am. We drive very slowly over the cobbled mews and within minutes we have arrived at The Royal Free Hospital; it feels like déjà-vu. Daniella offers to stay with me, whilst we take Michael to the wing for elderly patients and those suffering from dementia. There will be a full-blown assessment. As soon as Dr Patel returns to his office, and the Social Worker departs, Michael asks for Kathleen. He keeps saying that he needs her, she understands him, she is his wife. Daniella takes me out of the ward and sits me down on one of the plastic blue chairs near the Nurse's Station. She hands me a box of tissues. I can't hold back my tears anymore; they just keep rolling down like the rain from a leaking gutter. My phone buzzes. It's Kathleen. She wants to come to the hospital. And is her job safe? Am I going to pay her in cash or make a bank transfer? I think she only cares about the money. I don't think she loves Michael like I do, even if I am struggling to show it at times.

We walk back into the ward. There's a curtain drawn around Michael's bed. He is having a blood test. A nurse appears with the sample and checks the information on the sticker with the notes on her clipboard. A male nurse appears with a small beaker. Daniella explains that they need a urine sample. I know but it seems churlish to say that I do. There's an awful commotion emanating from behind the curtain. There's a poltergeist on the other side, kicking and pushing, whilst the male nurse tries to help Michael lower his trousers. I knew he would resent having another man anywhere near his genitals. The male nurse comes out of the cubicle, vociferously shaking his head. He wants me to try. I don't want to. Michael is proud and sensitive about these things. But the male nurse insists. He calls me by my first name. I am being cajoled from all sides. Even Daniella takes me by the arm and encourages me to follow him into the cubicle. She says the sample is necessary and it would be better if the request came from me. She tells Michael that I am here, and makes sure that he knows it is me. But lately he hasn't known who I am so why should now be any different? He's wearing blue jeans, with buttons, which was obviously a mistake on my part. I didn't anticipate today's procedures. The others leave the cubicle to give us both some privacy. It feels strange to be with him now.

I kneel down on the floor, beside the bed. I slowly unbutton his trousers and slide them down his thighs. The patient looks down at me and calls me Sophie for the first time in days. His penis quickly becomes erect; I think it recognises my scent. I know that I do not look attractive today. I am unprepared for his volcanic ejaculation as he *comes* so quickly. The sticky white semen attaches itself to my neck and face. He stands with his hands on his hips, proud to be a full-blooded male. My husband's sperm and my tears are intermingled. I am still holding the beaker. I don't think it is physically possible for him to pass urine now. I don't want the male nurse to come back in yet. I try to wrestle with Michael's jeans but I can't get them back up; it's as if his sperm is acting like some sort of gluing agent. I let my knees give way and slide to the sticky floor so that my hands slip under the curtain into the outside world that is the ward.

Daniella immediately pulls me away from the cubicle as the male nurse pushes himself back into it. He promises to be discreet.

I feel as though I have been contaminated. There's a washroom at the end of the ward; I realise it's for the patients but I can't face being seen in the corridors. I sit on the lavatory and cry until I am totally spent. My tears must be bankrupt. I sit for what seems like hours but it can only be a matter of minutes. I am calmer now. I bend my head towards the basin, which is too low for me as it's designed for wheelchairs, and let the water from the tap drink onto my hair. It is far from satisfactory. I press the hand dryer but the air is barely hot enough and it stops after twenty seconds. My peace is short-lived as someone is banging on the door. An elderly man is trying to reach the lavatory whilst his yellow urine trickles down his emaciated leg. I say I am so sorry and I burst into tears again. Why couldn't Michael just piss in a bottle? I apologise to the elderly man again. He doesn't have dementia. His only offence is his age; he is 97 on Saturday. I have no desire to be that old.

Chapter 31
The Truce

The hospital will keep Michael under observation until Friday. At least I know that he will be safe there. I return to our house to find Kathleen reading the *Daily Mail*. I feel affronted as the old Michael wouldn't allow it in our house. She immediately gets up and makes me a cup of tea. I think this is the beginning of our truce. I am so relieved. I sit down opposite her and wrap my cold fingers around the hot mug. She offers to hold the fort over the next few days. She says I need to rest and see my children. I feel irresponsible for leaving Michael but equally torn for abandoning my children. It's a *lose lose* situation.

We talk for what seems like hours. She tells me her life story and I tell her mine. I have no idea whether she is telling me the truth. I do though. I can be naïve that way. Kathleen softens her voice and promises to support me. I am so overwhelmed by the milk of her human kindness that my tears are free to saunter down my face once more. I thank her for sorting out the wardrobes; I mean it now. I ask her to reorganise the kitchen and she slaps me on the back saying it would be her pleasure. The slap hurts a little. I don't think she knows her own strength.

Relieved and tired, I go upstairs. I don't know where to sleep. I wander into my own room and pack up my things, enough for three days, and place the small travel bag near the door. I turn the bed down and see that the fitted sheet isn't clean; there's even a stain on Michael's side that I don't want to investigate. I strip the whole bed and struggle to hold the sheets and duvet cover in my arms. Kathleen is there like a genie. Nothing is too much trouble for her. She wrestles the washing from my arms and hurls it down the stairs like a rugby ball. She stuffs everything into the washing machine. She shows it no mercy. I tell her there's no need to be my housekeeper; I'm not paying her to do that role. Kathleen insists. The whole house will be shipshape by the time I come home. And Michael might even be in it to welcome me too. The thought of this brings me out in a cold sweat which I conceal beneath my bulky wintery clothes.

In the morning, I struggle to lug the bags, including my own small one, to the front door and order the Uber for Hove; it will cost a fortune but I can't manage the train. The Uber arrives but the driver remains stubbornly behind the wheel. The cases weigh a tonne. Kathleen, my saviour, picks up Olivia's in one hand and Eddie's in the other and dumps them unceremoniously on the ground. She knocks on the driver's window, giving him a bit of a fright. She bundles me into the back seat of the car, pushing my head down as if I have been arrested. The driver thinks she is my mother. I wonder how she will spend the next three days. She has the whole house at her disposal. I haven't locked up anything. Not even our bank statements. I am not sure why I have adopted this cavalier attitude towards my privacy; it's so unlike me.

The Uber driver is surly and silent; this suits me as it means I can use the car as a temporary office. I have nearly two hours at my disposal. I phone the hospital and eventually get through to one of the doctors on the unit where Michael is being held *against* his will. He has been temporarily sectioned. The doctor explains that the hospital will probably only keep my husband for a few days though he could be held for two weeks; they will alter his medication and conduct a series of tests. He informs me that Michael has been prescribed risperidone; it will be injected into the muscles initially and taken by mouth thereafter. They haven't started the treatment yet as he is still being assessed. I send a text to Kathleen, immediately updating her. It's an antipsychotic drug, apparently. I knew she would know. The doctor reassures me that Michael will be well looked after, even though the Royal Free is no place for him; it's a temporary solution to a long-term problem. I am not sure I can deal with the word long term as I am already struggling.

He needs to be admitted to a home with specialised care; they speak to me as if I don't already know this. I can visit anytime other than between 7 am and 10 am. The doctor passes the phone to a nurse. I give her Kathleen's name, saying that she is temporarily the "next of kin" whilst I am in Sussex; however, I remain the first point of contact. It's just that she will be the primary visitor. The nurse finds this a bit odd. There is an outside chance that Michael will be admitted to a care home, if the psychiatrist and the other doctors feel that this is appropriate. It is not a foregone conclusion. I am not sure what to say to the twins or to my parents. I think I will just tell them he's in hospital. Nothing serious.

This has been the longest February I have ever known. It is still a bleak midwinter in Sussex. The Brighton sea looks grey and gloomy; the seagulls have lost weight and everything fun has been boarded up or is closed until the Spring Bank Holiday. The silent Uber driver delivers me to "Shingles" and I collapse into my father's open arms; it's the most wonderful feeling to be protected and loved by someone like him. He immediately tries picking up Eddie and Olivia's cases but they're too heavy; he's not the robust man that he used to be. Eddie bounds down the stairs like a hunting dog. He hugs me energetically, and tells me that I have shrunk. My mother and Olivia rush in from the sitting room to greet me; I feel like royalty. I suggest we go for a walk into Brighton; it's easier to talk about sensitive issues when we don't have to make eye contact.

We walk up the broad promenade initially four abreast. I

update everyone at once. Repeating myself doesn't improve Michael's situation. I resist the temptation of using the word "sectioned" in front of the twins though they sense that I am holding something back. We drink coffee in one of the small cafés in the Lanes; it isn't busy and I wonder how they break even in the winter. I steer the conversation away from Michael and towards Chamonix. After warming up, we walk towards the shopping mall. My father hates it in there as he finds it claustrophobic. My mother enjoys shopping. We break off from the *boys* and indulge Olivia who is always grateful and remains beautifully unspoilt. She takes three items into the fitting room at North Face in addition to a set of thermals for both her and for Eddie. She is a twin, after all. I seize the opportunity to update my mother. She mentions the local care homes again. I explain that we may not have that luxury anymore; it may all be taken out of my hands.

In the evening, I call the hospital again. I leave a message with someone. It is not convenient. A nurse calls me back at 7.35 pm She has just started her night shift. Her name is Elsa. I explain my situation and say that I will be back in London on Friday. I can tell that she is reading the notes from the computer in the Nurse's station. Michael has had a "good day" and is "adjusting". I almost laugh when she says this. No one visited him. He has been asking to see his "duck". She has no idea what he means but I think Michael's Staffordshire roots are hard to eradicate. Not that I want to. It was always part of his charm. Eddie is desperate to speak to his father. I give him the number and explain that it's not so easy. Maybe it would be better in the morning. He is a little suspicious of me, and begins to ask awkward questions that I simply don't want to answer. It is like extracting teeth but mine aren't coming out. I want to protect my children from the unbearable truth, even though I know that they're young adults. I will wrestle with my conscience later.

On Friday morning, my parents, Eddie, Olivia and I drive

to the North Terminal at Gatwick Airport. It's an emotional parting. I remind Eddie and Olivia to look out for one another. I always say this. My experience of life, and of my students' lives, has made me wary and uneasy. No one is invincible. I am told to stop worrying. My parents and I return to the house where I tell them the uncomfortable truth. They clearly think Michael's confinement will do *me* good; as far as my father is concerned, it can't be long enough. He hasn't forgiven him. I have partially recovered whilst here and I am pleased that I look less of a wreck and more my old self.

Sheila and Henry drive me to Brighton Station and escort me onto the train; it feels as though I am off to boarding school. I sit at a table for four. The other three chairs are occupied by a mother and her three young children. They have iPads; snacks; water bottles and games but they are still "bored" and invade my space. I look out of the window, ignoring them instead of engaging with them. The mother is young and looks desperate. I'm daydreaming when she asks me if I have children. Parents always ask this at school; it's as if a teacher without children can't be truly empathetic. I disagree. I tell the young woman that I have twins. She mistakenly assumes that they are younger than they are. I let her believe this. There is no point correcting her. We talk a bit about how to fill up the half-term which is academic now as it's Friday. When we arrive at Victoria, I help her gather the children's various items and walk behind them as they step off the train.

Victoria Station is heaving. I manage to catch a bus but it's standing room only. I look out of the windows, taking in the sights as if I were a tourist. It feels as though I have been away for ages. I dread going home. I don't want to face the reality that is waiting for me. I text Kathleen. I expect she knows I will invade her space soon enough. I get off the bus near Swiss Cottage and walk past the swanky new Central School of Speech and Drama building. I wish I could reinvent myself, and my life. I reach the front door which opens before I put my key in the lock. Kathleen is there, wearing my apron. She tells me I look worn out and calls me a "poor thing"; this is not what I want to hear. Besides, I have been well cared for over the past few days. She takes my travel bag from me and immediately starts unpacking it, pulling out my pink underwear. *Really?* she says. Her tone is patronising. I say it's absolutely not necessary but she is instantly offended, shoving the little grey travel case back in my direction. I haven't learned how to manage Kathleen yet. She is different from any other member of staff that I have ever supervised. I apologise, distressed that I have offended her. I put my hand on her hand and say I am sorry again. I say I am lucky to have her in my life and in my home. She flinches at the word "my" but pats me on the head, sending me off for some "rest". She will bring my toiletries upstairs in a few minutes. I put my hands in my pockets to check that my mobile is there; I don't want her reading my texts. I go upstairs and poke my head through each room, just to check that they're tidy. I needn't have done this. The house looks as though it's ready for its first Airbnb customers. My bed has clean sheets and a new duvet cover; it's Olivia's but how was Kathleen supposed to know that? It doesn't matter anyway. I throw myself onto the bed and sob into the pillows.

Kathleen appears at the door. She is omnipresent. I'm like a stroppy teenager again, telling her to go away. She comes in regardless and perches on the side of the bed. I turn my puffy face towards her. For some inexplicable reason she bends down to kiss me on the forehead; it's an unwelcome gesture that makes me tingly and edgy. Her breath smells of alcohol. I don't know what her tipple is but she's clearly drunk too much of it. My mobile buzzes in my pocket. I take it out and try reading the text from my mother under the duvet. Kathleen reminds me that she is still here. My behaviour is rude and ungracious, apparently. I pull the duvet right over my head and tell her to get out.

I wake up fully clothed in my bed. My mobile and I were bedfellows; it's now down to 3% and utterly useless to me. I take a long shower and return to the bedroom, wrapped in a large white towel. Kathleen is downstairs, clattering about with pots and pans. I think she is making a cooked breakfast. I won't eat any as a matter of principle. I get dressed and potter downstairs. I am adopting a nonchalant mood before I have to become Mrs Responsible and visit Michael. A bowl of piping hot porridge is thrust in my direction. I politely refuse it. I'm not hungry. I say I can't find my charger. Has she seen it? She denies all knowledge and assures me that it will turn up. She slaps me between the shoulder blades, by way of reassurance. I want her to keep her hands to herself; I don't believe I have encouraged her attention.

I leave the house ravenous. I don't take my mobile with me as it's on 0%. I feel as though I have lost my right arm. I buy a café latte from Starbucks and take it with me into the hospital. I'm too early and the staff won't let me see Michael until he is more "presentable". I am told to wait with the other visitors. I can read a magazine while I am waiting. I am not used to being told what I can and can't do all the time. I am usually the one giving the instructions. I chat to another woman. She is much older than me, and very frail. Her husband has had hip surgery and is recovering on the ward. She has been happily married for sixty-three years. I know my marriage won't last this long, even if I wanted it to. I start to feel resentful again. I feel as though the world has conspired against me. What did I do to deserve this unhappiness? I wallow in my own wretchedness, unphased by the comings and goings around me. Eventually, a nurse makes an announcement. We are "allowed" to visit our loved ones.

Michael has been moved to a temporary ward which has a sign above the door: "Secure Unit". A nurse presses the keypad and lets me in. We immediately enter a large square room with an upright piano in the corner; a few chairs and tables and a television. It doesn't feel much like a hospital ward. There are about six patients in the room, one of whom is Michael. He is not the youngest. I walk next to the nurse as she escorts me to the other side of the room; it might as well be an ocean. Michael is sitting on a plastic chair, talking to another patient; she's a woman about my age. She even looks a bit like me. I ask the nurse if I can talk to Michael. And if the other woman will mind? I don't want to upset anyone. She may not understand. Estelle is led away to another area of the room and given a doll to clutch instead of Michael's hand. I sit down on the empty chair that was previously occupied by the mirror image of myself. I don't know what to say. I feel awkward and out-of-place. The nurse comes to rescue me. She says my reaction is normal. Lots of people are overwhelmed by the situation. I feel slightly uncomfortable and look down at the floor. There's nothing to focus on; it's all white.

I ask Michael whether he likes the food here. He says he doesn't. And whether he has seen the view of Hampstead Heath. He would rather walk on it. I talk about the twins and tell him that they're probably in Geneva right now and will be in Chamonix by tomorrow. He doesn't know where these places are but he would like to be with them. He wants to know why he's at King's Cross. *Are we catching the Eurostar?* I don't think the room looks much like St Pancras. I try to reassure him that he will be coming home on Monday; it's in two days' time. He asks me if his wife is coming back too. I think he means Estelle. Once again, I am lost for words. And my eyes are full of tears. The nurse, who is hovering nearby, leads Michael to the little nurse's bay in the corner, and says she's going to administer the dose of the risperidone. I try to hold his hand but he wants to be with Estelle. She's not allowed into the bay. I am. But I turn away as the needle enters his buttocks. She tells me that's it for another two weeks, though the doctor will advise if my husband is to take anything in pill form. There will be a meeting on Sunday morning. One of the consultants is coming in especially. He won't be happy about it. The nurse indicates that there are more needy patients than Michael. She thinks he will be discharged. I think she has no idea what he's like.

I wander around M & S Food Hall, next to the hospital, and buy some strawberries imported from Egypt and a litre of milk. The strawberries remind me of better times: summer holidays and picnics with the children. At home, I put the milk in the fridge; there isn't much in it. Kathleen obviously doesn't like spending her own money. I leave £50 on the counter, with a note, saying "Please buy the essentials. Budgens is cheaper than M & S" but I scribble out the last bit, given where I have just been. I take out my laptop and start preparing for the Governors' meeting. I can't quite believe that I will be able to make it; after all, the nurse is threatening to discharge Michael any day now. A mobile vibrates; it's mine. I had completely forgotten about it. The interloper has obviously found my charger. I have a horrible feeling that she has trawled through my messages. My password is too obvious.

I click on my Amazon icon and check the orders; the nanny card was "signed for" whilst I was in Sussex. I hope the package wasn't opened. I feel sick and scared. The house is tidy and I can't see any boxes or even the post for that matter. I wonder where she has put it. I start opening all the drawers in the kitchen and toss out the old examination papers. Nothing. I make quite a mess as I systematically undo the interloper's good work. I check the sitting room and the downstairs coat cupboard and shoe rack, just in case she has piled things up there. There isn't even a speck of dust. I walk up the stairs. It has been ages since I have spent any time in Eddie's room. It has never been this tidy and it smells of Kathleen, not my beautiful son. There are two empty wine bottles in the wastepaper basket along with an empty box of throat sweets. I'm surprised she hasn't put the evidence in the recycle bin; that's remiss of her. My Amazon package is in the bedside drawer. It is unopened.

She has stashed it away along with three letters and one utility bill. Everything is addressed to me, except for the utility bill which is still in Michael's name. I am not sure what to do. If I reclaim the correspondence, she will know that I have been snooping around; but if I don't, when will I have time to install the hidden camera? I sit on the bed and think about my dilemma. I hear the key in the lock downstairs. There is no time to think anymore. I close the drawer quietly and tip-toe out of the room empty-handed. I creep into my own room and lie on the bed. I pretend to be asleep.

The interloper calls me from downstairs. She's been shopping (with her own money) and quickly unloads the items into the fridge and into the cupboards. I know she has called me twice but the door is closed and I think that if I were asleep, I might not have heard her. I can hear her heavy footsteps pounding up the staircase. She knocks loudly on my door; this is a first. She normally barges in. She's holding my package and some other letters. She has been keeping them "safe" for me. I pretend that she has woken me from a strange dream but I can't remember what it's about. I ask her to give me some privacy. It has been a difficult day. She demands information from me, mostly about Michael and what I expect from her. She complains about the state of the kitchen and offers to go to the Royal Free. The interloper manages to say all these things in one breath.

On Monday, I cycle into school. I find it quite difficult as I have had nine days off. I can't believe how tired I am on arrival. It's no distance and it's not even up hill. I pop into Principal Peter's office to explain what's happened and what I think is about to happen. I clarify that it might be difficult for me to attend the Governors' meeting tonight but I have done the preparation. I will email all the documents by noon today. He looks fed up. He complains about my poor attitude and isn't as sympathetic as I had thought he would be. He mentions the possibility of my sabbatical. "It may be time," he says, with his low and distinctive Canadian accent.

I teach most of the morning, oblivious to what's going on with Michael. I successfully compartmentalise my problems, filing them into boxes, and only retrieving them on a need-to-know basis. I have a scheduled meeting with a dissatisfied parent of a Year 7 girl. She was in all the teams in her Junior School but since she has been here, she hasn't been selected for anything, not even the netball squad. I am not sure what this has got to do with me. When the mother comes in, she's much more contrite and courteous than her email. I am extremely sympathetic. Olivia was often on the bench. Too short, like me. I offer the lady tea but she doesn't want any. She just wants her daughter to be in the squad; it doesn't matter if it's the D team. I promise her that I will lean on the Sports Department even though I know that they will resent me for this. I still have some authority in this school even if I have no authority at home anymore.

After the meeting, I teach for the rest of the morning. The students are all the better for their half-term break. I'm about to make a personal call from my office when Liam knocks and enters simultaneously. He pulls up a chair and gives me the "heads up" about my "precarious job situation". It is vulnerable. I should take some leave while I have the chance. I shouldn't wait to be dismissed. I have been naïve and stupid. I had no idea that other people thought I was incapable and unprofessional. I am not sure if I want a sabbatical yet. I am not even fifty. I don't make the personal call and, instead, respond to all my emails; plan a couple of lessons and drink two glasses of water. I need a clear head. Fearful that someone might catch me peeping at my mobile, I take it with me to the staff lavatory and lock myself in. There are five messages from Kathleen. Michael is being discharged this afternoon. I have a voicemail from the hospital which explains that although they have their concerns, in their view, my husband can return home with the carer but be readmitted in a fortnight for further tests and another observation day. I am not thrilled. It means that I am stuck with Kathleen for a bit longer.

I force myself to attend the Governors' meeting which is held in the Randolph Room. There is a green tablecloth (the same colour as a snooker table) draped over the tables which have been shaped into a U. Each place has been marked out with a glass; an agenda; a branded pen and two bottles of water (one sparkling and one still). I can see where our money is spent. I am the first to arrive. I need to look as though I am keen even though I know that I should be collecting Michael from the hospital. The Chairwoman arrives shortly after me; she removes her pumps and changes into black heels. She is elegant in a Thatcherite sort of way though greyer, taller, thinner and plummier. She always wears shocking pink because she can. I am reminded that even Margaret Thatcher developed "classic dementia." No one is immune. The Chairwoman and I exchange pleasantries and sit down to look at the agenda which we have already received by email. She has thin scar right across her neck; this is the first time I have noticed it. Throat cancer, I suppose. And to think, she has survived that and still become a Chair of Governors. Principal Peter and Liam arrive next, followed by two parent governors and two lay governors. They're all wearing suits. The meeting is lengthy. Nothing is allowed to slip beneath the radar. It ends at 8.30 pm and I am grateful that I have my bicycle as the buses are practically obsolete at this time.

When I reach my house, I see balloons flying at the entrance; it looks as though we are hosting a children's party. Kathleen doesn't open the door on my arrival; instead, she is sitting next to Michael, pretending to watch television with him. He looks up at me and calls me Estelle. I roll my eyeballs at the interloper who doesn't give me the satisfaction of responding. She makes me feel guilty for reacting this way. I am losing my patience with that woman but I know that I will lose my job if I don't hang onto her. I think she is well aware of her power over me. I chastise myself for having all the wrong priorities.

I feel faint with hunger and want to eat. The kitchen is spotless again. She has tidied up or thrown my papers away; I am not sure which yet and I am beyond caring now. I make myself scrambled eggs on toast and sit at the kitchen table on my own, half-listening to the down-market programme they're not really watching. Michael was always rather discerning when it came to watching television; more than I ever was, in fact, but now he is reduced to her level. It saddens me to see it. The interloper-cum-nanny finally gets up to go to the lavatory. I seize the moment and instantly remove the Amazon package from my backpack and discreetly read the instructions for the hidden camera; it's straightforward enough, even for technophobes like me. I stand on the kitchen chair and unscrew the smoke alarm; remove the battery and replace it with the nanny card. It is easy. I hear the loo flush before I have finished screwing the cover back on. I just hope she washes her hands.

Chapter 32
Voyeurism

I have turned into something of a voyeur though I am embarrassed to admit that this week's tranche of daily episodes of *Michael & Kathleen* have been disappointingly dull! I really need to install a few more hidden cameras as just having the one in the kitchen is limiting to the point of tediousness. I have been dipping in and out of this soap opera in between lessons and management meetings. There is no sound but I have had no recourse to engage a professional lip reader, yet. It has been nothing but a string of coffees; cooked breakfasts; reading the *Daily Mail*; an occasional game of Jenga and long stretches of viewing empty chairs at the vacant kitchen table. According to Michael's *Life 360*, which I monitor each evening, he has been to scheduled medical appointments; two visits back to the Royal Free; one trip to Waitrose and several excursions up to Waterstones and back. I didn't have Kathleen down as much of a reader; after all, she spends about ten minutes on each page of her tabloid newspaper. I am grateful that she is with him though. It's either her or a residential care home. It is only a matter of time until he is in one. I know this. But it is also hard losing a little bit more of your husband with each hour that passes.

After a full week at school (something of a novelty for me these days) I am easily persuaded to join some of my colleagues at Jak's Bar in South Molton Street. I need the outing. It has all been so intense and miserable both at home and at work. We tend to congregate in the first-floor bar as the other areas are designated for cocktails or food, neither of which any of us can afford. We really should find an alternative venue.

Benedict starts rolling up a marijuana joint. Principal Peter turns a blind eye; after all, we are not at work now. I have never been a smoker but I have enjoyed the occasional spliff in my twenties. I am woefully out of practice but it seems like a good opportunity to reignite the old memory. I follow Benedict down the stairs and out onto South Molton Street. I don't want to be with the big shots upstairs. No doubt my days are numbered anyway. There are a few iron chairs strewn across the pavement outside the bar and several hard-core drinkers and smokers leaning against the building. Benedict is still wearing his suit trousers but has left his jacket at work. He looks younger in his burgundy Yale sweatshirt. I can't remember whether he did a postgraduate there. He lights the spliff and inhales and exhales. He looks like James Dean. We are an unlikely pairing. He takes another drag and hands the neatly rolled joint to me. It has been years since I have indulged. Years. Michael never approved. He always took the moral high-ground when we were at university. I am not even sure if I still know how to inhale. We stand there for ages. Neither of us judges each other. It is a lovely experience.

I eventually convince myself that it's time to go home. It is very dark; slightly wet and it feels late. I am a reckless rider and almost cause a bus to swerve into a lamppost. I am freewheeling down the streets of Mumbai: flashing lights and the occasional cow comes in and out of my path. I know that I am tripping. The three joints we smoked have gone straight to my head. I reach the outside of what looks a bit like my house and press my face against the glass with my hands on either side of my ears. It is drizzling and I am damp. Michael and Kathleen are eating popcorn in front of *Supermarket Sweep*. How low can you go? I can't believe they have revived that programme. I fumble around for my keys but am too impatient to actually use them; it is easier to bang on the window. The couch potatoes are both shocked by the sudden disturbance. The Irish potato opens the door but blocks my entrance. The English potato remains on the sofa. *I am not thinking of bringing that dirty feck-in bicycle in here. The feck in floor has just been polished.* This is the first time I have heard her use expletives. I am bold in my heightened state and am rash and irresponsible again. I can't help myself. I know that I am better than this. The tyres leave little track marks over the Irish potato's white fluffy slippers. I bend down to touch the tiny kaleidoscope images which are coloured by the uplighters in the sitting room. I tell her that they're "pretty". I'm a little giddy and struggle to get up. I think I am going to be sick.

Other people are allowed to enjoy their Friday nights; get drunk, smoke dope, be foolish. I am not. *I should be ashamed of myself! What kind of example am I to my children? My pupils? What use am I to my doting husband?* I say that's a good word. I have got the munchies. I'm so hungry I could eat her feet. I clamber up her stout legs and head straight to the kitchen. I put the radio on and impatiently test out each station until music is played; that's all I want: music, food and love. I don't know why but I have a craving for cheese. I take out a block of mature cheddar and a triangular chunk of Stilton. I hack them both as if they're firewood. I don't use a chopping board. I have no idea where anything is anymore. The kitchen has been totally reorganised. Michael is oblivious to my entrance and my munchies. He sits in a zombie state, chomping the popcorn and drinking beer. I'm sure she has dosed him up on something but whatever it was, it wasn't in the kitchen. Even in my altered state, I know that much.

Kathleen isn't pleased with me. I knew our truce couldn't last. She is a tyrant. A Trunchbull. A Mr Brocklehurst. I am Matilda and Jane Eyre rolled into one. I don't know what I am doing. I have eaten too much cheese: cheddar and Stilton; it's not a good combination. I will probably develop a migraine. And nightmares. I can barely crawl up the stairs. I am reminded of Matt and I yearn for him to rescue me. I am on all fours, like a toddler, and only just make it to the lavatory where I throw up in spectacular style. Bits of carrot and salad (from lunch time) and the cheese (just now) are sprayed against the white tiles around the toilet bowl. It is a disgusting sight. I am not sure if there is more to come.

I am semi-conscious of a large shadow behind me. *Proud of yourself? Look at the state of you! How can you hold down a responsible job? I wouldn't be surprised if you're sleeping with that eejit of a Principal of yours.* I am not proud of myself and I am not sleeping with anyone. I tell her this but she isn't listening. I am an idiot telling a tale. All I can hear is Kathleen's abrasive caterwauling piercing into my ears. Her lecture about responsibility is never-ending. I have to give it to her, mine are usually much shorter. I turn on the radio and swivel the dial so that the volume literally drowns out her sermon. There's a scholarly programme on called *The Art of Innovation*. I have missed the first part. It's incomprehensible erudition. I am drunk and high. She says it's "pretentious claptrap" and that I am too "thick" to follow it. I am certainly too drunk and too doped up to follow anything at the moment. I tell her to stop following me around with her bad breath. I am a hypocrite.

I catch sight of myself in the mirror. I have streaks of mascara down my face; vomit in the ends of my hair and dirt in my nails. It is a bit of a wake-up call. I am no longer high. I have reached a new low. Kathleen drags me in the shower cubicle (fully clothed) and switches on the cold tap; it's freezing and I feel as though my scalp is burning with the icy water. I don't know why I can't get out. The woman shows me no compassion. I suppose I deserve it. I will feel better afterwards, that's what she tells me. After a few minutes, she yanks me out of the shower and is too heavy-handed with the towel. I am a helpless wet puppy: bedraggled and dripping onto the bath mat. She escorts me into Olivia's bedroom where she helps me change and get into bed. I am only half-conscious of what is going on. I lie down, relieved to be horizontal, and try to imagine my life before Michael's dementia. I can't remember it.

On Saturday morning, I wake up very early with what feels like a hangover. I have a cotton mouth and dry eyes. I go to the bathroom but can barely urinate. I am horribly dehydrated. I am wearing pink kickers and one of Michael's shirts. I have no recollection of putting this on. I wander into my own bedroom to find Michael sleeping. I snuggle up next to him and pull the duvet up to my chin. He wakes up, looking confused, but is pleased to see me. My throat feels as though it's going to crack. He says I look awful and I thank him for his honesty. We even laugh a little. It feels strange and comforting to be with my husband. I know this moment won't last but I am desperate to savour it. We lie together for at least an hour.

Later on, when we have breakfast, I give Kathleen the rest of the day off; this will also give me time to hide another camera in the bedroom. She huffs and puffs her way around the kitchen but the ranting has stopped. She knows I am worse for wear but I am sober and sensible now. I won't be pushed around by her today. I owe her £400. Michael is behaving fairly normally. He wants to go for a walk. We escort Kathleen down to a cashpoint on the Finchley Road and I take out the maximum amount: £250. I will have to get the rest out tomorrow. She grabs the money from me and stuffs it into her garish gold and red purse. She has a date with Primark.

I hold Michael's hand in mine and try to keep up with his long stride. We don't go to Ronnie's as I am not in the mood to meet anyone else. I feel as though I have "dope" tattooed across my forehead. We buy two russets from the grocer's and a newspaper from the corner shop. It's like old times. I ask Michael whether he would like to walk up to Fenton House; it has a pretty walled garden. We used to take the twins there for the annual Easter Egg hunt. We walk up to the top of Hampstead High Street, munching our apples. Michael has the *Times* tucked under his arm. I pull out my National Trust card and explain that we are both members although Michael doesn't have his card on him. The elderly volunteer waves us both through. I love Fenton House. It used to belong to a merchant – a successful one – and was subsequently bequeathed by Lady Binning in 1952. She was the last resident and owner. I often meander around these lovely houses, imagining what it must be like to live in them. Michael asks me when we're moving in. I pretend that it's some time in April. He will have forgotten about the house by then. We wander around, admiring the collection of paintings and porcelain, and end up in the garden; this is where I feel at my happiest. I need to breathe in the fresh air, especially after my appalling behaviour last night. I still feel a little worse for wear.

By 1.30 pm Michael is ravenous and I am too. I think carefully about where we can go without drawing too much attention to ourselves. Café Rouge is no longer an option. The greedy landlord wants to turn the restaurant into flats. We walk back down the hill and opt for Chez Bob in Belsize Park; it's next to the Everyman cinema and is always buzzing with atmosphere. It's also noisy enough to mask any embarrassing conversations. The waiter ushers us to a small table for two; it's in the corner, which suits me. We open up the menu and I start reading bits of it out loud. I am not sure why I am doing this. Michael snatches the menu from me, saying that he can choose for himself. He orders three puddings. I order the sour dough with smashed avocado. We don't talk much. He works his way through the chocolate brownie, the cheesecake and the vanilla ice-cream. The bill is brought to Michael. He pulls a handkerchief from his trouser pocket; it's full of his snot and is most unhygienic. He wants to settle the bill with it. It is almost funny in its absurdity. I remove the handkerchief and say they only take debit cards these days. He looks a bit affronted, which I ignore, and I take over and pay the bill.

When we get home, Michael needs a rest; this is helpful because I don't want him wittering on about the hidden camera, just in case he realises what I am doing. He lies down on the sofa and closes his eyes. I envy his capacity to easily fall asleep. I pick up Olivia's little Brighton teddy bear and try to find a way of inserting the nanny card into its jersey. I take it upstairs and put it on the window sill in my room; it has a good view of everything. I test it out from my laptop and am pleased to see that despite my weed and alcohol induced hangover, I am still able to function.

I sit down at the kitchen table and send Eddie and Olivia a long text and two pictures of Michael and me at Fenton House. We look like a normal couple; it's a picture that they will be able to show their friends or co-workers. Nothing to be embarrassed about. I take the opportunity of the peace and quiet to phone my parents; they're recovering from a long walk on the Downs. I admire their positive attitude. I only tell them about our trip to Fenton House and how well the twins are getting on in Chamonix. I don't remark on Kathleen's mistreatment of me nor do I confess to my dalliance with illegal substances. Ignorance can be bliss sometimes.

The daylight fades and the night closes in. I need to wake Michael up before Kathleen comes home, otherwise she will accuse me of being a lazy and neglectful wife. I gently nudge him. He stirs a little and opens his eyes. I am not sure if he recognises me now. He is always at his worst after a nap. He is a bit dozy but parts of what he says make sense. *Has he been a good boy? Will he get a reward today?* He repeats this several times. Kathleen has obviously been patronising him in the way that she attempts to patronise me. We agree that he deserves a reward. He wants chocolate. But I think he has eaten too many sugary desserts in the restaurant. Michael becomes quite agitated and irritated with me. We start to argue; it's not a pretty sight. I sit back down on the sofa and try taking his hand in mine. I try to be kind and patient but he is exasperated with me. I am a "hussy". I have never heard him use this word before. I know that it's one of Kathleen's. I vow to cross-examine her later. I will treat her like one of my adolescent pupils. She won't get the better of me this evening.

Kathleen walks in on cue. She is armed with four brown Primark bags, all of which are bursting at the seams. She has spent all the cash that I gave her. I offer to help her with her bags as she helped me with mine last week. *You? I don't think so. You couldn't lift a pound of turnips.* I don't really know why I put up with her rudeness. I was so confident that I would be able to rebuff her insults and yet here she is, immediately belittling me. Michael is still asking for chocolate. He is rummaging around the old treats' drawer; we haven't used it since the twins were about eleven. It's strange how his memory works, or doesn't work. He insists on receiving his *reward* and it has to be in chocolate form. Kathleen stands on one of the kitchen chairs and picks up a bar of Cadbury's chocolate from the top cupboard.

The chair creaks a little; I hope that it will give way under the strain but it remains stubbornly upright. She hands it to Michael and ignores my comments about his lunch. *And whose fault is that? He has got to stick to his routine. It's not my fault he married a little hussy.* And there it is: that word. I knew it came from her. I stand up to Kathleen this time. She has no right to speak to her employer like that; it's a sackable offence. She threatens to report my marijuana felony to the police. I'm just waiting to find some hard evidence on her. It can only be a matter of time.

Michael is becoming quite attached to Kathleen; it wouldn't surprise me if she manipulates him into changing his will. I need to stay in the driving seat. I don't trust that woman.

Chapter 33
No News is Good News

Winter has finally abated and spring has appeared. We break up in three weeks' time and with the twins away and Michael being looked after, I have managed to get through the past fortnight relatively unscathed. Principal Peter has not raised the subject of my sabbatical recently. I have a free period so I log onto my webcam to see what's going on in the latest episode of *Michael & Kathleen*. The kitchen is currently unoccupied. I am expecting something dramatic to happen but nothing does. The webcam is also functioning in the bedroom; this is a relief, as I am sure that the interloper invades my personal space as often as she can. But still nothing. All's Quiet on the Western Front.

Emily pops into my office; it has been a while since I have had to talk to her about her classroom management. She has a Year 8 pupil with her. Lucas has been using his mobile in her lesson and has uploaded a film of her onto YouTube. The puerile boy has been boasting about his technical brilliance in class. I immediately find the one-minute upload and see that it is totally humiliating. The boy has filmed her breasts from above; they're practically falling out of her blouse whilst she has been helping another child with his homework. I am forced to watch it twice, so that I can see who the other culprits are. Lucas has not acted alone. I use the internal phone to contact Liam; he is more technically astute than I am. He comes very quickly. He isn't busy or he is a voyeur like me; either way, it doesn't look good. I am not sure a Deputy Head should be so easily available.

Lucas is sent out of the room and is asked to wait in the corridor. He slumps onto the floor, stretching his legs out for passers-by to trip over. He is skating on thin ice. The three of us watch the YouTube clip. I have viewed it three times and it is three times too many. I feel sorry for this poor young teacher. Emily is in tears. The clip has already been viewed by 43,000 people and the numbers keep rising. Liam manages to get the offensive video taken down within minutes. But everyone in Year 8 has seen it and the vast majority have shared it with several others. Liam says "boys will be boys" which I think is unhelpful. I phone Lucas' parents and asked them to collect him at 2.30 pm. He will be suspended for ten days. Emily cries pitifully and confesses that she can't face returning to her classroom. She is mortified. I give her the School Counsellor's number and inform her that she is entitled to three free sessions. I send her home to "convalesce" and end up covering her remaining two periods. I let the students watch a film (something educational) which I know is a cop-out but I don't have time to prepare anything myself. When I return to the office, I see that I have six missed calls from Eddie.

I close the door and put a "Silence: Exam in Progress" notice on the glass panel; this is the only way I can guarantee no one will disturb me. Until now, no news has been good news. But Eddie's desperate messages which are devoid of content have filled me with fear. What has Olivia broken? Why can't he elaborate on a text? I hope I can get through. Which hospital is Olivia in? I make the call. Eddie answers straight away; it sounds as though he is in an airport. He isn't. He's in Geneva University Hospital. Eddie is crying so much that I can barely make out a word that he is saying. I tell him to slow down. I am here. She was flown by helicopter from Chamonix. I tell him to sit down and stay on the line. I am worried that he will collapse. He is in a complete state. Eddie listens to my clear and calm instructions. It feels good to be back in the driving seat but bad to be in this particular one. Olivia has suspected meningitis. I Google meningitis as we speak. I ask him if it's viral or bacterial. He says it could be the former but they suspect it's the latter. Either way, it's worrying. It's every parent's worst nightmare. The symptoms started with a severe headache last night. She couldn't work this morning. She developed a stiff neck and couldn't turn it to the left or right. Olivia complained that the chalet lights were too bright; this rang alarm bells with the one of the guests who happens to be a junior doctor in Geneva. I want to know if she has a rash or pimples. Eddie said she had pinprick pimples on her legs.

It's only Monday evening but it is obvious that I won't be working for the rest of the week. I leave the sign on my door and rush over to Peter Principal's office. He's on the phone but waves me in. I am too flustered to sit down so I pace around his characterless room until he says he will call the person back. I tell him about Olivia. He is sympathetic and concerned. I'm not to worry about setting cover. Harry-the-Harrovian will do that. But my erratic attendance will have consequences. He reminds me that the option for a sabbatical is still open and that he strongly recommends that I take it. I phone my parents' landline. They offer to fly to Geneva instead of me but I reject this offer. I want to go. I want them to remain on standby for Michael, just in case something happens. I send Kathleen a text, asking her not to make any arrangements this week. I will fill her in when I get home. I offer her an additional £100 for the inconvenience as she will be on duty 24/7. I start searching for flights. I am lucky. The British Airways flight isn't full. I don't book a hotel room. I text Eddie my itinerary and send lots of kisses. I will phone him again later. I will be with him in less than twenty-four hours.

At home, Michael is already changed into his pyjamas; it's only 6.30 pm Kathleen says he is worn out. They've had a full day. I hand him a blanket (which is permanently on the sofa) as he is a little exposed but he says he's too hot and doesn't want it. I am no use to him now. Kathleen makes dinner. I don't think I can keep a curry down tonight. She is easily offended. I just want to be with my children. I take out a black holdall from the under stairs cupboard. I am not sure how long I will be away so I pack enough clothes for a week. I lay everything out onto the bed; I have always packed this way. I take a couple of adapter plugs out of the drawer and pack a spare mobile charger in case I forget it tomorrow morning. It will be a very early start. The holdall isn't particularly heavy so I carry it down the stairs by myself. I leave it in the hall, near the front door, but make sure that it's not in anyone's way.

Kathleen is still dawdling in the kitchen. I ask her if she has ever treated a patient with meningitis. We sit down opposite each other. She regales me with a dreadful story about a little girl who lost her leg. Her description is horribly graphic. I tell her that I don't want to hear it but she insists on continuing. I want to leave the table. My hearing is muffled; my vision is blurred and my legs feel weak. I know I am on the verge of fainting. Kathleen props me up a bit and forces a glass of water down my throat. *I knew you were a fainter. I know the type.* I am in no mood for confrontation. I allow myself a little time to recover before I get down to business. I send her images of my passport; my insurance documents and the details of the hospital. I do this all on WhatsApp. I also remind her that Michael has an appointment with the psychiatrist on Thursday. She will have to take him there. I can hear her mutter something under her breath. Something about my being useless anyway but I pretend I can't hear her. What's the point? Olivia is more important than my pride.

Michael is still resting on the sofa. I ask him if he wants to come up to bed with me. He rejects my offer, much to the amusement of Kathleen, and says he's busy. He has work to do and deadlines to meet. He almost sounds sane. I shrug my shoulders and head upstairs. I am still feeling a little nauseous. I brush my teeth, set my alarm, lock the door and go to bed. It's short lived though as I wake up at 3 am and can't resettle. I start Googling the NHS website about meningitis; it's clear and informative but terrifying to read. I just want to be in Geneva. I can't be there soon enough. I decide to leave the house early so as to avoid Kathleen. My holdall is ready. The Uber arrives within ten minutes. There isn't much traffic at 5.30 am so I have hours to kill before I can even check in. The time passes sluggishly. I send Eddie text after text. I also send messages to my close friends, most of whom instantly reply. They can't believe it. Rosie says I have been dealt a misère hand.

The flight is quick. The captain announces the punctual landing as the conditions couldn't be more perfect; besides, we are the first scheduled flight of the day to arrive in Geneva. At least one thing has gone my way. I take a taxi straight to the main University Geneva Hospital and report to the reception. The building looks more like a state-of-the-art five-star hotel. I am confident that Olivia is in good hands. But I am desperate to see her. I can barely hear the instructions that are meted out to me. When I reach the isolation wing, I am not allowed beyond the waiting room. I enquire after Olivia and ask if Eddie is here. A middle-aged nurse greets me and takes me to a room with a table and four chairs. She immediately inspires confidence. I just want to see my daughter but am told that I will do, soon, but not until they have ruled certain things in or out. The doctors are still conducting tests. Olivia has a very high temperature; a severe headache; is suffering from dizziness and is over sensitive to the light. She has all the classic symptoms of meningitis. I ask about the tumbler test; it's one of the few things I know about, but she shakes her head and tells me to be patient. Eddie appears within minutes. He looks frazzled and exhausted. He is father, brother and son combined. It is too much responsibility for a young man.

Another nurse comes into the room with two glasses of water and a plate of biscuits which remain untouched. She asks me to sign a consent form for a lumbar puncture and hands me a hospital biro, indicating the place where my signature is needed. The middle-aged nurse explains that the lumbar puncture is used by doctors to confirm the diagnosis of meningitis and to check for signs of what is causing it. Her English is perfect. She starts to clarify how the test is conducted. It can take up to thirty to forty minutes. I know that Olivia is as squeamish as me so I also hope that she isn't fully conscious of the process. The nurse continues to speak. I hear the letters CSF but I don't catch what they stand for. I am desperately trying to be strong for Eddie; after all, I am his mother. He should be able to defer to me now. But as the nurse explains in vivid detail that a needle is passed between two vertebrae at the lower end of the spine, containing the CSF, I am deaf and blind again. Kathleen is right. I am a fainter. I always have been. I am quite comfortable lying on the floor though truthfully, I have no idea where I am. I can hear someone say "Sophie Boswell" and another lower voice calling me "mum" and "mummy". It takes me a few seconds for to realise what has happened. I don't want the attention; it's awkward and embarrassing. The focus has to be on Olivia. I say this out loud. A cup of sweet tea is brought to my lips. The nurse is kind and encourages me to sip it, even though she says she couldn't drink it herself.

We wait for an hour but it seems much longer. The staff here are kind and attentive. They have even assigned us a private room close to the nurse's station. But we are still not allowed to visit Olivia in person. Not yet. We are encouraged to rest as the test results will not be instantaneous. I cannot remember the last time I shared a room with Eddie. He reminds me so much of Michael. There are two single beds separated by accompanying night tables with lamps. He kicks off his shoes and lies down on top of the sheets. I know I should check into the webcam but I am too tired; besides, nothing ever happens. I am not missing Kathleen and I am sure that Michael isn't missing me. Eddie falls asleep quickly; he is his father's son. I put my mobile onto charge and read the BBC News on my app. British politics seems irrelevant to me. I only want to receive a positive newsflash about Olivia. I switch the main light off, leaving only my bedside lamp on. I watch Eddie's chest rise and fall with his quiet and regular breathing. I hope he has pleasant dreams. I leave the room and speak to the nurse on night duty. Her name is Nina and she's about twenty-five and pretty. She has a one-year-old daughter. I ask to see a picture. The baby is beautiful. She has large blue eyes and a mop of curly flaxen hair. Nina is tactful and mature for her age. She asks me to show her a picture of Olivia. She confesses that it's hard to see the real person beneath the tubes and cannulas. We talk for at least half an hour but we are interrupted by a most insistent bleep. She returns to the ward and I go to bed.

I spend most of the night awake. I try to sleep – I really do – but my insomnia is determined to keep me company throughout the night. Someone knocks on our door at 8 am. Eddie is still asleep. He must be exhausted, emotionally and physically. I am so sleep deprived that yet again I fear that I won't be able to cope. I am not sure what I am running on: fear, I think. I tidy up the little room and reorganise my things as well as Eddie's. He has only brought a tiny rucksack and has virtually nothing in it. The knock is harder and more persistent. I open the door to a cleaner. She empties the bin and cleans the en suite bathroom that we haven't used. Eddie wakes up when the woman leaves.

We walk over to the nurse's station and ask for an update. A consultant takes us to one side and sits us down. It's good news. The lumbar puncture result has confirmed that Olivia doesn't have meningitis but she does have septicaemia. I sob with relief but we are not out of the woods yet. I ask when we can see her. We follow the consultant and the nurse down a series of corridors until we reach Olivia's room. She is still in isolation though not in solitary confinement. We are advised to use plenty of hand sanitiser and are given surgical gowns and masks to wear. Olivia's bed has been slightly raised so that she can see us as we enter the room. She smiles weakly. Little tears appear from the corner of her eyes. I bend down to kiss her wet cheeks, trying not to touch the drips and cannulas inserted into her veins. The sheets are pulled up to her chest so I can't see the rash on her legs. She's attached to an intravenous drip and there are other devices and monitors which I don't fully understand. Eddie has a lovely bedside manner. I wonder whether he should reapply to study medicine instead of Biochemistry. I sit back on one of the two chairs and watch Eddie and Olivia speak without speaking.

The doctor wants to talk to me about the course of treatment. He indicates that the septicaemia is under control but they are wary of sepsis developing; this would be a complete calamity. I know so little about either that I just listen and nod my head. The consultant advises me to book a room in a hotel nearby. We will be here for some time. A nurse comes over with a wad of leaflets, one of which is for a hotel called the Adriatica. It's located in the Malagnou and Champel district which is about half a mile from the hospital. It has free Wifi and free bicycles. I thank her and accept her recommendation.

Eddie and I take it turns to visit Olivia as the nurse is worried that our combined efforts are too exhausting for her. I take out my laptop and book adjoining rooms at the recommended hotel. I am conscious that I haven't spoken to Kathleen, or updated her, or watched the webcam, and I can't do any of this in front of my son. Besides, he must want his privacy as I want mine.

We walk to the hotel using Google map to get us there. When we arrive, the façade is illuminated in pink in addition to international flags swaying in the light breeze. We walk up the elegant steps which are flanked by small fir trees; these lead straight to the reception which is old fashioned in its fussiness and different from the modernity expressed outside. The stripey chairs in the hall way remind me of antiquated pubs in Brighton. We take the lift up to the fourth floor and enter our rooms simultaneously. Mine is very tasteful: modern, chic, a well-dressed room with lovely touches and a large flat-screen television that takes up half the back wall. I'm also pleased to have a bath as opposed to a shower. I knock gently on Eddie's door to check that he's happy in his room too. His room is identical to mine except that he has a shower and not a bath. We are both content. We agree to meet for breakfast at 9 am I tell him he can have whatever he wants from the minibar; this is a first. I have spent my life telling the children the complete opposite.

I finally plug in my laptop and tune into home. It's late and I fear that I have probably missed all the excitement, if indeed there was any. I haven't even texted Kathleen, or phoned Michael. There hasn't been much of an opportunity until now. I go to the loo; run a hot bubbly bath and decide to soak in it until I have turned into a fragrant prune. I take advantage of the fluffy white towelling robe and even wear the oversized slippers, since they're provided. I return to the bed and lie down to watch my house. I flick between the kitchen and the bedroom. The kitchen is tidy. The chairs are tucked under the table and the only thing on it is a tabloid newspaper. I flick back to our bedroom. Michael's long body is under the duvet. He's wriggling around a bit and has his head buried under one of the pillows. I watch him for a few minutes and wonder if he is having a nightmare. Part of me desires to see his face; for him to look straight at the teddy camera. But he doesn't. I keep watching my screen, mesmerized by the image. My eyes are so tired that I tell myself to stop. I should take advantage of the hotel and sleep. What good will I be to either of my children if I don't recharge my batteries? I am on the verge of closing the laptop when I see a flicker of movement from the right -hand side of the bed. There's a large silhouette in the frame. It's very difficult to see the figure clearly, until she switches on the bedside lamp. The woman puts on a pair of white latex gloves. I am glued to the screen. What can she want these for? Her hands approach the bed and to my horror, she climbs in next to Michael.

Chapter 34
Night Nurse

My prurience is interrupted by a succession of childish knocks on my hotel room door. I haven't ordered room service. I reluctantly tear myself away from the greyish images. I look through the spy hole to see my son, Eddie, standing in the corridor wearing boxer shorts and a tee shirt (the one he has been wearing all day). He comes into the room and flops down on the single chair beside the bed. I close the laptop and give Eddie one of the white towelling robes from the bathroom. I make us mugs of tea, taking care not to spill the miserly miniature carton of milk supplied in long-life form. We talk for what seems like hours. He is anxious that the dementia might be hereditary. We have had this discussion before. The doctors have reassured me Michael's particular strain of frontal lobe dementia is highly unlikely to be hereditary. I remind Eddie that Michael's parents died in their forties so we have little medical history to go on. I resume my motherly role, giving him the love and reassurance that he craves. He is scared that his father won't recognise him when he gets home. I console him with white lies: we are eons from this but in all honesty, I don't know whether we are weeks, months or years from this cruel eventuality. He probes me for more details, both about Michael and Olivia. I am reluctant to share what I know, even though Eddie is eighteen. Eventually, I give him just enough information to send him back to his room. I am kind but firm. We both need to sleep.

I have clearly dozed off because I wake up with the bedside

lamps still on and the empty mugs beside me. I immediately reach for my laptop and look at the webcam. Michael is sleeping, soundly, and there's nothing sensational to report. I feel a sense of anti-climax. I am half awake and half asleep. I begin to question what I viewed. Perhaps I was imagining it? Deep sleep and I are intimate strangers. The image on the screen was neither light nor clear. I can't view it again; it's not a recording device. Even though it's about 3 am I take two green and white pills; they're my last remaining Night Nurse capsules. It seems a shame to waste them at this hour but I am desperate for some continuous sleep.

In my dream, we are gathered at the Hampstead Cemetery for Michael's premature funeral. There are hundreds of people there: his former work colleagues from Dayton Hardwick and Chase; his lanky brother has come down from Newcastle, complete with a carer; my children and some of our friends. Everyone is crying. I try to smile at Michael's brother, Ian. He looks young: thin, clean-shaven and boyish. I haven't seen him for years. He could be one of my students. Even in my dreamlike state, I am conscious that I haven't told him about Michael. He wouldn't understand though. He can barely speak. The skies are full of dark clouds which look ready to burst with rain. We are surrounded by willow trees, bending and swaying into our path. The branches protrude into the mourners, enveloping them with their delicate twigs, mostly bereft of their leaves. Small buds are reappearing; it's spring after all, though in my dream it could be any season. The rain begins to fall, landing noisily onto Michael's coffin.

I know that I am dreaming but I am on the periphery, observing the scene. I want to be part of it but I am on the outside looking in. Almost everyone is dressed in white with black carnations pinned to their jacket lapels or flimsy dresses. Everyone is drenched. Michael's former boss, the one who let him go so unceremoniously, gives a hollow eulogy. Even in my dream, I am angry with him. I want to approach him but nature intervenes. She springs up in the form of plants and tangled trees; they appear around my naked feet, twisting and whirling around my ankles like black ribbons on a ballet dancer. The rain teems down, as it does in films. The deluge comes down in Biblical proportions. Eddie is sopping wet, standing next to Olivia. Her cannula is still attached to her wrist and her insubstantial hospital gown is soaked. I cannot understand why she isn't wearing a proper dress. The willow trees bend towards her, sheltering her under their sympathetic branches. I find a navy suit jacket rolled up next to the trunk and place it over her shoulders; it's one of Michael's and it still has the dry-cleaning label pinned inside the pocket. I am startled in my dream to see Kathleen present. She is the only person wearing black and her ugly face is half-concealed by a delicate lace veil. There's a monstrously large red carnation pinned to her left breast. As with all dreamers, I am bold and confident, though my shoeless feet sink heavily into the squelching mud. I continue to defy my surroundings, approaching this duplicitous woman. I jab her portly chest with my sharp fingers and accuse her of abusing Michael. The half-veiled woman doesn't reply but her carnation bleeds slowly, until the flower droops and bends its head away from me.

After the burial, I find myself being drawn to the outside of The Flask in Highgate. I know it well. As with all dreamers, I am in possession of great knowledge and yet everything I know is void of meaning. I am alone again, running down a dark and empty corridor. It is nothing like the pub in Highgate. It is much more like a school though it isn't mine. My body is drawn to the noise and the familiar voices. The corridor is no longer empty. There are hundreds of scruffy students sitting on the floor, blocking my way. They are sitting on a red carpet. I leave muddy footprints in between their outstretched legs and am conscious of my untidy trail. I don't know why my feet are bare. I can hear muffled music; crowds of people drinking at a bar; a jukebox playing "Dangerous Woman" by Ariana Grande. I try entering– everyone I know is in there now – but my entrance is forbidden. I have lost my black carnation.

I wake up in a peculiar position on the hotel bed. I'm lying the opposite way around with the duvet half on and half off. It takes me a few minutes to re-orientate myself. I wonder whether Michael feels like this every morning: bewildered. I feel as though I will be exposed; that other people will know what I have dreamt. I look in the mirror to see a normal person facing me. I phone Eddie and suggest we meet downstairs for breakfast.

I phone the hospital from the hotel breakfast-cum-dining room. The news is good. Olivia is responding well to the intravenous medication. We are informed that the recovery can vary between three to ten days. I send Eddie off to buy some clothes for himself; there's a department store quite near the hospital. He has money; a debit card and common sense. I am sure he can manage. Besides, I want to speak to the nurses and the doctors in private. We pare off in separate directions but agree to meet at Olivia's bedside in two hours, or thereabouts. I am not specific. It is not school.

I arrive before visiting hours so I find a table near a socket and plug my laptop into it so that I don't run the battery down. Luckily my adapter is still attached. I don't feel as though I am in another country. One hospital canteen is very much like another. I have fifteen minutes before I can visit Olivia. I phone my parents. My father puts me on loudspeaker; I'm used to this but it makes me self-conscious. My mother knows that I am hiding something but I refuse to elaborate. Sheila and Henry simultaneously offer to fly out to Geneva. I decline again but ask them if they could come up to London for when we return. Eddie and Olivia will not be completing their work experience here.

When I reach the nurse's station, I am relieved to see the familiar face of Nina. She smiles, reassuringly, and I feel grateful that there is at least one person here in whom

I can confide. She escorts me back onto the ward where I am greeted by two doctors and another nurse. The doctor is concise and professional. He does his best to use layman's terms. We are almost out of the woods. Before I am allowed to see Olivia, I take the opportunity of explaining my husband's condition to the medics. I don't want their sympathy but I do want their understanding and their advice. Besides, I feel compelled to excuse his absence. The consultant isn't judgemental. He scribbles down a note and hands it to the more senior of the two nurses; it's a recommendation of a psychiatrist whom they will contact on Olivia's behalf. There will be no charge.

I sit down next to Olivia and stroke her hair away from her forehead; it's a little sticky and needs a wash. I take her soft hand in mine and caress it until she wakes up. I reassure her that she will be discharged within the week. She can see a counsellor if she would like to. Olivia nods her head. Little tears cascade down her cheeks. She asks me about her father. We talk wistfully about the old days and how unfair life is; I can't say that it isn't. Eddie breaks the sombre atmosphere by bounding into the room. He is armed with two shopping bags, one of which is full of clothes for Olivia. He is thoughtful twin. The three of us are closer than ever. I talk to my children quite candidly about the future. I mention Principal's Peter suggestion that I take a sabbatical. Even as I refer to it, I can hear my mother's words rankle in my ears. *You need to support your family; don't throw your career away; it's not necessary; be careful; just take three months off if you have to* and so on. My children are surprisingly rational and reasonable. They will support my decision either way. I wasn't sure what to expect.

Eddie proceeds to pull out various items of clothing including a lovely brightly coloured knitted cardigan; it's for Olivia and he won't be reimbursed for it. I leave the twins chatting quietly and ask Nina, who is still on duty, if there's a private room that I can use, just for a few minutes. I plug my laptop in again and look at the webcam. I still feel uncomfortable about leaving Michael with Kathleen. They're in the kitchen, chatting. It all looks very innocent. I decide to telephone her whilst simultaneously watching the screen. The image in the kitchen is much clearer than the one in the bedroom as it's bright and all the spotlights are on. I put my finger on her name in my contacts' list and wait for her to answer. I feel jittery and nervous, as if I am waiting for my students' examination results. Kathleen deliberately lets her mobile ring at least ten times. I watch her as she observes her phone vibrate on the kitchen table. Michael looks a little agitated but he doesn't open his mouth other than to eat toast. There is no sound on my webcam.

Kathleen is civil. She asks after Olivia and says all the right things; however, there is no sentimentality in her voice and I doubt she means anything she says. I am annoyed with her for letting the mobile ring unnecessarily and decide to be more assertive. I ask to speak to Michael; after all, he is still my husband. She places her hand across his mouth without touching it. He is still chewing. He nods his head as if he is complicit in her ridiculous game. There is a long pause whilst Kathleen *pretends* to fetch him from the sitting room. I have to force myself to go along with this farce for fear of blowing my cover. I wait, patiently, for the next episode in this soap opera that is my life and theirs. I update Michael about Geneva and inform him that Olivia is making a good recovery. We will all be home soon. I am not sure what he understands but his responses are normal and polite. Either that or they're a reflex action.

As I talk, and he listens, I watch that odious woman hovering over his shoulder. *Have I been to Geneva? Is it in England? Should I be there?* His unassuming questions make him sound like the simpleton that he isn't. I wait a few seconds until she walks over to the sink. I ask Michael if he is free to speak. Is there something he wants to tell me? Does he feel safe? I practically whisper these words down the line as I am fearful that Kathleen is still in earshot. I repeat: are you all right? But this is too subtle for his disorientated state. I simply ask: is Kathleen hurting you? As I say this, I watch both Michael and Kathleen. She is inches away from him, washing something up in the sink. He props the mobile up with his right shoulder, wedging it under his right ear; simultaneously, he starts rolling up his left sleeve. I'm certain that he is about to reveal a bruise or an injury but Kathleen pounces on him, grabbing her mobile before he utters another sound. She looks straight at the camera that she doesn't know is there. She tells me that he is fine. I should stop fussing. Michael rolls up his sleeve, revealing a red welt on his wrist. His mouth is moving but I can't quite hear him as she has decided to boil the kettle for added interference. I can hear her sounding off in the background: *If you're so worried about your blessed eejit of a husband, I suggest you come back to London you fecken' blonde bimbo.* I have been a bimbo. I should have been more circumspect; locked my papers away; taken more precautions. I am not sure why I didn't. My ineptitude doesn't even make sense to me. I put it down to stress. My life is no longer ordinary. I am not as resilient as I thought I was.

I have heard enough. I end the call and end her contract. My parents will have to come down sooner than I planned.

I will pick up the pieces when I get home.

Chapter 35
My Temperance Level

It is the end of March and the end of term; it couldn't come soon enough for me. I have written my sabbatical email in draft form and propose handing it to Principal Peter, in person, after his final assembly or at tonight's staff party. It seems only fair. He knows it's coming. We have talked about little else since I returned to London with the twins last week. Olivia is still convalescing but she is well enough to receive a succession of visits from her lively friends.

Even at forty-nine, I heavily rely on my parents for their help. They have been staying in an Airbnb in a rather grand house in Daleham Gardens, just around the corner from our mews house. I never imagined that Sheila and Henry would feel so comfortable in North West London. They are Sussex folk, through and through. Whilst I have been back in school, they have engaged and paid for an army of helpers, both for Olivia and for Michael. I know that he has deteriorated further but he is no longer as angry as he was and his outbursts and temper are much reduced though his aggression is still latent. I remain careful around Michael. He doesn't always know what he is doing, especially first thing in the morning. It's not easy sharing a bedroom with someone who occasionally forgets who you are. It's as if I am an imposter in my own home.

I like to think that he's pleased to see the back of Kathleen but I shall never know. He refuses to talk about her and says he doesn't know who she is. Or to use his own words: *I don't' think I know this woman. Did I have sex with her?*

My parents have invited Olivia, Eddie and Michael over for an informal supper. Eddie and Olivia walk on either side of their father. I pop in for a quick drink but am returning to school, by bus, for the party. *It's good to see that you have made an effort with your appearance, at last. You look lovely.* These are my mother's and my father's respective comments. I look at Michael for his approval but it isn't forthcoming. I am not sure what I am to him anymore or what he is to me. My father opens a bottle of white wine. He makes a toast to our good health; I can't help thinking that this is tinged with irony.

I catch the bus into town. I wish I could take the Jubilee line; it would be so much faster. I know this aversion to the underground cannot go on. I need to address my demons. I am armed with a printed copy of my email-cum-letter; it's suitably contrite and grateful. I finger the envelope in my handbag and resist the temptation to re-read its content. It's too late now. I just hope I have the confidence to hand it in. When I arrive at Bond Street, I can see that the entrance of our school is flanked by silver helium balloons. It's quite a spectacle. There's even a red carpet up the short staircase to the front door. Someone ought to be a professional party organiser. I change into my heels and put my trainers into a small black tote-bag. I walk up the red carpet, turn my head to the non-existent paparazzi, and continue into the hall where I am immediately plied with champagne. I am bemused by the sudden decadence; there wasn't a hint of it earlier in the day. Abbas is dressed in navy suit, blue shirt and a yellow tie. He looks like a lawyer or an investment banker. I am not sure he knows how to dress to party… My other colleagues are less formal but they've all made an effort, even Liam, who is inclined to dress down for parties as he says he lives in a suit five days a week. The atmosphere is convivial. We start congregating in the Randolph Room; it has many uses and this is one of the more enjoyable ones. I stand with the other members of the SMT. We gaze at and comment on the twenty-somethings; they're all dressed to party though I still can't quite get my head around young women wearing dresses and trainers. Olivia has done this for years. I'm offered another glass of champagne. I have a low temperance level but I tend to forget this after a couple of glasses of fizz. Besides, it's my last day until September. What can possibly go wrong?

The ceiling lights are dimmed as the colourful disco bulbs rotate around the panelled room. It's dark enough for the more self-conscious members of staff to lose themselves in the music. I dance with Abbas (who can't) and Liam (who can). In between dances, I am encouraged to imbibe more than I should. And I am already feeling wobbly and giggly. The 70s, 80s and 90s music is exchanged for rap and some modern stuff that I don't recognise; it's an ugly sound that drives a few of us oldies away. Abbas leaves at 10 pm on the dot. I retreat into Peter Principal's office. I don't switch on the light as there's enough emanating from the corridor. I am alone, at last. The music is still pulsating; it's offensive now and I am beginning to regret not leaving earlier. I take my "sabbatical letter" out of my handbag and place it under the telephone. There's no going back. Peter Principal must either be careless or trusting; either way, it is expedient for me that he has left his computer switched on and his password appears to be "password"; this contravenes all the advice meted out to us last term. I have an overwhelming desire to know if he has lined up my replacement and if so, whom? It is odd that he hasn't told me. Perhaps I won't approve of his choice? I have a quick look at the contents of his double in-tray. There's a copy of my timetable – which has been highlighted – and a few notes in Liam's distinctive handwriting. There's a memorandum from one of the Governors and a few randomly printed out emails that look personal so I don't read them.

I can hear a series of heavy and light footsteps coming down the corridor in my direction. I hold my breath and press the button on the monitor making it instantly dark. The male and female footsteps retreat into what sounds like my office. I am too scared to follow them in; besides, technically, it's not really my office anymore. I turn the monitor back on and resume my search. There are hundreds and hundreds of emails; even more than in my inbox. I am getting nowhere.

Naughty, naughty, naughty... I push the chair back against the wall behind me and hide under the desk. I can't quite believe I am doing this. *Come out, you know you want to.* I tell the voice to go away. I know it's not Principal Peter's voice but I also know that I shouldn't be snooping about in his office. I'm still crouching under the large desk; its modesty panel doesn't quite reach the floor so I can see the voice's feet, pacing up and down. *Come on. Out. I need to lock up.* It sounds plausible. The door closes and I can hear the lock turn but the feet are still inside the office. They're wearing trainers, not leather shoes, and the feet are huge and smell of sweat. I crawl out from under the desk and sit awkwardly onto the swivel chair that I had been sitting on earlier. It's still very dark. My visitor hasn't turned on the light and I don't think he's going to. The tall figure is nothing more than a silhouette; it approaches me and stands between the desk and the chair; there's barely room to swing a cat, let alone his one. Joe is no longer the friendly school caretaker. He is a hefty, vigorous man. *I won't tell if you don't tell.* His erect penis is making a huge bulge in his scruffy jeans. *No, I say. No. I shouldn't have been nosing around. I know that. Come on, Joe. Let's be sensible. It's my last day for ages.* But he insists that we play Cat and Mouse for a few minutes, whilst I try to extricate myself from his misguided embraces. I am beginning to have one of my panic attacks. The large looming figure isn't sympathetic and is getting impatient with me. Within seconds, one of his rough hands is grasping my neck whilst the other is unzipping his flies. He rubs himself up and down until he comes all over me; it's disgusting. I can't shout or scream. All my self-defence training has evaded me. Besides, am I really doing to stab him in the eye with a biro?

Joe pushes his penis back into his stained trousers. He isn't finished with me though. I am still on the swivel chair, trapped behind the desk. My new red dress is damp with his sticky sperm. At least he hasn't raped me. I say: *I am too old. I am nearly fifty.* I plead with him and say I'll do anything for him. I'll help him find a better job. But he likes his job. He doesn't want another one. And I'm not too old. He is older than me. He takes his eyes off me for a second. carpe diem: seize the day. I get off the chair and scramble over the desk, taking off one of my shoes so that I can use it as a weapon. I jab him in the chest with the heel and bash him over the head; it should really hurt but it doesn't make much of an impact. We wrestle a bit and I make my way over to the door. My dress is torn; my hair is tangled and dishevelled; my tights are laddered and even though I can't see myself in the mirror, I know that my black mascara has run down my cheeks. I start banging on the glass panel of the door, hoping that the owners of the male and female giggling voices I heard earlier – the ones in my office – will hear my shrieks and cries. Panic sets in again as I fear the worst. I have injured my hand with all the bashing and banging.

We can both hear the familiar plodding feet of our Principal. In an instant, Joe tidies himself up and unlocks and opens the door. He grabs the First Aid kit from the wall and opens it, yanking out a white bandage which he expertly unravels. He starts wrapping it around my bleeding hand. He is quick and professional. I begin to think he is wasted as a caretaker.

Principal Peter appears. He towers over both of us, bending his head as he enters his own office. He sees the letter that I placed under his telephone and opens it whilst he stares at Joe, my bleeding hand and the well-applied bandage. *I hope that doesn't hurt. How on earth did you manage that on your last day?* I reply: no comment. And feign a weak smile. *I thought you should know that your predecessor, Elizabeth, is returning to hold the fort in your absence. I have managed to persuade her to come out of retirement. But you must promise to return in mid-August, when the results come out. I need you, Sophie Boswell. Try not to get yourself arrested between now and then.* He has a dry sense of humour but the irony is not wasted on me. I have been somewhat reckless since Michael's diagnosis.

I stagger down to the bus stop and manage to catch the 13. I normally sit on the top deck but I feel vulnerable so I don't. I sit near the driver instead. I have about twenty minutes to come up with a plausible story for my wrecked appearance. I get off at Swiss Cottage; cross over the Finchley Road and pass the hideous Tavistock Centre and up Daleham Gardens and turn into the mews. It's very dark and very late. I am hopeful that I will get home unnoticed.

Fortunately, everyone is in bed though Eddie's bedside lamp is on. I stand under the shower for ages, removing any trace of Joe's odour and fluids from my bruised and battered body. I screw up the dress and carefully place it into a plastic bag, dumping it in the corner of the bathroom, hoping that I remember to bin it tomorrow morning. I comb my hair into a parting, brush my teeth, put on a night-shirt, drink a large glass of water and clamber into bed next to my slumbering husband. He stretches out his arm and pulls me in beside him. We are like two bent spoons. I have forgotten what it's like to be loved and cossetted.

Tomorrow is another day.

Chapter 36
Spring Forward

It feels a little strange being the Fab Four again. Each of our three bedrooms is occupied by its rightful owner; the fridge is well stocked; the cupboards are bursting with a variety of exotic teas and there's a healthy mess in the sitting room: books; magazines; iPads; mobiles and chargers; countless pairs of shoes and hoodies not to mention a recycling bin that is practically overflowing. The mountains of clutter are welcome. We're *almost* a regular, nuclear family. And the best thing is still to come: an unexpected week on a cruise ship, paid for by my parents.

Sheila and Henry have never been on a cruise. They're not "cruise people", whoever they are, but for the first time in their lives, they have booked for us to join them for a week around the Mediterranean in mid-May. The twins took a little convincing; they're probably "too cool" to be seen on a large commercial ship; however, the thought of a free and allegedly luxurious holiday, coupled with at least five stops to places of interest, was enough to convince them to join us. Besides, we all need a little distance from the misery that has invaded our lives like the destructive virus that it is. Michael may not remember this holiday but we are determined to make it a happy experience for all of us. I have been reading people's views on TripAdvisor: some are most encouraging whilst others are damning. I will reserve my judgement.

My colleagues have returned to school for the Summer Term. Elizabeth Keller, the retired deputy head, has made herself comfortable in my office, so Abbas tells me. She's an English specialist so she can take over my timetable though I appreciate that there have been quite a few changes to the GCSE syllabus since she retired. She's old school, which might be a good thing. I am not sure whether *all* the students will warm to her but at least they should achieve the grades that they deserve. When I was on maternity leave, all those years ago, I felt resentful that someone occupied my office and stole my beloved students from me; this time, it is different. I see my replacement as an angel of mercy. I have even left Diet Coke in my office fridge though Elizabeth probably doesn't touch the filthy stuff. The sixty-eight-year-old lady is a little like my mother: firm; professional, has silvery grey hair in a tidy bob, wears her dark suits well and speaks with a clipped, slightly old-fashioned accent. Principal Peter has given me some reassurance about my job prospects though this came with a long lecture about paying for suitable help or finding a decent care home for Michael. He isn't wrong. He has told me categorically that Elizabeth won't be displacing me for long as the polymath is far too busy. I hear she organises and attends various U3A groups which comprise Loving Literature; a German conversation class and Art and Architecture. She walks, swims al fresco, plays golf and has taken up Pilates. She also has six grandchildren. I am grateful that Wonder Woman has a fulfilled life as I am not ready for early retirement.

I cannot pretend that things are totally uneventful at home. Michael is prickly about being given instructions. Each day, I lay out his clothes on our bed, hoping that he will get dressed without making a drama out of it. It is never straightforward. He wears odd socks, even if I leave a pair out for him; his tee shirts are worn inside out or back-to-front; his boxer shorts or Y-fronts are taut over his trousers. He is my Superman. I can see that he is losing his coordination. Buttons remain a challenge. We avoid them where possible. We have abandoned shirts for now though I will be packing a few for the cruise. The travel agent has advised my parents to do as much "fine dining" as possible, so that they can avoid the large canteen; besides, it will be a nightmare keeping track of Michael. I hardly need Old King Hamlet's ghost to come and tell me this.

Eddie and I fetch the cases out of the loft and dust them down. Olivia removes the old luggage tags from Croatia. That was the past. This is the present. We are all thinking the same thing but none of us says it out loud. Michael and I will share a case, as will the twins. We have been advised that the cabins don't have much storage space, unsurprisingly, so we need to pack prudently. Eddie is worried that Olivia will bring twice as much as him. I advise him to pack first! The Day Centre in West Hampstead is closed for an industrial clean; apropos of this, I am going to encourage Michael to help me pack as this was his speciality in the past. The prospect, however, fills him with anxiety and dread. He is convinced that I am sending him to a care home. Our conversations are constant battle grounds though I have learned to be less confrontational and more conciliatory.

I ask Michael to choose some clothes for our holiday. I open his underwear drawer for him and suggest this is a sensible place to start. I say it quietly and casually, so that it doesn't sound like an instruction. He takes everything out and unceremoniously dumps his socks, boxer shorts, some pants and even vests that I never knew he owned, onto the bed. Without prompting, Michael continues to ransack every drawer, gathering piles of clothes from his cupboards (all of which were labelled by the dreaded interloper). Our bed is tantamount to a jumble sale. I let out a little sigh; there's no malice in it, only frustration. It's a pity that I have not learned to curtail my emotions. He is quick to lash out. I sit on the edge of the bed whilst he continues raiding the wardrobes.

I want to stop him but I reign myself in as my directions will be misinterpreted as officious; I will be yelled at and censured for being a nagging and interfering wife. I don't need this aggravation, especially before we embark on our trip. This acquiescent behaviour doesn't come naturally to me. Years of being assertive in the classroom have probably turned me into a bossy control freak. I no longer know my true self. I will be an actor playing the role of a Stepford Wife. It might be easier that way. I thank my tetchy husband for his efforts and run downstairs to alleviate the agency carer, Aleksandra, from her date with her Americano. Could she take Michael out? Just for a bit? She reluctantly removes herself from the chair and follows me back up the stairs. Despite his reservations about my erroneous plot to send him away, Michael stuffs his clothes into the case, along with some random items of mine. It's a far cry from the old days when he used to take charge. Everything had to be meticulously folded, colour-coordinated and bagged. Nothing was allowed to be loose. I used to accuse him of suffering from OCD though in reality I knew I was lucky to have a husband like this. I encourage Michael to go out for a walk with Aleksandra. She's pretty and blonde. He takes little persuasion. But I tell the young Polish girl to stick to the roads and not to wander off onto the heath. Michael isn't going to turn into a werewolf but even men with dementia have "needs". I tell her to get back within the hour. No later.

I empty the case and start all over again. I let out a loud sigh, deliberately, as a retort for having to stifle my earlier one. I carefully sort Michael's clothes into colours and fabrics and then do the same with mine. I fetch a few plastic bags from the kitchen and start shoving things into them. I zip the case up and drag it onto the floor; it's not too heavy and, if push comes to shove, I will be able to carry it up and down the stairs myself. I open the folder with all the printed material about the forthcoming holiday. In the past, Michael used to do the checking in for all of us; order the Uber and basically take control. Now I have to do everything myself. It is not particularly onerous. I have organised many school trips in the past; this can't be so different. I check through the details. I am paranoid that I will make a mistake. We are staying in Rome for two nights and catching a train to the port from there. My parents are flying from Gatwick. We are flying from Luton. We will meet them at the apartment in Italy. Safety in numbers.

A taxi drives the four of us to Via Labicana in Lazio, Rome; it's a stone's throw from the Colosseum and it has incredible views from each of its many windows. We have rented a three-bedroom apartment which has its own kitchen-diner, sitting room and two small Juliet balconies. My parents arrive a few minutes after us. We allocate the largest bedroom to them; after all, this is our way of saying thank you for the cruise. Eddie and Olivia take the bedroom with the two singles which leaves Michael and I with the smallest room; it has a tiny bed. It can't be more than four-foot-six. I unpack our nightclothes and our toiletries; freshen up and change into lighter clothing. It's a little humid in Rome and much warmer than in London or Sussex. Everyone changes, except for Michael. No one wants an argument at this time of night.

We traipse around the narrow streets in search of both a shop to buy a few provisions and a restaurant in which we can eat a light supper. We find both though the prices are exorbitant. We are clearly staying in a touristy area; either that, or we're paying tourist prices. We eat too much bread whilst we're waiting, and sample the famous artichoke dish which none of us much like. I know that I must be a philistine as I'd really just like English Italian food. Eddie asks for a spaghetti Bolognese but the restauranteur laughs in his face; that's an English dish, Signor. You can have ragu. Michael orders a pizza which is met with derision. My parents are the only members of our family who order something sophisticated. They also drink a carafe of wine. The rest of us drink water.

We stroll back to the apartment, two-by-two: Eddie and

Olivia, Sheila and Henry, Michael and I. I am hopeful that we will mix and match over the next few days. We congregate at the glass dining room table at the far end of the sitting room. My father has brought his battered *Insight Guide to Rome* and put yellow post-it notes in its key pages. My mother has brought a pad and pen with her, and is poised, ready to take notes as if she were his secretary. She writes down a list of all the main sights and works out a route and a schedule. We are exempt from visiting the Vatican, this time, as the queues will be too long as we haven't made an advanced booking. Eddie and Olivia are speechless. I can see that this is not what they had in mind. They both ask for permission to wander around Rome by themselves. They don't really need to ask.

Even though I have shared a house with my parents in the past– mainly in their home in Sussex – being confined to a small apartment is a little too close for comfort. The constant loo flushing is a bit of a revelation too. I hope my father isn't developing prostate cancer. I sit on the bed, next to Michael, and make sure that he's wearing his pyjamas and has brushed his teeth. It's like being with an oversized child. I check the door to see if there's a lock. There isn't. Michael doesn't stir. He is thinking. This can only mean one thing: a series of questions to which I won't have all the answers. *Why am I here? Have I been here before? You need to give me time to adjust. I haven't lived up north for years. Is this our new house?* The questions are endless. I do my best to answer them quietly and methodically until he is satisfied that I am telling the truth. I open up the white linen sheets and encourage Michael to get in between them. His legs hang over the end of the bed; I know he will struggle to fall sleep like this. I pop back out to the sitting room to inspect the sofa; it's quite long and bends round into a U shape. He might be more comfortable on that. Michael is offended and refuses to budge. *You're just trying to get rid of me. You can take the sofa.* He is unnecessarily aggressive. So much for our Roman Holiday. I already want to go home. I remind myself that it's the dementia talking. The man I have loved for so many years isn't really here anymore; he's the imposter now and I am not sure how much longer I can last in this relationship. I feel as though I am imprisoned by love. I'm the one who needs time to adjust, not him.

It's about 5 am by the time I have realised that sleep and I are not going to be good bedfellows. I wander into the sitting room and gaze out of the window at the illuminated Colosseum; it's a beautiful sight. We are lucky to be here. I feel light-headed, thirsty and tired. The whole journey was fraught with tension and incident. I'm pleased my parents were spared the embarrassment that travelling with my husband now entails. I sit down at the glass table and read through my mother's itinerary for the day; it looks exhausting and I am already anxious at the prospect of making sure that Michael doesn't wander off. It's supposed to be a holiday, not the Duke of Edinburgh Award. I make myself a cup of tea; it tastes odd. The water is too soft. I flick through my father's guidebook and try to take in the advice meted out in it. A gentle hand is placed on my shoulder; it's my mother's. She can't sleep either. We sit on the sofa together, arms around each other. *I know it's difficult, darling. If it's all too much today, do your own thing. We want everyone to be happy, especially you.* I give way to her kindness and descend into tears. It's not the first time and it won't be the last. This is my life. I am reassured that it won't last forever; that Michael's decline is rapid. I must be brave, for the children. I know that she is right. I allow my mother to take over.

Chapter 37
The Cruise

We board the ship via a long gangway which zigzags its way towards the legal polluting monstrosity that sits on the dark blue water at Port Civitavecchia. Michael has insisted on carrying our case, as opposed to dragging it along on its wheels, but my father claims that it's good for him to get some exercise. I cannot argue with that. Henry pulls my parents' case along with some effort. My mother has packed an outfit for each day with shoes and accessories to match. I'm depending on her to lend me a bit of everything as I always pack too little.

Initially, we are told to congregate at our fire stations. Ours is H and it's in a place called the Carousel Lounge. We are packed into this place like sardines in a tin. Some of the elderly passengers are wearing white face masks. There are very few seats available. I notice a group of young people taking up most of a sofa. I give them one of my institutional stares, shaming them into rendering their seats up for my parents. I insist they accept. I realise I am being bossy again. Our drill is led by a young man called Tommy. He's a total drama queen and creates a theatrical performance out of the most humdrum of experiences. I admire him for that. We chat a little and I establish that he was a pupil at Arts Educational in Chiswick; this doesn't surprise me. He's one of the actors/dancers on the ship. We say we're looking forward to seeing him in his "spectacular" show though in reality we are unlikely to see it. My parents detest musical theatre. I am not allowed to: I'm a teacher, after all. I have VIP seats at every show whether I want these or not.

Once the drill is over, we are informed that our cabins are ready. We are on Deck 7 and our three cabins are all next to each other: 701, 703 and 705. We walk down the stairs from Level 10 to Level 7. There's a sign indicating which way the cabin numbers work though each corridor looks like the other. Even the doors are the same colour except for the one near the stairs; that's blue. It's not a lavatory, as in the care homes that I saw earlier in the year. It's just a blue door. It says "staff only". My father leads the way, striding down the corridor. He spies his case outside one of the doors and greets it like an old friend. I suspect he was worried about the shopping trips that my mother would insist on, should the damn thing not arrive in time for the ship's disembarkation. I take out the blue and white credit card which is labelled with the ship's name and it press it against the censor on the door. The red instantly flashes into green. We're in.

The cabin is very well designed. The bed is a surprisingly good size and it has lovely little bedside cabinets on each side in addition to a love-seat sofa, a vanity desk, a hairdryer, clever space saving cupboards and an en suite shower and lavatory. The storage space is remarkably good. I am quite excited. Our stateroom also has a balcony which overlooks the lifeboats though we can also see the sea. I am not complaining. I go straight onto the balcony and stand at the railings looking out onto the busy port. My parents are one step behind me, sliding their door open too. We can all see each other's balconies, with just a little stretch of our necks. I find it quite comforting though I tell myself that privacy will be somewhat restricted unless we keep the sliding doors closed.

The ship disembarks at 6 pm. We have had plenty of time to unpack; or rather, I have. I have left Michael on the balcony where he can relax. I slip quietly out of the room, putting the lock onto the latch, and walk into Eddie and Olivia's room. I want to check that they have settled in. Theirs is a carbon copy of ours except that, much to my relief, they have two single beds. It's a bit cosy but I know that they will respect each other's privacy when required. They have an understanding that only twins can have. We chat about how we're going to keep their grandparents happy whilst also not compromising too much on our own holiday. I stress the importance of timekeeping as ships have been known to depart without all their passengers. Lateness isn't tolerated. I can hear myself again: dishing out instructions. I make a silent promise to myself to stop. I wonder whether Michael's control over me facilitates my control over others. It's not *Wuthering Heights*. Michael isn't Heathcliff and I'm not Cathy. I am hopeful that this holiday will be a panacea for all our trials and tribulations.

I return to our cabin and join Michael on the balcony. I pour us a glass of sparkling water from the complimentary bottle on our vanity unit. We drink a toast to our future even though I know that he doesn't have one. He looks quite hand-some in his blue polo tee shirt and his white chinos. I wonder how long it will take for this illusion of a husband to make his dementia known to the other passengers. My thoughts are interrupted by a friendly knock on the door; it's our maid, Lally, who is looking after our corridor for the dura-tion of the holiday. She's about forty; from the Philippines; is married with two young children and is desperate to save up enough money for her future. I don't enquire further. I invite her into the cabin and admire her handiwork. She has sculpted an elephant out of the white towel. It's in the room, so to speak. Funny. She says nothing is too much trouble for her. She is here to serve. I want her to enjoy *serving* us – if that makes her happy – but I regret to inform her that my husband has a mental illness. I've said it. She is disappointed in me; it's as if my disloyalty reflects gravely on my charac-ter. I don't doubt it but I say it to protect her, not because I am callous or mean. I am being practical.

In the evening, we meet at the bar on Level 10 as there's

a live band with a rather good singer. My parents are dancing along with two other couples. They're at least ten years younger than the others. They're all very light on their feet. They're a different generation; the ones that learned to dance as opposed to jiggle around to the beat. Michael and I sit down at a little table as if we're on the set for *Cabaret*. A few moments later, Eddie and Olivia join us. They both look lovely. I remark on their efforts and they blush simultaneously. Olivia tells her father to take me onto the dancefloor. No, I say. I think we're about to go into dinner. I love to dance but I don't want to make a spectacle of myself, especially on the first night of the cruise. She is most insistent, dragging her father up by the wrist until he gives way to her prettiness and pleading. Why don't you dance with your father? I say it with a teasing smile but she joins our hands together and leaves us to it. The dancefloor has too much space. I feel exposed. Michael can't dance. He's jerky and lopsided. He never was much good anyway but now he is worse. I pull him closer to me, so that my face rests against his blue shirt, and just let him hold me close. He embraces me tightly and says he won't let me go. We dance to our own tune and it's all right. I wish this moment of happiness could last us my lifetime.

During dinner, we manage to keep a conversation going. My parents are adept at this, regaling us with information about each of the five stops; the currencies in each country; whether we need our passports and so forth. They assume their positions as the patriarch and the matriarch of our family; I'm more than happy for them to do this. It is too exhausting being in control all the time. We eat well though we eat too much. There are endless courses which arrive at very short intervals. We drink excessively, taking full advantage of the drinks package that my parents have generously bought us. I can see that Olivia is definitely tipsy, as am I, so I encourage Eddie to escort his sister back to the cabin. They can go to the 18 to 30 disco another night. My parents agree. No one dares to disobey them.

Michael and I saunter down the confusing set of corridors until we find our cabin. He has absolutely no idea where we are. Lally is prowling around, having turned down our sheets and left us little wrapped chocolates on the bed. I ask her if she can put something distinctive on our door, so that it's easier for us to recognise. She says she will think of something and I thank her. I lock the door from the inside. Anyone could think our cabin was theirs though I am sure we are secure in ours. Michael starts stripping off his clothes, leaving them strewn on the tiny space of carpet that is in front of the bedside table. His little area is a mess. I tell him that it's not Lally's job to pick up after him; not like that, anyway. He's not Prince Charles. I don't know why I bother. He doesn't know who I am talking about and in the end, I have to tidy up after him anyway. It saddens me to see him this way. Michael was always so considerate. Unspoilt. Fun. He was always a bit northern and sometimes defensive with it, accusing us southerners of being posh and spoilt. But we were equals in our marriage: husband and wife. Not man and servant. I capitulate, eventually, and take pity on the man, even though I'm a little unsteady on my feet. I vow to abstain from alcohol tomorrow. I leave Michael sitting on the little sofa, pretending to read the information sheet, and take a shower, knowing that he is safe in our cabin.

Afterwards, I stand on the balcony. It is lovely to be able to see the stars and planets in the sky. I don't know which is which. Michael used to know; I miss his intellect. There is no light pollution here, other than the tiny little lights emanating from the orange lifeboats several decks beneath us. My father is sitting on the balcony, sipping a whiskey. *We heard your shenanigans,* he says. I apologise and stretch my hand over the divider between our balconies so that he can share his drink with me. So much for my abstention.

I stay out there for about an hour, staring up at the full moon; its reflection glows brightly on the inky water. I press my face against the sliding door, hoping that Michael will be asleep. I can't see him in the cabin. I suddenly feel anxious and have to suppress the anxiety attack that is about to force itself on me. I check the shower/loo – he's not there either. I look under the bed, where we have stashed the case, and I check inside the cupboards. I know it's daft but I half expect him to jump out at me like Cato in *Inspector Clouseau*. I am disappointed that he doesn't. I return to the balcony to see if my father is still there but he isn't. My parents' cabin light is off and the curtains are closed. I look on the other side. There's no sign of life from Eddie and Olivia's cabin either. It must be later than I thought.

I am not sure what to do. I know that one of the symptoms of dementia is restlessness. Michael might be suffering from cabin fever. He can't have gone very far. In my panic, I exit the room in my nightshirt and bare feet. I am definitely not dreaming this time. I run down the corridor, calling for Michael. No one responds. I run up the stairs, back to the bar. Very few people are still there. A waiter, wearing a wine-red waistcoat, approaches me with his little round silver tray. I don't want a drink. I want my husband. I describe him down to the last detail but realise that he's not wearing the clothes that he was in earlier. He may be wearing pyjamas. *Like you*, says the waiter. I explain that it's an emergency. The waiter advises me to liaise with the staff on duty at the Customer Services desk; it's on Level 3.

There's only one Night Manager on duty. He's called Juan and is from South America. The only British people are the passengers. Amazingly, the cabin staff are from all over the world. They all speak a different version of English. Juan is helpful and sympathetic but he isn't unduly worried about Michael's disappearance. It's a common phenomenon on cruise ships, especially at the beginning of the week. Passengers drink too much; they get lost and disorientated; it's completely normal. He can't use the tannoy as it's 2.30 am but he will circulate an urgent memorandum to all the crew. He tells me to wait at one of the tables at the far end of the circular lounge opposite the help desk. I sit down on my own. I have left my mobile charging in the room and only have the key-card with me. I wonder if I should wake up the twins or my parents. I can't work out whether they would want me to or not. None of us will be much good to Michael if we all lose a night's sleep. I suppose I am getting used to sleep deprivation.

Juan is on the desk phone, rabbiting away in Spanish. I can only make out the odd word but I hear him say Michael's name. The call is evidently about my lost husband. I am restless. There's too much adrenalin flowing through my arteries. Eventually, Juan gestures me to come back to him. Michael has been found. I follow him and the other member of staff down towards the life boats. Michael is leaning against one of them, dressed in his blue stripy pyjamas. There is an empty beer bottle next to him. Fortunately, Michael is asleep. Juan and Jamie, the other man, drag my husband onto the deck where they prop him up between their shoulders. It's a mild night but they're keen to bring him indoors. Michael is significantly taller and broader than both of his rescuers; they struggle to support his weight. I offer to help but they say they can manage. We enter the lift and I push the number 7 for our floor. It takes a moment for me to re-orientate myself; after all, we haven't even been on the ship for twenty-four hours. Juan and Jamie drag Michael's lank body all the way to our cabin. Lally has stuck red and blue balloons down on each side of our door; it is no one's birthday but it will certainly be easier to find our cabin now. The two members of staff are totally out of breath. I apologise profusely and offer them twenty euros each. After a little hesitation, they accept. I assure them that this gesture will be our little secret.

I roll Michael into the bed, making sure that he's in the recovery position. I kiss him gently on the lips, savouring his scent. I still love him. I enter the bed from the other side, pulling the sheets right up to my neck. My eyes well up and the tears fall down, saturating the pillow. The ship moves swiftly and silently through the black water onto its first destination: the port of Messina.

We dock at 8 am and are encouraged to start disembarking shortly after that. We have been given a newsletter sheet which includes essential information about returning to the ship on time, local taxis, excursions to Taormina and other general facts including the weather. It will be a maximum of 22 degrees and sunny: perfect for sightseeing. We meet for breakfast – which is a buffet in the main dining room – and discuss our day ahead. My father accompanies Michael to each of the food stations until he has everything that he wants. He chooses an unusual combination but he's not alone in this; most of the passengers on the ship are desperate to get their money's worth. I bring a tray of coffee and tea over to our table. All is well. My parents suggest that we all take a daytrip to Taormina as there's not much to do in Messina, given half of it was rebuilt after the earthquake. We disembark from the ship and are immediately accosted by the many travel reps who have sold "tours" to our chosen destination; the thought of spending 90% of our time sitting on a coach whilst the same information is said in four different languages is our idea of pure hell. Instead, we flag down a taxi driver whose mini bus can accommodate us. We agree a price and hire Giovanni for the whole day.

Taormina is delightful. Its Greek theatre, charming piazzas and pedestrianised streets enable us all to relax and enjoy being on dry-land. It feels safe here. The six of us wander down the main street, Corso Umberto I, until we reach the Teatro Greco and Duca di Cesaro gardens nearby. We do our best to avoid the other cruise ship passengers, most of whom are being herded like cattle from one main point of interest to another. After visiting the Greek Theatre, we decide to split up. My mother, Olivia and I make the most of the quaint little shops. My father, Michael and Eddie, tell us that they will visit the San Agostino church followed by a bar

C. S. Brahams

that serves ice-cold beer. It is a good day. No one gets lost or pickpocketed. We even eat a delicious Sicilian-style lunch: caponata and a mixed salad. I have enjoyed the opportunity to bond with my mother and daughter. I send the menfolk a text, to see if they've had an equally good time. Eddie replies with images of beer bottles.

When we return to the ship, we have to go through security again. Michael is a little confused as it's not dissimilar to the airport, though much more confined. I take his arm and loop mine through it. He smiles and says *"We are happy, aren't we?"* We lie down on the bed together and I read the newsletter out loud; it has a list of all the onboard entertainment, most of which has no interest for us. The evening show, however, is a condensed version of *Mamma Mia*. I think it would do us good to see something light and uplifting. I send a text to the family WhatsApp group. I am mindful that the show clashes with our dinner reservation. I feel as though I have to ask permission to be excused but no one minds at all. We are at liberty to enjoy our holiday in any which way that we choose.

Michael and I wander down to Level 3 where the ship's theatre is situated. We are surprised by its size and grandeur. It's smarter and more modern than many of the theatres in the West End though we both know that the standard of the performance might not live up to our expectations. We sit in the middle of the middle row. There's no escape. Unusually for us, we order soft drinks. We chat a little. Michael seems much more like his old self; it's a relief to be with him in this state; I hope that it will last. The theatre lights dim. There's a medley of Abba songs, all of which we recognise, followed by a whole cast dance spectacular; this is all before the show really begins. The jokes and links from one song to another are as corny as the film but it's so tongue-in-cheek that we don't care. Besides, the performers are from all over the world so the humour is enhanced in ways that we didn't anticipate. We emerge from the theatre singing "Dancing

261

Queen" and "Thank You for the Music". Michael has come back to me, albeit for a few minutes. I wish our happiness could be preserved like honey.

For the first time in a while, I don't worry about what everyone else is doing. And I am not anxious about going to bed with Michael. We seem to have found peace. Perhaps the cruise is just what we needed.

Chapter 38
360 Degrees

The holiday thus far has been a success. We are cruising along to our penultimate stop: Dubrovnik, Croatia. We were here less than a year ago – bathing in blissful ignorance – and now we are all too aware of the fragility of life. As we walk into the beautiful Old Town, we take in the charm of our surroundings. Its pedestrianised streets accompanied by its marble and light-coloured stone buildings and churches, make it one of the prettiest places on our itinerary. Despite being damaged during the armed conflict in the 1990s, it remains a striking place. Unfortunately, thousands of tourists flood the city, many of whom have stepped off their humungous cruise ships; however, we quickly learn to keep our "hotel-on-the-sea" quiet. The locals resent their presence with a vengeance.

As we battle with the plethora of visitors, it is noticeable that Michael is becoming increasingly agitated. The merest brush of the shoulder results in heavy sighs and the occasional swear word. We all ignore his outbursts. Life is too short. We edge slowly down to the small harbour. The twins are keen to visit Lokrum Island as they want to see the large medieval Benedictine monastery there; at first, I'm bemused by this sudden interest but apparently part of the attraction is its association with *Game of Thrones* which neither Michael nor I have ever seen. Interestingly though, the locals say that Lokrum carries a curse: whosoever claims Lokrum for his or her own personal pleasure shall be damned! Eddie admits that it is where *Game of Thrones* was partially filmed; he wants his chance to pose imperiously on an iron throne. Olivia is equally enthusiastic. It's worthy of Instagram, apparently. The boat ride only takes about ten minutes until it reaches the quaint harbour of Portoc Bay. We wander around, taking in the fragrant smell of the eucalyptus trees and enjoy watching the many peacocks and peahens wandering freely on this sanctuary of an island. It's a special place. No one is allowed to stay here overnight, not that we can anyway. There are neither hotels nor houses here, just a couple of restaurants and cafes. We deliberately avoid the nudist beach ahead, even though the boatman said it had the best vantage points for swimming. In the old days, Michael and I *might* have dared to go there. But definitely not in front of either my parents or our children. Instead, we head towards the uneven rocks, in the direction of the sea. We all want to swim in the rolling waves but I fear the conditions are a little too thrilling for my parents, even though both of them are strong swimmers.

Another family is a little ahead of us. We follow their trail, zigzagging across the rocks until we reach the metal swimming pool style steps that are carved into one of the rocks; these lead straight down into the sea. The husband, wife and their son, who can't be more than about eleven, reach the steps a few moments before us. I wonder why the boy isn't in school but I don't ask, of course. I quickly learn that his name is Luke. Everyone in my family group starts divesting themselves of their clothes; we are all wearing our costumes underneath them. I look down at the intrepid scene: crashing waves attacking the jagged rocks. It looks treacherous. I suggest to my parents that they may want to guard our things instead of swimming but they are offended. Besides, if the young boy can swim here, so can they. I am not worried about Michael; he's by the far the strongest swimmer amongst us. He gingerly walks down the steep steps, turns swiftly and plunges into the cool rough waves. It's good to see him so joyful. The family of three are quick to follow, though Luke, spurred on by his parents, looks petrified. I shadow the skinny boy as if I were *in loco parentis*. Teachers are never really on sabbatical when it comes to children. Eddie and Olivia are seconds behind me and my parents follow them. The bay is hemmed in by massive pointy rocks; if the steps were not carved into them, people wouldn't dare swim here. I am beginning to regret my cavalier attitude to this expedition. The bright sun disappears behind a large dark cloud. The sky unexpectedly looks ominous but the effort to enter the water outweighs the desire to exit it.

It is too deep to stand and too rough to relax but I swim up to Michael and kiss him gently on the cheeks. I tell him that I love him. I am sorry for not being able to cope better with his illness. He doesn't know what I am talking about. *I'm feeling fine. Invigorated.* In some ways, I'm glad that he is entering this phase of his dementia – the state of not knowing – though I am dreading the next stage in which he will lose the ability to swallow, talk or walk. I don't know how families cope. The illness is as relentless as the tide but it shows no mercy. Michael will exist but he won't really live. I hold onto Michael who treads water for the both of us. We are happy and distracted, looking at each other with a renewed intensity that has been absent for many months.

Refreshed, my parents swim back towards the steps. My mother first, closely followed by my father. He is protective of her, shadowing her every move as she struggles up the steep steps back to safety. I watch Henry and Sheila until they're safely back onto dry land. I'm relieved. Olivia and Eddie have had enough too. They make light of the steps which I am secretly dreading. Michael and I stay in the water, probably against my better judgement, but he is so content here that I can't bring myself to terminate his happiness. I am responsible for him now. He can't make decisions for himself. Not really. We allow ourselves to be thrashed about by the waves though I fear that we have remained in too long. Luke and his parents are swimming precariously close to the jagged rock. I think they're reckless and irresponsible. The boy is too young. The waves are loftier now, and the rain has started teeming down. There's going to be a storm. The boy's parents ascend the steps first, leaving the child hanging onto the bottom step which is submerged in the water. Each step is too far apart, even for an adult, but much more intimidating for a child. They should have put him in the middle. He starts to panic. His weak arms can barely hold his weight. *Come on, Luke. You're nearly there. Keep going. Three more steps and you can have an ice-cream.* It is not for me to judge but I cannot help but watch him closely whilst I desperately try to keep my head above the water.

A huge and unforeseen wave crashes into Luke's little body with such force that he falls back into the water. He is barely conscious. It is every mother's nightmare come to fruition. I can barely watch. Michael instinctively swims quickly over to the child, scooping him up in his muscular arms and lifting him towards the steps. He manages to hand the child over to the boy's father, whose arms are stretched down towards his son. He is safe now. There's a round of applause from above. Fifteen to twenty people come forward, clapping and cheering my husband: the hero. He is embarrassed and confused.

We should get out too. Michael doesn't want to. Perhaps he is savouring the moment in private? It is hard to know what he is thinking these days. He lives in a different world from me. I wonder whether I should stay in the sea with him; after all, he isn't well. I tread water, near him, but he points towards the steps and tells me to get out. He sounds authoritative, as if he were in the office. Instinctively, I obey him. I don't know why. I start clambering up the steps, eager to reach the dry land. The sea has sapped the energy out of me. I wrap a gaudy beach towel around myself and start jabbering away to the parents and the boy. Luke has survived his ordeal. I tell my children that they can be proud of their father. Luke's parents want to thank Michael and take us out for dinner at the very least. I tell them it's not necessary but his grateful mother adds me to her contacts on her mobile. She promises to be in touch. Michael is a star in her eyes. I am momentarily distracted, caught up in her tangled world of emotions. Nothing feels real anymore. The weather is quickly deteriorating. The sky and sea are in cahoots together; they make for an ominous pair of thieves, robbing the sky of its sun and energy.

I urge Michael to get out of the water but he's reluctant to comply. The storm is whipping up; most of his fan club has dispersed, and my family and I are the only ones left on the serrated rocks. The others are busy getting changed, even though the exercise is somewhat futile. I get dressed too, and drape my towel around my shoulders. I am only distracted for a couple of minutes.

The rain is substantial though the ambient temperature is still warm. The swimming conditions are dangerous, even for the best of swimmers.

I'm too late.

Michael's thick dark hair is matted with blood. He has hit his head against one of the rocks. The angry sea sweeps his lifeless body against his unyielding murderer, back and forth, until it becomes wedged under the steps. It doesn't feel real. He can't be dead. He can't be...

I scream; it's a piercing, shrill sound that would not be out of place in the opera The Exterminating Angel. I don't recognise my penetrating voice. But I am not as loud as I think I am. I must be in shock. I unthinkingly dive into the water where the blue has turned to deep red. I struggle to pull Michael's lifeless limp body towards the steps. Eddie dives in after me; Olivia after him. My mother calls an ambulance; my father calls the police. We are all inextricably linked.

I cry for my beloved husband: my hero. I cry for my doting children. I cry for every woman whose husband has dementia. But I am also drowning in guilt.

I have spent my life compartmentalising my problems. But not this time. I can't do it. I have to let other people help me. I am full of regret. I know that I could have done things differently but hindsight would be exterminated if he existed in person. I know I would shoot him.

People talk of resilience. I have even killed this topic with my PowerPoint presentations. What does the ordinary middle-class person know about resilience?

The grief and guilt envelop me like a shroud.

The Epilogue

There isn't even a hint of funereal weather. It is gloriously sunny and the heavens are shining down on us.

We stand together at the Hampstead Cemetery, dressed in black. The reality is very different from my nightmare. There are no carnations, no white dresses and no sign of Kathleen. My parents are here. They look older and frailer than before. They hold each other's hands and stand in a dignified silence, close to me and next to Eddie and Olivia. We are united in our grief. It feels surreal. I cannot believe that I am burying my fifty-year-old husband, the father of my children. I feel as though my soul extricates itself from my body; it's as if I am having an out-of-body experience.

I am overwhelmed by the sheer numbers of mourners. Not only have most of Michael's former colleagues come but so have mine. Principal Peter, Liam, Abbas, Emily and even Benedict are all here. Most of our friends have turned up. Rosie and Emma have come with their husbands and all their children. And many of our children's friends have made the effort to support them. Gabriella, our GP, is standing next to our neighbour, Matt. I know that Michael would be humbled by the large turn-out.

I'm not sure if I believe in the "undiscovered country" but it would be reassuring to think that heaven existed. When we were at university, we were both atheists. But as we matured, and attended funerals over the years, we have wanted to believe in something though we rarely spoke about the possibility of an afterlife. We didn't expect to confront it this soon. I look around the graveyard and make a mental note of everyone who is standing here in Michael's honour. The counting helps me hold back the tears.

Back inside the intimate chapel, several people want to express their views about Michael's moral character and his many achievements. The vicar speaks first. We are not churchy people. But he has done his homework and does my late husband justice. Afterwards, Eddie and Olivia share the podium together; they're brave and funny, sweet and affectionate. But as Olivia brings their joint eulogy to a close, her voice quivers. She looks at the coffin which is covered in flowers and a wreath of white roses. Olivia whispers "my daddy: the hero". The chapel echoes with her voice. In my eyes and ears, my daughter morphs into Bobbie in *The Railway Children*. She's on the platform, shrouded in a silvery vapour. My eyes are full of misty salt water. I am no longer able to contain my emotion. I finally submit and let the tears roll down my colourless cheeks. The whole congregation is reduced to loud sobs. I put my arms around Olivia and Eddie. In time, we will learn to forget the horrors of this year and remember the wonders of the years that preceded it. He was a good husband and an even better father. Various former associates of Michael's talk about his generosity at work; his charm and his intellectual prowess. He was popular, well liked and well respected. It is not easy hearing these compliments when so many people deserted him during the last few months. But I am not one to hold grudges. It's no one's fault. I stand with my grown-up children; they're on the cusp of true independence. In a few months' time, they will be undergraduates at university. And I will return to the job that I once loved.

Michael is buried with care, prayers and love. We sing his favourite hymn and mine: "I Vow to Thee My Country". And, despite the many occasions that I have sung this hymn at school, this time, it reduces me to tears and I cannot stop the incessant flow. I wonder if my love did stand the test, and if my love ever faltered. I know the answer. But don't judge me too harshly. I sing as loudly and proudly as I can though it is difficult to enunciate the beautiful lyrics in my fragile state. My parents, Eddie, Olivia and I stand in a line, holding hands.

I know that Michael will live on in his children.

And instead of being remembered for his dementia, we will look back on him as our hero.

About the Author

C.S. Brahams was educated at Queen's College, Harley Street and MPW, Kensington, after which she read English, Russian Studies and Linguistics at Durham University. She qualified as a teacher of English from the Institute of Education and later gained an MA in Management from UCL. She is an experienced teacher of English, former Vice Principal and Head of Sixth Form. Catherine is currently a School Governor and School Inspector. Although she has written articles, both for internal and external publications, this is her debut novel. Catherine is married to Lawrence and they have one daughter, Alice.

The author would like to express her gratitude to Jackie Miller and Sue Haskel for their kind assistance with the plot development. She would also like to thank her parents, Diana and Malcolm Brahams, for proof-reading the novel. And finally, the author is very grateful to her close friend and cousin, Rosalind Saker, for her continued support, good humour and friendship throughout the writing process.

Lightning Source UK Ltd.
Milton Keynes UK
UKHW040716310720
367482UK00003B/845

9 781913 340827